SHADOW WITCH

THE WITCHES OF HOLLOW COVE
BOOK ONE

KIM RICHARDSON

FABLEPRINT

This book is a work of fiction. Any references to historical events, real people, or real locales are used fictitiously. Other names, characters, places, and incidents are the product of the author's imagination, and any resemblance to actual events or locales or persons, living or dead, is entirely coincidental.
FablePrint

Shadow Witch, The Witches of Hollow Cove, Book One

ISBN-13: 9798672663142
[1. Supernatural—Fiction. 2. Demonology—Fiction. 3. Magic—Fiction].

BOOKS BY KIM RICHARDSON

THE WITCHES OF HOLLOW COVE
Shadow Witch
Midnight Spells
Charmed Nights
Magical Mojo
Practical Hexes
Wicked Ways
Witching Whispers
Mystic Madness
Rebel Magic
Cosmic Jinx

THE DARK FILES
Spells & Ashes
Charms & Demons
Hexes & Flames
Curses & Blood

SHADOW AND LIGHT
Dark Hunt
Dark Bound
Dark Rise
Dark Gift
Dark Curse
Dark Angel
Dark Strike

SHADOW
WITCH

THE WITCHES OF HOLLOW COVE
BOOK ONE

KIM RICHARDSON

CHAPTER

1

*"**I** don't love you anymore."*

Okay. So, those were definitely *not* the words I was expecting to hear coming out of my—now ex—boyfriend's mouth. I had hoped for a "You look beautiful today," or "Those jeans make your ass look great," but I would have settled for a "Pass the salt."

Turns out, the douche had been sleeping around on me for the past three months.

Ouch.

Yes, I'll admit it. It had hurt like he'd taken a knife and stabbed me in the heart with it and then twisted the knife around in my gut. The not-in-love-anymore sucked, but the betrayal was worse. I had a "temporary" meltdown moment, which consisted of me throwing a mug at his head followed by a milk carton, the TV remotes, an orchid (I felt terrible about the orchid later), and anything within arm's length. I never hit him with any of those, but hearing his squeal and seeing him squirm and duck was satisfying enough.

Though I *had* noticed a change in John's behavior, his declaration had come as a surprise.

Yup. He was sleeping with us both at the same time. Real classy. The thought made bile rise in the back of my throat. It was the worst deception ever. The guy didn't even have the balls to tell me *before* he jumped into bed with another woman.

I had cried that night, but not as much as I thought I would. I was even more surprised that the anger had quickly turned to numbness… and then nothing. I realized then that his sleeping with someone else (I did not care to know her name) had severed whatever feelings I'd had for him. Like a switch. They turned off. Completely.

I would not let myself fall in the depths of despair for a man who didn't love me, or any man. I deserved better.

So, the next morning, I'd packed a bag, stuffed with only the necessities that fit in my one suitcase, and grabbed the first Greyhound bus out of New York City.

It didn't help that I was broke—way down in the crapper broke. That's what happened when you tried to follow your boyfriend's lifestyle with a graphic designer's salary. He was a lawyer on his way up the corporate ladder, and me, I was fifty thousand in the hole from credit card debt and personal loans and had no idea how I was going to pay it back.

I'd always paid my portion of the rent, food, and bills. I was just too damn proud to admit I couldn't even afford my half.

I'd fallen in love with John when I met him in a pub in Manhattan five years ago. I was finishing my BFA in Design at the School of Visual Arts and living with three other roommates in an apartment the size of the school's bathroom.

We dated for three months. And when he asked me to move in with him, I said yes.

At the time I hadn't realized it was the biggest mistake of my life—not in terms of the relationship but finances. I'd really put myself deep in debt.

I let out a long breath and shifted in my seat, staring at the beautiful landscapes of rolling green hills that wound in and out among thick, tall trees and sparkling lakes and ponds. I was furious with myself to have let it go this far. The only good thing that came out of this was I couldn't dig myself any deeper in the crapper. So I hoped.

This was my rock bottom. There was only uphill from here, and I would climb my way out. I swore it.

The seven-and-a-half-hour bus ride from Manhattan to Maine had seemed like a lifetime as I stared at the window, contemplating my life choices and seeing five years of my life flash by me. I'm not going to lie. I dipped here and there into a bit of depression. It was hard to admit that the man I thought I was going to spend the rest of my life with thought I was garbage and not important enough to remain faithful.

But as soon as I caught a glimpse of the Atlantic Ocean, a strange calm came over me. I sat straighter in my seat as I saw the rugged coastline dotted with lighthouses and picture-perfect seaside villages painted in every color of the rainbow.

My heart sped up with excitement. If I could have rolled down my window, I would have stuck out my head and let my tongue loll like a dog's.

A large wooden sign with a picture of a lighthouse overlooking the ocean and peppered with seagulls came into view: WELCOME TO HOLLOW COVE. And below that, in a handwritten font: *Beware. We will turn trespassers into toads!*

I jerked in my seat as the bus came to a halt.

"This is my stop!" I said happily to my seat-neighbor as I stood up. She was in her sixties, and her wrinkled face pinched, looking annoyed that she had to get up and move if she didn't want me to climb over her to get out. Which was exactly what I'd do if she didn't move in the next three seconds. I might even use a few elbows too. Maybe a knee.

Taking her sweet time, the woman got up and moved out of my way. I rushed out of the bus, looking forward to getting the blood flowing back into my legs. My butt was numb from sitting for so long, and I was pretty sure it had flattened. No kidding. I needed to get out and breathe in the fresh air. After I grabbed my suitcase—the only one with duct tape holding the sides together, which the driver kindly left on the side of the road for me—I wheeled it around and started my journey toward Hollow Cove Bridge.

Fire hydrant red metal beams glimmered in the late evening sun as I made for the bridge, my suitcase's wheels squealing loudly like a dying animal.

Hollow Cove Bridge sounded grand and huge, but in reality, it was a two-minute walk across the tiny two-way bridge that separated Hollow Cove from the rest of the world—the human world, that is. It was a tiny patch of land, surrounded by water and many other things.

5

As soon as I stepped on the bridge, I felt it.

An influx of energy rushed from my toes all the way to my head, my skin riddling in goosebumps, and then it left me.

Magic.

My pulse leaped and my breath quickened. An ordinary human wouldn't have felt the waves of supernatural energy that I'd just walked into, power so terrifying and exhilarating and exceptional that I nearly fell to my knees and sobbed.

But I wasn't ordinary.

With a new hop to my step, I trudged along the bridge, pulling my suitcase behind me. The water below the bridge stirred, the surface reflecting in the sun with thousands of brilliant white lights.

"Tessa? Is that you?" called a woman's voice the moment I stepped off the bridge.

A plump woman in her early sixties marched my way. Her long, flowing dress of loud patterns in a mix of burgundy and purple billowed around her as she neared. Her dark hair was pulled back in a tight bun, showing off her bejeweled glasses sitting on a small nose. At the sight of me, her dark eyes intensified, framed by layers of caked-on mascara, and her smile was infectious.

"Hi, Martha." I slowed to a stop since the woman had purposely positioned herself in front of me to block my way.

A familiar wave of energy hit me, sending a swirl of prickles along my skin as the power crested. A mix of rose perfume and the scent of lavender rolled off her. But it did nothing to hide the scent of pine needles, wet earth, and leaves mixed with a wildflower meadow—the scent of White witches.

Her eyes widened in delight. "Oh! I knew it was you! I just knew it! Knew it! Look at you. You haven't changed a bit—except that you lost a bit of weight. Are you feeling okay, my dear?"

"Yes, I—"

"I can't wait to tell Liz that you're back," she prattled on, a long red fingernail pointing at me. "She'll be so jealous I saw you first. Oooh! Can't wait to see the look on that witch's face when I tell her." She placed her hands on her wide hips. "When was the last time you were here?"

"Fi—"

"Five years ago," answered the large woman. "Wasn't it?"

I sighed. "Yes." Perhaps I should stay quiet since the witch was answering her own questions.

Martha narrowed her eyes. "Your mother's not here, darling. She left two years ago. Not for the first time that witch ups and leaves in the middle of the night. Like a thief that one. You know what I mean?"

My chest clenched. "I know."

Her face took on a sloppy pity look. "Oh, dear. Did you have another quarrel? The two of you never seemed to get along. Pity, as you're her only daughter."

"Pity that she's my only mother." I frowned. The nerve of this woman. The more I stood here, the more I understood why my mother never wanted to live here permanently.

Martha was nodding slowly, gossip forming behind those gaudy glasses. "How old are you now?"

"Twenty-nine."

"That's when wrinkles start creeping up on you." Martha's eyes flashed. "You can't have those, hon. Before you know it—you'll look like a hag."

"I thought beauty came from the inside?"

A narrow smile curved her lips. "Beauty comes from the inside. The inside of my salon."

"Right."

"You look like you've been crying." Martha took a step forward, her eyes so round I could see all the whites. "You've had a lover's quarrel. Haven't you? Yes. Yes. It's why you've come back!" She was practically squealing in delight at the prospect of my heartbreak.

The woman was a menace. But it was also my cue to leave.

"I've got to go," I told her. "My aunts are waiting for me. Nice to see you, Martha." The witch opened her mouth to say something, but I'd already made my way around her. I didn't care if it was rude. I was not here to talk about my life to the town's gossip queen.

"When you're settled in you have to swing by my salon!" called Martha. "I'll give you my 'two for one special' on my facial hair removal spell. Nose hairs free!"

Nice.

I rushed down the cobblestone road, my suitcase bumping along behind me. Shops lined both sides of the street, their windows packed with their latest products and whatever was on sale. Bottles and boxes of potions and charms sat in the windows beside tottering piles of spell books and rolls of parchment.

I moved past a shop with a yellow door and a sign that said POTIONS FOR ALL AFFLIC- TIONS and another that read GET YOUR FREAK ON and HAVE A BOOTYFUL DAY!

All around me, Hollow Cove was just as vibrant and strange as the last time I was here. Not because of the colorful residents—okay, maybe just a little—but because it was the only town for miles where the paranormal lived.

To the human eye, Hollow Cove was just another coastal town with its quaint shops and nosey residents. To us, it was where you'd see a nymph take out her trash, a werewolf mother scolding her kids in the park that pulling the wings of pixies was not a good idea, where trolls manned their pubs and brewed their beers, and where witches sold their potions and their spells.

If you were human, chances were you couldn't see the supernatural. And that was just fine and dandy to the town's people.

"Out of sight. Out of mind," was what my aunts used to say.

Two women outside Wicked Witch & Handsome Devil Pub watched me as I went by. The shorter one shook her head, her voice rising to reach me. "Her mother kept moving around and around. Dragging that poor child all over the country. The child can't be normal after that kind of dysfunctional upbringing. She was trying to shake the witch out of her, that's what."

Child? I thought about stopping and telling this stranger what this *child* was capable of, but I didn't have the energy. I ached from traveling. And what little energy I had left was needed to keep my legs moving.

I hit the town square just as shop owners and customers were coming out, closing for the day. Heads turned my way. They pointed and gazed open-mouthed, whispering excitedly as I rushed by.

Don't look. Don't look, I warned myself. If I made eye contact, I was in for it.

As I passed another block, I glimpsed eyes on me—the same ones I'd seen a few moments ago. I looked up, and there was Martha, whispering something into the ear of a short man who looked familiar.

How the hell did she get there so fast? Didn't matter. Now everyone knew I was back, with some tragic, made-up scandal no less. The more scandalous, the better. Wasn't it always the case in small towns?

I moved swiftly through the streets, aware of every glance shooting my way. I kept my head down and walked as fast as I could without it being considered a jog.

"Tessa! Wait!"

Martha again.

Now I was running.

It was the most awkward run of the century, pulling the suitcase behind me. But I would rather risk looking like a giant idiot than discuss my personal life right now. I wasn't in the mood, and it was no one's business but my own.

The walk to Davenport House from the bridge was usually a half-hour walk. At a run, I'd made it in ten minutes.

Davenport House was a massive farmhouse beauty with a black metal roof, white wood siding, and a glorious wraparound porch supported by thick, round columns. It was one of those houses that made you do a double-take and triple-take, stopping whatever you were doing to take a look. It was *that* awesome.

The enormous house stood on the edge of a cliff looking out toward the ocean, three floors of majestic views furnished with balconies. The property sat on twenty acres of land and waterfront and was built by the first Davenport witches.

I stood for a moment, taking it all in.

I hadn't set foot in Davenport House in more than five years. Memories came flooding in, bits and pieces like flipping through an old photo album. My mother often took me to Davenport House, well, when we were in town. This house had always been my "happy place" as a child. It was so big, I'd often get lost in it, on purpose of course. So many doors and secret hideaways, it was a kid's dream.

Now, looking at it after all these years... it looked perfect. And I mean like it was *newly* built. I couldn't see a single flake of old paint on the siding, not even a crack on one of the many windows or a warped plank of wood from the porch. It looked... well, it looked brand spanking new. But the house was over two hundred years old. The salt from the sea was enough to do some serious damage to the wood siding, but the planks were smooth, as though they'd just been sandblasted and painted.

"Weird."

I let out a lengthy sigh and made for the stone path leading to the front of the house and flanked by rose bushes and Annabelle hydrangeas. A wind blew, carrying the scent of the ocean mixed in with the fragrance of roses. Red geraniums and purple petunias draped from the flower boxes that hung over the porch's rail.

My legs felt like jelly as I yanked my suitcase up with me and stood by the wide birch front door with a stained-glass window portraying the image of a witch flying on her broom next to a full moon.

An engraved metal plate next to the door written in large bold letters read: THE MERLIN GROUP. And just below that written in smaller letters: Magical Enforcement Response League Intelligence Network.

Yup. It was good to be home.

And with that warm feeling in my gut, I turned the doorknob and stepped inside.

CHAPTER

2

"Hello?" I called as I ventured inside. "Is anyone here?"

I jerked as a ripple of energy washed through me, causing the hair from my ponytail to rise, and I smelled the scent of stale coffee.

"I don't remember that," I mumbled, as the energy left me in a rush.

I shut the door behind me and looked around. I stood in the large foyer with lots of polished wood paneling and thick oak moldings. An enormous iron chandelier hung from the tall, twelve-foot ceiling. To my left was a winding staircase that twisted up to the higher levels. Picture frames from the Davenport family stared down at me from the walls. Their faces were so solemn that some even looked angry, and I always wondered if they did that on purpose to scare away intruders. It was creepy. Witches were masters of creepy.

I was still holding on to my suitcase as I waited to hear one of my aunts' voices answer me. All I got was the wonderful scent of freshly baked pumpkin cookies. My favorite.

I heard a thump, a curse, and then a pair of short steps. A second later, a woman stood in the hallway across from me. She was small and fit with her white hair wrapped around the top of her head in a messy bun. She wore a long flowing pale blue skirt with a linen white blouse whose sleeves she'd folded up to her elbows. The lines at the corner of her blue eyes deepened with her smile, and I could see her face was spotted with flour.

"Tessa!" said my aunt. Something orange flew from her wooden spoon and hit the wall as she jerked excitedly. "House told me you were here. Ooh, thank the cauldron you arrived safely."

"Hi, Ruth," I said. I wasn't being rude. None of my aunts wanted me to call them auntie. Said it made them feel old.

Her bare feet slapped the dark hardwood floor as she ran—yes ran—at me. More orange goo slopped on the walls and the floor as she wrapped her arms around me. I rested my chin on the top of her head as I hugged her back, taking in the floral smell of her shampoo.

Ruth let go of me and peered up at me, her blue eyes intense. "I know all about it. You don't have to talk about it now if you don't want to. But I'm here if you want."

"Talk about what?" I hadn't told my aunts about John's cheating ass, but I suspected that somehow they already knew.

She cocked an eyebrow. "We'll talk about it later."

"Okay."

"Leave that." Ruth flung the spoon again, sending what I realized now was pumpkin cookie batter all over the cream and blue Persian rug. "House will take your things to your room. Come to the kitchen," ordered my aunt as she skipped down the hallway and disappeared in the kitchen.

I felt another slip of energy in the air, and then my beat-up suitcase rose off the floor and hovered for a moment before floating up the staircase as though an invisible butler had taken it.

I knew Davenport House was magical, but I'd forgotten so much. I laughed. "Now I remember why this was my favorite place."

After I'd peeled off my shoes—because after having them on for so long, they were practically embedded in my skin—I followed my aunt down the long hallway toward the kitchen. I practically moaned as my bare feet contacted the cool hardwood floors.

To my left was the large parlor or living room with a massive fireplace that could cook an entire cow, if my aunts actually ate meat, which none of them did.

"Would you eat your pet dog Spot? Or Kitty the cat? No, of course not. Flesh is flesh. We don't eat flesh," my aunts had once told me. Followed by the remark, "If it has a soul… we don't eat it."

I stepped into a kitchen larger than the apartment I shared in New York City. The white shaker cabinets reached all the way to the ceiling above a large range that could hold a few cauldrons. The white subway tiles offset the ten-by-six wood island standing in the middle. Mouth-sized orange cookies speckled with chocolate chips covered most of the island counter. Pumpkin cookies.

I was going to get SO fat.

Ruth caught me staring, or rather salivating. "Go ahead. Take some. I made them for you."

She didn't have to tell me twice. I grabbed a cookie and took a bite. "Wow. Better than I remember."

Ruth beamed. "Can I get you something to drink?"

"Water?" I said between chews and swallowed. I looked at the cookies, remembering all the years I was careful not to surpass my daily caloric intake to stay slim for John.

John… John was gone. Yes, it rhymed. And yes, I grabbed another cookie and shoved the entire thing into my mouth.

"Here." Ruth gave me a glass of water and pulled out a chair for me. "Sit. You must be exhausted after your trip." She made her way to the counter and whipped the contents of a large ceramic bowl. "When I was your age, I traveled to Boston with Gerry. I thought I would pull out my hair. I've never liked long trips. Makes me anxious. Makes me want to pee every ten minutes."

I laughed as I took a sip of water and sat. "It wasn't that bad. The scenery was nice." I didn't want to have to tell my aunt I was too broke to afford a plane ticket. "Thanks for letting me stay here. I promise I'll make it up to you. As soon as I can afford my own place, I'll be moving out."

Ruth laughed. "Stay here? You're a Davenport witch. This is your home. Just like all Davenport witches. Here. Have another cookie." Ruth tossed me a cookie like she was playing softball.

I caught it, surprised at my own reflexes. "Thank you." Even if I was a Davenport witch, it didn't feel right to stay here without contributing in some way. "You know I won't stay if I don't help."

"I seem to remember that conversation on the phone," said my aunt.

"I have two websites to design and three more book covers. So, I can help with groceries and the utility bills—"

"Here they come!" shouted Ruth making me jerk, my heart pounding.

There was a sudden "ting" and the oven door burst open. A cookie platter shot out of the oven, hovered for a second, and landed on the kitchen island with a plop. Inches from my face.

I let out a breath. I'd forgotten how strange this place was.

"It's good that you're back, Tessa." Ruth's shoulders were stiff as she emptied the platter of cookies onto the island. When she spoke next her voice was low and serious. "Things are changing in Hollow Cove. Something's happening."

I swallowed the last of my cookie. "What's happening?"

The kitchen's back door flew open.

A tall woman, about five-ten, strolled into the kitchen. Her long gray hair was tied into a braid that reached the middle of her back. She wore a pantsuit, light gray that matched her gray hair. Her deep scowl disappeared at the sight of me.

"Tessa! You're here," she said as she came for me, her face bright with a genuine smile.

I slipped off my chair. "Hi, Dolores," I said and hugged my aunt.

"I know all about it," said Dolores as she let go of me, her cynical eyes grave. "You don't have to talk about it if you don't want."

I bit the inside of my cheek so I wouldn't laugh. "Thanks." I was right. They knew. Great.

"Dolores? Is it as bad as we thought?" asked Ruth, her toes wiggling as she shifted from foot to foot like she had to pee.

Dolores let out a long sigh. "Worse."

I looked from Ruth to Dolores. "What's happening?"

"You tell her." Ruth pointed her wooden spoon at her sister. "You're better at explaining than me."

Dolores put a hand on her hip while using the other one like a baton as she spoke. "We have to discuss your job."

I frowned. "You want to learn about graphic design?" My aunts weren't exactly computer savvy. But hey, if they wanted to learn, that was fine by me.

Dolores pointed a finger at me. "Your *other* job."

Uh-oh. My brows reached the bridge of my nose. "My *other* job? I don't have another job."

The tall witch looked down at me. "Of course you do. You're a Davenport witch. And as a Davenport witch, you have responsibilities. Obligations. To your family and to Hollow Cove, just like the witches before you."

Here it comes. "Such as?"

"Such as working for the Merlin Group."

"What?" I looked at Ruth and she clamped her mouth shut, her eyes wide and staring at her sister. I felt my blood pressure rise aided by my anger. "This is why you asked me to come. Isn't it?" Now it was all making sense why they'd been so thrilled when I told them I was broke and needed a place to crash.

Dolores frowned at me. "Now, you listen here, Tessa—"

"You wanted me to come here to join your demon-banishing group?" My voice was hard, and I immediately regretted it, but it was too late. Now, I felt like a giant asshole. My frustration wasn't geared toward my aunts. It was geared toward me. I was grateful they were letting me stay here, and this was not how I wanted to show them.

"Not just demons," interjected Ruth. "Hill giants, zombies, soul eaters, wraiths… every monster you can imagine. Well, just last week we banished a harpy that had eaten—"

"Ruth," growled Dolores, and Ruth clamped her mouth shut again.

Dolores fixed her eyes on me. "Your place is here with your family. Not with that cheater John in New York. But here. With us."

My mouth fell open as heat rushed to my face. "How did you know about that?"

Dolores's face softened. "You don't understand, Tessa. We need you—"

There was the sudden bang of the front door closing and then the sounds of voices conversing somewhere in the hallway.

"Beverly's here," said Ruth, looking slightly relieved.

I narrowed my eyes and crossed my arms over my chest. They were going to gang up on me. I knew it.

A beautiful woman sashayed into the kitchen, her blonde hair perfectly styled, straight and brushed against her shoulders as she neared. She had that Marilyn Monroe vibe with a snug white dress that accentuated all her curves, and she had plenty to go around. Her red shoes matched her red lips as she smiled.

Wrapped around her arm was a man in his sixties, handsome in the Marlon Brando type way and wearing an expensive suit. His face was blank, and so were his eyes. Weird. He looked… he looked *spelled*.

"Oh, hi, Tessa, darling," said Beverly, her green eyes glistening. "When did you get in?"

"Just now," I began, my eyes still on the man. Strands of drool ran from his mouth to the floor. Not good.

"Who's this?" asked Dolores. "Your date?"

"This here," said Beverly, as she patted his arm, "is Tom-the-cheater. Tom was caught cheating on his wife."

"With you, no doubt," laughed Dolores, making Ruth snort.

Beverly gave her sisters a murderous look. "Five other women, am I right, Tom?"

Tom nodded and said in a dreamy voice, "Yes. Yes, that's right."

"I told him I'd show him the house," informed Beverly. "Well then. Come on, darling."

Beverly yanked the man forward with one hand while she opened a single white door opposite the kitchen, which I remembered led to the basement. I also remembered that I wasn't allowed in there. Which only intensified my curiosity. The door opened with a squeak.

I leaned to see the inside, but Beverly was hiding it with her body. I knew she did that on purpose.

Beverly turned to Tom-the-cheater as she smiled brightly and said, "Bye, bye, darling."

And with that, she pushed the man through the threshold and slammed the door shut. There was a surprised yelp, followed by the sound of someone falling down the stairs.

The walls of the kitchen shook, and the floor trembled like an earthquake had hit us. The lights flickered on and off, and then a loud sound erupted from the basement, a rumbling that sounded a lot like a massive burp. And then the house settled.

"Uh. What the hell was that?" I was very aware that Tom-the-cheater might be dead of a broken neck.

Beverly beamed at me. "So, what did I miss?" She wiped her hands on her dress as though the mere touching of the man had soiled them.

"Tessa doesn't want to join the Merlin Group," said Ruth, looking worried.

"Hey, I never said that," I protested, seeing how quickly they changed the subject of poor Tom-the-cheater.

Dolores put both hands on her hips. "You never said yes either."

I clamped my jaw shut, feeling an ambush in the making.

Beverly raised her hands in the air and moved to the fridge. "What does it matter? She has no choice." She pulled out a bottle of white wine and poured herself a generous helping.

"I do have a choice," I said, not appreciating being discussed as though I wasn't there. "Even if I said yes," I began, "I haven't prac- ticed in years. I don't remember it. I don't even think I *can* do magic. I'm all magicked out. I'm completely drained."

"That's what Ed said to me last night after our date," said Beverly with a sexy smile.

Dolores's face took on a softer edge. "You *can* do magic. It's not something that leaves you because you haven't practiced in a while. It's *in* you. It's in your blood."

"You're born a witch, Tessa. Like us," said Ruth, smiling. The age lines in her face made her look even more comforting and kind.

"And," continued Dolores, "unlike your mother, who showed no real magical skill, you have a *great* gift. A powerful one. We've all seen how you can manipulate the energies, how the power of the elements responds to you."

"You have?" *Because I surely hadn't.*

"We did." Beverly came around and set her glass of wine on the kitchen island. "You've got it, darling."

"With some practice, it'll all come back to you," encouraged Ruth. "You'll see."

I let myself fall back in my chair. "What did I get myself into?"

"Tessa, listen to me," said Dolores, all business again. "The Merlin Group needs new members. After your mother left—"

"Abandoned," snapped Beverly, her cheeks flushed and looking angry for the first time. "Say it like it is, Dolores. Don't sugarcoat it for her."

"She was never that invested." Ruth took a cookie off the counter and took a bite. "It's not her fault. It was never her calling."

25

"No, but running around the country with a musician who can't even afford to feed his family is?" snapped Beverly.

"She did what she could," said Ruth her eyes sad. "She never had the gift."

Dolores rubbed her temples. "Look, Tessa." She squared her shoulders and came closer. "We're the only ones left. And in case you haven't noticed, it's not like we're getting any younger."

"Speak for yourself," said Beverly as she traced a hand down from her breasts to her hips. "Tom-the-cheater said I didn't look a day over thirty-nine."

Ruth spit out her cookie and put her hand to her mouth.

"Thirty-nine?" laughed Dolores. "I think you're confused with the number of men you've been with this week."

My lips parted as I stared at Beverly. I thought she'd be angry, but she just smiled wickedly and took another sip of her wine, as though her sister had just complimented her.

My eyes fell on Ruth. "You said something was happening here. What kind of something?" Judging by the sudden tension and the anxious looks from the three witches, it was bad.

Ruth looked at her sisters before answering me. "It's big," she told me, her eyes round. "And bad."

"Your vocabulary astonishes me, Einstein," commented Dolores.

I darted a nervous glance around the sisters. "So, it's evil, I take it. Something evil is here?"

"There's more to it than that." Dolores took a calming breath. "The Merlin Group's mandate is to protect our community, to protect Hollow Cove. As White witches, we have the means and the power to do so." Her dark eyes searched my face. "We need your help, Tessa. I wouldn't ask if it weren't important."

"More like *desperate*." Beverly picked a chocolate chip from a cookie and popped it into her mouth.

I looked at my aunts, seeing some of my mother in each of them. She had Dolores's dark eyes, Beverly's body, and Ruth's naïveté. My mother had let me down more often than I cared to remember. But I wasn't my mother. And I wouldn't abandon them, like she did all of us.

I could tell this was important to them. "Fine, I'll join your group," I said before I changed my mind. Might as well agree to it, seeing as it was the least I could do since they were letting me stay here without paying rent.

"Good," said Dolores, nodding her head. "That's fantastic, Tessa."

I shrugged. "Happy to help. But I'll need a refresher course in White Magic 101. You know what I'm saying?" I laughed. "I'm a little rusty with all things magical. Maybe we can start tomorrow."

"There's no time for that." Dolores had that severe cast again.

I shifted in my seat, not liking the sound of that. "And why's that?"

Dolores looked at me and said, "Because we've got a case for you *tonight*."

CHAPTER

3

When your family asks you to do something for them, make sure you read the fine print before you agree to it.

I was not expecting to be working a case for the Merlin Group the moment I got off the bus and was supposed to be relaxing and trying to piece my life back together.

Worse, I was especially *not* expecting to be staring at a dead body.

Even worse than that, you couldn't really call it a body. There wasn't much of it to call it anything. It was more of a slop, a bloody mess of innards and bones of what used to be someone.

Bright yellow light spilling from a hovering globe illuminated the scene with all its gruesome details. My Aunt Dolores had supplied the witch orb, making me jealous. It just hovered there like a miniature floating sun. I wanted one of those.

Ruth's cookies were doing a fine job of wanting to rise from my gut and spew out all over the crime scene. That wouldn't exactly be the best first impression on my very first case.

I gritted my teeth, reeling in my nausea. I was a Davenport witch, damn it, and we didn't puke in front of the town at the sight of an unholy mess on the ground—not unless we really had no choice.

And yes, I do mean *all* the town's people. I could make out at least twenty curious onlookers. Some I recognized, like Martha, and some were just faces in a crowd. A little girl of maybe eight or nine years old stood next to Martha, her long blonde hair pulled back in a ponytail. I thought it strange that the girl's parents would let her witness something like that. But then again, this was Hollow Cove. Anything went.

A guy about my age with a mess of brown hair that was sticking up on all angles like he'd just stepped out of bed appeared next to me. He smelled of beer with a touch of sulfur.

He whistled and said, "Gives a whole new meaning to the words Sloppy Joe. Doesn't it?"

He laughed, hands in his jean pockets. His skin was as pale as a white sheet under his black leather jacket, but his features were flawless, sculpted, and handsome. It was very distant, but the smell of sulfur hung around him.

He was a vampire.

He caught me staring at him. "You're Tess, right? The new blood in town?"

The way he said blood made me shiver. I wasn't sure I liked him. "Tessa." Right now, I wasn't here to make friends. He better not get in my way.

"I'm Ronin." He raised his hand but lowered it at the scowl on Dolores's face. He also lost his smile.

I sighed through my nose, feeling the earth thrum through the soles of my boots. The air was packed with thick energy that made all the hairs on my body rise, like static electricity. The only other place I'd felt a surge of power like that was at Davenport House.

"Do we know who this is?" I turned and looked over my aunts' faces, standing over what was left of the body. Yes, I know, identifying the bloody mess was a stretch, but someone here had to know who this person was—that's if this individual was from Hollow Cove and not some poor, straying human.

"We don't know yet," said Beverly, her face grim as she kept rubbing her arms like she was cold. "They didn't have any ID on them. Right, Dolores?"

Dolores pressed her thin lips together. "Not that we found, no. This could be anyone. Ronin. Stop that."

Ronin pulled back his finger that was an inch from touching a puddle of blood. "What?" He shrugged as he stood up, smiling. "It was calling to me."

I frowned. Damn vampire.

"Could be a human who wandered in here," said Ruth, as though reading my thoughts. "It wouldn't be the first time a human got lost, took the wrong turn on Ocean Side, and ended up here."

"But it doesn't explain why they were killed this way," said Dolores, her voice tense.

"A demon did this." Martha came forward and took a drag of her cigarette. She caught me staring and added, "I smoke when I'm nervous." Her eyes moved to the body and then back at my aunts. "Look at this. It's like acid was poured on the body. Like in that Alien movie."

"This wasn't an alien, Martha," said Dolores, sounding a little annoyed.

"More like the poor bastard ingested a bomb," said Ronin.

Martha took another long drag of her cigarette. "This is the work of a demon. I know it. I can feel it in my bones."

"A demon?" said a voice. I turned around to see a short, pudgy man with gray hair, a bow tie, and large brown eyes marching his way toward us. I recognized him as the same man I'd seen Martha talking with earlier. "We have a demon loose in our town!" he shrilled. "What are we going to do? Your wards are supposed to protect us. It's why the town pays the Merlin Group." He pointed a chubby finger at her. "For. Protection. Protect us!"

"Calm down, Gilbert," said Dolores, a tired look on her face. "We don't know if the attacker was a demon."

Gilbert threw up his hands, his face darkening. "No? Just look at this! Look what they did. What else could do this?"

I could think of a few half-breeds. A deranged werewolf, a rogue vampire, a grumpy troll, even a Dark fae could have easily killed this person and made it look like a demon did it.

Half-breeds were a race of mortal creatures that had once been human and had been subjected to one of the demon viruses, which then turned them into the different demon races—vampires, werewolves, faeries, leprechauns, witches, shifters, and trolls, to name a few. Half-breeds had demon blood running through their veins, which gave them supernatural abilities and made them stronger and deadlier than humans.

As a White witch, I knew my ancestors had also been subjected to demonic blood. But unlike our cousins, the Dark witches, who borrowed their magic from demons, we used a more natural approach. We drew our power from ley lines—a series of networks through which magic energy flows throughout the world—and the four elements—earth, air, water, and fire.

The only thing that separated White or Dark witches was how they used their magic.

Still, I kept my mouth shut. Not because I feared the townspeople would think I was nuts, but because I knew everyone in Hollow Cove was a half-breed.

"We're all in danger!" cried Gilbert, making other townspeople clutch one another in fear. "It's still out there. Don't you get it! It's hunting us. They can kill us in our sleep! In our beds—"

Dolores slapped Gilbert across the face, and I jerked back as though she'd hit me. "Calm down, Gilbert," she said, her voice surprisingly calm. "Your hysterics aren't helping. You're scaring everyone. Control yourself."

The tiny man's face went bright red. He opened his mouth to object. Then with a pop, he collapsed into a large barn owl and flew away, leaving a few tawny feathers floating to the ground behind him.

If I weren't a witch, I would have probably fainted. Seeing as I was, I was fascinated and a little envious. I'd seen my share of shifters growing up, so no surprise there. Witches could also change their bodies with a transfiguring spell, but that took hours to prepare and it was equally dangerous. If you didn't get it right, you might end up with half your body transformed and the rest of you… not. Yeah, not a good look.

Okay. Gilbert was a shifter. Interesting. Judging by his reaction, I doubted he was capable of this gruesome murder. I moved my gaze to the cluster of townspeople. Martha was on her second cigarette, blowing the smoke into a poor woman's face who looked green and about to puke. Next to them was a young couple, werewolves, by the smell of wet dog that drifted from them. Then, the rest all got jumbled together with different animal scents. I couldn't differentiate the weres from the shifters or even the witches. It was like stepping into a zoo.

The one thing they had in common was they all twitched with that same nervous energy. They were scared.

"Finally, someone with enough balls to shut the old man up," said Ronin, staring at my aunt Dolores like she was his new best friend.

"He won't forget that." Beverly gave her sister a raised brow.

Ruth made a pout. "He probably won't let me buy the devil's claw I've been waiting for. His store is the only one that carries it in Maine."

Dolores raised her chin. "I'm not sorry I did it. But if he's right… it means…" Fear shifted on her features as she flicked her gaze over the crowd at something in the distance.

"What?" I looked over the crowd for something out of place but saw only the shadow of buildings.

The three sisters exchanged an uneasy sidelong glance between them. It had lasted only a few seconds, but I'd caught it. Something was definitely wrong, and they weren't sharing.

"Tessa, you stay here and keep an eye on things," ordered Dolores, her expression hard and all business again. "There's something we have to do. Ladies?"

The three of them picked themselves up and walked away from the crime scene.

"Hey? Wait a minute." I ran after them, my heart throbbing in my chest. "Where are you going? You can't just leave me here… with *them*," I added in a whisper, though I was sure most of them could hear our conversation.

"You're a Merlin now, Tessa," said Dolores. "It's your job to protect the town, just like us. Whatever did this might still be out there."

I searched my aunts' faces. My gut instinct told me they were hiding something, and I would find out what that was.

I clenched my hands into fists. I wasn't about to run away scared, especially not with an audience. I'd given them my word. I would see it through.

"Fine," I said, hardening my resolve. "What do you want me to do?"

There was the slightest hesitation before Dolores said, "Find out who that person was and whether they were part of this town. It's important."

I nodded. "Okay. I can do that. And you? You're off to do some serious magic. Aren't you?"

Beverly gave me a small smile. "Something like that."

"It'll take us till morning," said Ruth as she waved. "Don't wait up."

I watched as my aunts left together, mumbling to each other and leaving me alone with the slop of the dead and a bunch of strangers. That meant either they trusted I could find helpful information, or they wanted me out of the way while they did real magic.

I needed to up my game if I wanted to stay in Hollow Cove and become a real Merlin like my aunts. I'd barely been here two hours and there was already a murder.

I had a feeling my life was about to get seriously complicated.

CHAPTER

4

Someone cleared their throat behind me. "Bummer. I think they just ditched you."

I turned around to find Ronin standing way too close, so close I could see the witch orb's light reflecting in his eyes, which were brown with golden specks, and smell the musky scent of cologne on him.

I glared at him. "You don't know anything."

"I know what my eyes see," answered the vampire, smiling. "And that, right there, is them ditching you."

What the hell was his problem? "What do you want?"

He perked up. "I can help."

"Thanks, but I've got this." I stepped around him and made my way back to the remnants of the dead. The crowd of onlookers were watching me, their eyes expectant like they thought I'd figure out who this person was and who had killed them just by standing here. I was not thrilled my aunts had left me alone with all these strangers.

Still, I had to show them I could do this. I *would* find out who had become a splatter of tomato soup, and I wouldn't stop until I figured it out.

I stared at the red mess, racking my brain for anything I could remember reading about demons and other supernatural creatures that would leave a body in that state. Maybe I'd Google it when I got home. You'd be surprised what you could find on the web.

Ronin moved to stand next to me. "Aren't you just a *little* glad this isn't you?"

I let out a sigh. "Isn't there a pint of blood with your name on it waiting for you somewhere?" I offered, wishing he would just go away.

"I don't drink blood."

I cocked a brow at him. "A vampire who doesn't drink blood? Now, that's a first."

"Half-vampire," corrected Ronin, his eyes on the bloody mess on the ground. "Mom's a human, dad's a vamp."

I stared at him for a moment longer. Half-vampires weren't a new thing, but they were rare since most of the babies died of complications shortly after birth. But for the few who survived, other vampire clans would destroy the child if they learned of it, all of which made Ronin special and interesting.

Seeing as he wasn't going away, I knelt for a better look and grimaced as the powerful smell of bile rose to my nose. "Smells like it was regurgitated."

"Like whatever ate him or her vomited it back out?" asked Ronin. "Nice."

"Can't be sure. But it smells like it." And I was also betting that whatever creature, monster, or demon did this, was big.

"You're going to need a huge straw to suck it all up," said Ronin as he knelt next to me, smiling like he was imagining me doing just that.

Right. Did my aunts expect me to clean this up? And then what? What did they expect me to do with the remains? I started to sweat, feeling like an idiot. Did I bag it? No, that didn't seem right. And you could just forget the straw. Yup. I thought I was about to throw up.

"Okay. Everyone, get back. Back, I said," ordered a voice.

I looked over my shoulder. A broad-shouldered man with tousled black hair weaved his way through the crowd, and I found I couldn't stop staring. There was a lot to see—a lot of him to admire. He walked with a confident strut and a predatory gait. His T-shirt did nothing to conceal his flat stomach and his powerful thighs were clearly evident under those snug jeans.

With a square jaw and perfectly straight nose, he looked about thirty-five, maybe younger, and familiar somehow. Maybe I'd seen him once when I was here before. Funny how I couldn't remember someone so very, very pretty. I had to tell my jaw to close because I didn't want anyone to see the new girl with her mouth hanging down, staring at this sexy-as-hell man. Because that would be creepy. He probably had a giant ego to match those bulging bicep muscles. I knew guys like him. They dated models or women who groomed themselves just as much as they did and cared more about what they looked like than anything else. Just like my ex.

Yeah, I didn't need that in my life right now.

Two burly men, both built like they spent most of their free time at the gym, moved behind him. One was fair, the other dark, and both had that predatory manner just like the first one.

I pulled my eyes away but not before I noticed how everyone was giving the man a wide berth. "Who's that?" I asked Ronin, seeing as he was still next to me, still a little too close.

"That's Marcus. He's the town's chief," said Ronin after a moment.

I raised my brows. "Like chief of police?"

Ronin nodded. "Yeah. He's kind of the boss here."

My gaze went back to the handsome chief. He was definitely not human. Vampire maybe? A shifter? He was way too hot to be a witch, but I could be wrong. He could be a witch-hotness-anomaly. "He's not wearing his uniform," I said and only then realized how loud my voice was.

Marcus's head snapped my way. Gray eyes framed with dark eyelashes focused on me.

Oh. Crap.

Marcus stepped around the bloody mess on the ground and walked toward me. "Who are you?"

"Tessa," I answered, not sure I liked his tone.

"Do you have a last name, Tessa?" he ordered, again with the tone, and stared at me with eyes that were hard and unyielding like stone.

Yup. I liked him as much as I liked ticks.

"How's it going, Chief?" said Ronin, and I knew he was just trying to smooth the mood a little. Didn't seem to work.

"Last name," Marcus commanded again, like I was his servant.

43

If he thought he could scare me with his hard stare, he was in for a surprise.

I shrugged, keeping my eyes on the chief. "How about you give me yours, and I'll give you mine," I answered, making Ronin snort. The half-vampire was growing on me.

Marcus's eyes narrowed, and he closed the distance between us until I had to look up at him.

"You're tall," I observed, and Ronin snorted again.

The chief's face hardened. "I make it my business to know everyone in my town. I want to know who you are and why you're here."

Jeez. Why are the pretty ones always so nasty? "*Your* town? I thought this was Hollow Cove, not Marcus Cove." *Oopsy*.

"I like her," expressed Ronin, all smiles. "She's entertaining. Let's keep her."

Marcus let out a breath. "Last name. Or I'll have you arrested."

My mouth fell. "For what? Breathing?" The nerve of this guy. If I knew how to spell him, I'd choose a deflatable spell, to deflate all those muscles and his ego, and give him a lanky twelve-year-old boy body. Yeah. The thought made me smile.

The big man pointed to the blood and guts. "Maybe this is your handiwork. I don't know. I don't know you."

I balled my hands into fists. "It's not. I'm here to help. To figure out what happened and to protect the town." Yes, I was new and had no idea what I was doing or how I would protect the town. But so what? This guy was really pissing me off.

Marcus kept staring at me and then his eyes widened, something flickering behind them. "You're Tessa Davenport." It wasn't a question.

I put my hands on my hips. "Yeah. So?"

Marcus's jaw clenched. "You should leave. I don't want you here."

A slip of anger lit through me. He was just asking for me to punch him across the face. "Is it against the 'law,'" I made quotes with my fingers, "that I'm standing here?"

Marcus blinked. "No."

"Then I'm staying, *Chief*." I heard Ronin laugh as I turned away from Marcus and made my way around the dead body, looking for clues. That's what I guessed I should be doing, though I had no freaking clue how to find clues—pun intended. And yes, I knew that sounded bad.

I caught Martha's eye, and the witch gave me a thumbs up. I was not going there.

Kneeling as close as I would let myself get to the slop of remains, I could feel Marcus's gaze on me, but I wouldn't give him the satisfaction of a look in his direction. I wasn't here for him.

I was here for my aunts. I told them I would help them with this case, and that's exactly what I was going to do. He would not scare me away.

"Marcus doesn't like me either." Ronin was next to me, staring down at the blood. "He's jealous because I've got better hair. Are those fingers?" He pointed to three small cylindrical shapes resting in the pool of blood and guts.

"Those are definitely fingers." I stared at what I thought was some flesh with hair. The scalp maybe? Yikes. *Don't throw up.* "He doesn't scare me." I didn't want Marcus to see how this scene was affecting me because it was.

Ronin flashed me his perfect white teeth. "So, what are we looking for?"

I couldn't help but notice he used the word "we," like we were a team or something. "Anything that'll tell me who this person was." My aunts never mentioned that I couldn't ask for help, and right now, I needed it. "If I knew, I would be a little closer to finding who did this and why."

"His name was Avi," came Marcus's loud voice. The bastard had been listening in on us.

I looked across from me to the handsome but seriously irritating chief. "And you got all this just by looking at this splatter of blood and guts?"

Marcus's gaze was locked on the blood. "Werewolves have a distinctive smell. Just like each person here does."

I was impressed, but I kept my face blank. He had to be a werewolf or a shifter to have that kind of keen sense of smell. The guy was good. I pegged him for a werewolf, which meant his buddies were probably werewolves too.

"You sure?" I asked. The chief didn't answer, and I took that as a yes. It also saved me the time and effort of going around door to door to see who was missing in town. Too bad he was being such a dick. He could've been useful for other information as well.

A name was better than I'd hoped. I stood up. "Thanks."

Marcus issued a sound like a growl. "You should leave."

My temper went into overdrive. "What is your problem?" My voice rose, aware that everyone had gone quiet around us. Ronin took a step back from me. Smart vampire.

Marcus smiled coldly. "You. You're my problem."

"Really?" I cocked my hips, my face all smiles, but my guts were having a wrestling competition. "Why's that, hot-stuff?"

Just like my ex, he knew all the right buttons to push. But he didn't even know me, so that made it worse. So much worse.

Marcus crossed his arms over his sizable chest, no doubt to show off all those hard, bulging muscles. "You have no investigative skills. Clearly, you don't understand what you're doing. You're not even a real witch," he snarled, his brows furrowed.

"Dude. You're *way* out of line," said Ronin, and I was surprised by the anger in his voice.

Marcus ignored him, his attention never wavering from me. "You're just going to get in the way. There's nothing you can do to help this town. Just like your mother."

My lips parted, and I frowned, my heart thrashing. "You know my mother?" When he didn't answer, I continued, "I don't work for you, Chief. I work for the Merlin Group."

Marcus laughed. "Just like your mother did until she left—in the middle of a case. More trouble than she was worth." He gave me a hard stare. "Your mother is a waste of space."

Something inside me snapped.

A rush of energy overflowed my aura. My breath caught, a force hammering inside me as I homed in on Marcus.

I didn't speak a word of magic. I didn't even conjure a spell.

I just… let go.

My instincts hit, and I raised my hands. A gust of wind flung through my palms. It hit Marcus in the chest and the big guy went rocketing back like he was hit by a missile. He let out a windy grunt as he hit the hard pavement fifty feet away.

I wavered a little as a slip of dizziness hit. I knew this was payment for using magic. All magic required it. No witch could do spells indefinitely. That would most certainly be deadly. Magic always took what was owed—a piece of the witch, a bit of aura—and made it its own, aiding in the spell.

But I barely felt it over the pumping energy of my anger.

"Screw you, Marcus."

I turned on my heel, grabbed the still-hovering orb, and left.

And that, ladies and gentlemen, is an exit.

CHAPTER

5

I'd waited until six in the morning for my aunts to show up. I wasn't even tired. I was so damn mad at Marcus, I thought I might spontaneously combust into a ball of witch fire.

And let's not talk about what *I'd* done. In front of *all* those people, no less. I was sure assaulting the chief was something that would definitely land me a trip to the town's jail.

I waited. But he never came. Neither did his buddies.

Damn. I was deep in the crapper. Neck-deep. Hell, make that fully submerged in the crapper. I was swimming in it.

But... wait for it... I'd done magic! Yay, me.

Take that, Chief Marcus.

I remembered casting spells as a kid and experimenting with enchantments, my aunts' pendants, lighting candles with just a word, stuff like that. Usually in secret, since my mother was against my using magic. She said I was better off not practicing it because magic only led to bigger problems.

But tonight had been different.

I'd never just thought about pushing someone away with my mind—and had it actually work. I was betting it had something to do with me being in *this* town.

Hollow Cove had some serious magic mojo.

"The whole town is talking about it," said Ruth as she put the kettle on. Sunlight filtered through the kitchen windows. The lines around her eyes and mouth had deepened since the last time I'd seen her, and strands of her white hair fell around her face. She looked tired, worn out. They all did. "You're even more popular than the summer solstice parade." She beamed.

Dolores sighed across from me at the kitchen table. "It poses a serious problem for us."

"To me," I said. "Not to you."

"You're part of this family," said Dolores. "What happens to you affects us."

"It shouldn't. You didn't do anything. I did." Now I felt like an idiot. I didn't want my aunts to suffer because I'd lost my temper. "I just… lost it, after what he said."

51

My little incident with Marcus was the first thing that came out of my mouth the moment they'd arrived back at the house. They'd all listened attentively, barely blinking as I recalled my superpower experience. I'd expected them to react, but they didn't.

Beverly carefully tucked a strand of her blonde hair behind her ear. "Marcus got what he deserved. The Durands have always been way too opinionated for their own good. Proud, pompous know-it-alls." She gave me a wink. "I'm just sorry I missed it."

I shrugged. "With my luck, it'll probably pop up on social media later today."

"Well," said Beverly, "don't blame yourself, darling. He shouldn't have said what he did about your mom. That was wrong."

"Very wrong." Ruth's eyebrows knitted together. "I know a few impotence spells that can last up to three months." She smiled wickedly. "I can curse him with some embarrassing STDs too, if you want. Say the word, Tessa, and it'll be done."

I laughed at the mischievous gleam in her eye. It was a good look for her. "It's fine, really. But thanks. I'll keep those in mind if ever I need them."

I swallowed hard. What Marcus had said about my mother hurt, not because it was false, but because most of what he said rang true.

Dolores hit the table with her palm, making me jerk. "What's done is done. No use in discussing it anymore. It's in the past. We all need to move on from this."

"You're absolutely right, Dolores," agreed Beverly. "Stress gives you premature wrinkles. You don't want those. They're a real pain to glamour off your face."

Dolores gave her sister a hard stare and then turned her gaze on me. "You did good, Tessa."

"How's that?"

"You got us a name," answered my aunt. "Now we don't have to fuss around town to get answers. You saved us a lot of work."

I didn't mention that they could have just asked Marcus too. Or maybe they preferred not to get him involved. There was some history there. "Did you know him? Avi?"

"We know his parents." Beverly grabbed a chair and let herself fall. "A delightful werewolf couple. Accountants. They're going to be devastated by the news. He was their only son."

"He was about your age," said Ruth as she sprinkled herbs in a steaming mug. "So sad what happened to him."

Sad? The dude was a slop of chunky tomato soup. "But *why* did it happen? Why him? Who would do this?"

Dolores rubbed her eyes, looking worn out. "Demons. We felt a lot of their residual demonic magic all over town."

I sat straighter in my chair. "Demons? I thought they couldn't enter the town? Because of the wards?"

"Usually, they can't," said Beverly as she picked at her perfectly manicured red nails. "But someone tampered with the wards that protect the town."

Dolores drummed her fingers on the table. "We think Avi was just… in the wrong place at the wrong time. A victim of circumstance."

Poor bastard. A pounding headache started behind my eyes, no doubt from the lack of sleep. "So, the wards are back up?" I now understood where my aunts had gone last night.

"Everything's fine," answered Dolores, and I couldn't help but notice how she didn't really answer. She gave me a brief smile. I could see the strain in her eyes and hear the tiredness in her voice. They tried not to show it, but they were exhausted. Putting the protection wards back up had cost them a lot.

They needed help. They needed me.

I cast my gaze around them. "Does this have to do with that 'evil' you said was here?" I asked the question though I knew the answer already.

The three sisters looked at each other, a silent communication passing between them that only decades of spending a life together could create. Dolores spoke next. "Yes."

"And it's happened before?"

"Yes."

"Are you going to tell me, or do I have to beat it out of you like I did Chief Marcus?"

The sisters laughed.

Then silence stewed again for a few moments. "Did your mother ever tell you the history of Hollow Cove?"

"A little," I breathed. "I know it's a paranormal community. It's where we can live in peace without having knucklehead humans come at us with flaming torches."

Dolores was nodding. "Yes. Yes, that's all true. But you see, Tessa. Hollow Cove is a special place. The town is—"

"Wired," giggled Ruth.

"Wired?" I asked.

"Powerful," said Dolores. "Magic everywhere. In the earth. In the air. The trees. Even the buildings."

Like Davenport House. "I know there's magic. I felt it tonight. I felt it the moment I stepped on Hollow Cove Bridge." The same I'd felt since I was a kid.

Dolores's voice took on a serious tone. "Which makes Hollow Cove magically potent, powerful... and very attractive to... *others*."

I tensed, and a chill ran through me. "Others? What others?" I didn't like the sound of that. "Do you mean demons?" I knew demons couldn't live on our side of the planes, not indefinitely. Not unless they figured out a way. I seriously hoped they hadn't.

Dolores shook her head, her frown lines deepening. "We're not sure." She took a moment, her bent fingers scratching at something on the table's surface. "Hollow Cove has always been a center of attraction for those who seek power. But the town always managed to drive those away who would hurt the town or its people, forming alliances with other supernatural communities and hiring witches to maintain the wards that protect us."

"Like the Merlin Group," I said, wondering how old this magical police unit was. Perhaps it was as old as the town.

"Exactly," answered Dolores. "But then for the past three years… strange things have been happening."

"Like demons killing and regurgitating half-breeds?" I said.

"Like that," said Dolores. "The wards that protect the town are being tampered with, and demons are slipping through. They're attracted by the source of power and magic in Hollow Cove like a hunger."

"Like a vampire is drawn to blood," said Ruth.

Not Ronin, I thought, but I kept that to myself. "So, what do you want me to do?"

"After you get some rest," said Dolores, "you will study wards, spells, hexes, and curses until you're blue in the face. Until you can set up your own wards to protect our town and yourself."

I blinked. "Me?"

Dolores was nodding. "Demons will sense your magic. You're a threat to them. They'll want to kill you."

"Awesome." I slumped in my chair, feeling exhausted without having done anything.

Beverly reached over and tapped my hand. "Don't worry, darling. I've had many who wanted to kill me over the years. But I'm still here. See?"

"The wives don't count, Beverly," commented Ruth, an eyebrow raised, and her lips curled at the corners.

Beverly beamed. "Of course, they count. A death threat is a death threat, no matter if it has breasts or not. It's not my fault I'm so *irresistible* to the opposite sex," added Beverly, flashing a dazzling smile. "I'm gorgeous. Who wouldn't want me? I would want me." She giggled.

I laughed, feeling some of my tension ease. At that moment, I realized how much I missed them and missed being here with the family I knew loved me.

"You need to rest. We have lots to cover." Dolores stood up, swayed a little, and held on to the backrest of the chair for support. "There's no better way to learn a craft than practice. You need to be ready, Tessa, because the threat is closer than we thought."

"It's right at our front door," said Ruth, her usual happy face wrinkled in concern.

I pushed back my chair and stood up. "I'm so wired. I'm not sure I can sleep."

"Here." Ruth gave me the steaming mug she'd been holding this whole time.

I stared at it suspiciously, especially at the orange flakes floating on the top. "What is it?"

"Drink it up," encouraged Ruth. "It will help you sleep." When I didn't, she added. "It's not *poison*." She bent over laughing, which was a tad creepy. "But it will taste like it."

Excellent. I tipped the mug to my lips and chugged the entire thing in two gulps. Better that way since I tasted it less. I swallowed and grimaced at the bitter taste that lingered on my tongue, but I'd tasted worse.

"Off to bed now." Ruth took the mug and pushed me out of the kitchen.

I don't even remember how I made it up the stairs, or why my feet never made contact with the steps. It was like I was floating. Either that, or Ruth had drugged me.

The drapes were drawn, giving the room a dark cast—perfect for sleeping. I hadn't had time to inspect my new room, which had been my mother's back in the day. There'd be time for that later.

I climbed over the four-poster bed fully clothed. As soon as my head hit the pillow, sleep took me.

CHAPTER

6

The next morning, or rather six hours later and midafternoon, I spent a few hours finishing up two book covers for two different clients—one a High Fantasy, the other a Clean Romance. Both were beautiful in their own way, and I was very proud of them.

Completing the final touches took longer than usual. That damned Marcus and his hot self kept interrupting my thoughts. He was crazy beautiful, but that's not what kept me from focusing on my work. I wouldn't let myself get sidetracked by another man, not after what my ex did. I was done with that. However, Marcus's open rage, his outright hostility and hatred for me, kept swirling through my thoughts.

I was pissed that the guy hated me because of who I was. Because of my mother.

What the hell had happened? What did my mother do to this guy to make him hate me when he didn't even know me?

His hatred for me had radiated from him in nearly palpable waves. I saw it. The whole damn town saw it. I wasn't embarrassed by it. I was way past that. I was just... angry. Furious at being treated this way. It wasn't fair. Maybe I was being stupid, but I believed in treating others with respect—until they pissed me off and then they were fair game.

Marcus had done just that and then some.

And then I'd upped and spelled his ass. I doubted I could conjure that kind of badass magic again. It had just happened. Driven by emotions, rage mostly. But it was something. I'd done magic. And it filled me with a new confidence.

"Thank you, Chief," I muttered. "You've been useful after all."

I sat at a dark mahogany makeup vanity, before an enormous window overlooking the ocean. It was equipped with a small mirror and chair and used to belong to my mother. I was now using it as my workstation. I'd dumped all the old perfume bottles, hairbrushes, eyeshadow palettes, lipsticks, and everything else that was on it into the top drawer. Makeup wasn't really my thing. A bit of eyeshadow, liner, and some mascara and I was out the door, sometimes forgetting to brush my hair.

These days, I honestly couldn't care less what I looked like. I'd draped a pillowcase over the mirror so I wouldn't have to watch myself work because that would be weird.

Dolores had come in a few hours ago and dumped eight large, leather-bound books on the floor next to me.

"Learn these," she'd instructed and had left the room like some obnoxious governess. She was more of a sergeant major, that one. I loved it.

With the two book covers finished, I sent my PayPal invoices and grabbed the first book. *White Magic and the Four Elements.* My pulse leaped with excitement as I began reading. It didn't take long to make connections, magical ones, as my memories came flooding in. The more I read, the more my mind opened as words and symbols started to make sense. In the next few hours, I'd finished *A Guide to Ley Lines; Wards for the Modern Witch; Spells, Hexes & Potions Encyclopedia* and *Know Your Monsters: Netherworld Demons Volume 12*.

But when my fingers found *Secrets of the Dark witch and Her Magic,* I was seriously in-trigued. More so that my aunt had left it for me.

"Look at you, my pretty," I said, and I felt my mouth stretching into a wide, half-crazy grin. I wasn't a Dark witch, but the more I knew about magic, the better prepared I'd be to face whatever this new evil was. Perhaps I could borrow a few tricks from my darker cousins.

I moved to my bed, stretched out on my stomach, and began to read.

The sound of the doorbell broke through my concentration. I looked up, noticing how dim the light in the room was and how I couldn't see the sun through my window anymore. Time flies when you're reading a good book.

The clock on my phone said it was half-past seven. "That explains why I'm so hungry." I closed my book and swung my legs off the bed. My stomach let out a growl that sounded like I had a baby tiger living in there. I was ravenous.

The smell of cooking had my mouth watering.

I moved to the double white dresser with a matching wood mirror. A single picture frame sat on it—a picture of my mother holding me in her arms when I was about four. It wasn't there yesterday. I knew my aunts did that on purpose.

I hadn't moved to the dresser to look at myself, well, maybe a little, but for something else. Something I remembered my mother doing when I was a kid. I decided to give it a try. Why the hell not?

I cleared my throat, feeling a little silly, and said, "House. What's for dinner?"

The mirror on the dresser shimmered and a plate of spinach and mushroom lasagna covered in a thick layer of cheese hovered where my reflection had been a moment ago.

I beamed. "Now, *that* I could get used to. Thanks, House." The mirror shimmered again, and my reflection stared back at me.

"Yikes. I look like a crack-whore." My hair was sticking out at the back in a big hair knot, I had dark bags under my eyes that I hadn't noticed before, and my cheeks were sunken, making me look like I'd aged ten years. That's what the stress of a bad and toxic relationship would do.

After a quick shower—apparently, every bedroom in this place had its own bathroom—I ventured downstairs. I followed the smell of that juicy lasagna with my damp hair bouncing past my shoulders.

The sound of voices wafted over to me and one sounded male. It sounded like Ronin. What was he doing here? I reached the end of the hallway and walked into the kitchen.

"That lasagna smells amazing—"

Dolores was leaning on the counter, her back to the sink.

And next to her stood Marcus.

It was like someone pressed my instant anger button, slammed it really. "What the hell is *he* doing here?" My voice rose to match my anger as the instant replay of what had happened last night flashed in my mind's eye.

My mother would never win any "Mother of the Year" awards, but she was still my mother. If anyone got to insult her, that would be me. Not him.

His gray eyes fastened on me, his jaw clenching. A black leather jacket hung over his wide shoulders that drew my eye down to his narrow waist. His blue jeans fit his long thighs perfectly, and the T-shirt did nothing to hide his muscled chest. If he thought he could hypnotize me with his perfectly defined body and his killer looks, he was a moron. I did not forget nor forgive easily.

If I'd known any cool martial arts moves, I would have ninja-flown across the kitchen and jump-kicked him in the throat. Seeing as I didn't, I resolved to give him my killer stare. Yeah, that ought to do it.

Dolores pushed off the counter. "Just… take it easy, Tessa. No need to destroy the kitchen."

Destroy the kitchen? Dolores was staring at me like I was a bomb about to blow. Her eyes moved to my hands.

I looked down at my hands and saw they were shaking. I hadn't even realized I'd balled them into fists. A thrum of magic pounded through me, energy pooling in my center as a quick influx of magic shifted. A ley line. I could feel the power of the ley line, but I had no idea how to tap into it. Which was good for Marcus's sake.

I let out a sigh through my nose, letting go of some of that pent-up anger. I saw my aunts' shoulders lower as I did.

Damn. I should have asked House who was at the front door. If I'd known he was here, I would have stayed in my room with my books. You could count on books. Books never let you down, and they were always there when you needed them.

What pissed me off, even more, was the guy looked just as peeved as I was. The nerve of this guy. This was *my* house.

"Here you go, Marcus." Ruth came into the kitchen from the room just off to the left, which was the potions room. She handed him what looked like a glass vial with a blue liquid inside.

What the hell? Why was my aunt Ruth supplying this creep with her potions? After what I told her he'd said to me, I hoped it was poison. A smile reached my lips. *Hello, chlamydia.*

"Thank you, Ruth," said Marcus as he pocketed the vial inside his jacket.

My heart was pounding, and not in a good way.

"Tessa," said Ruth seeing me standing in the threshold. "Come and sit. You must be starving after all that studying." She rushed to the stove and plopped a generous-sized square chunk of lasagna on a plate. Grabbing a knife and fork, she placed the plate on the kitchen table. "Come, before it gets cold."

I stared at Marcus, but he wouldn't meet my eyes. Good. He wouldn't get between me and my juicy, double-cheese veggie lasagna. No man's worth that.

Feeling the use of my legs again, I moved to the table and sat, tearing into the lasagna even before my butt hit the chair. It took every bit of effort not to moan as my taste buds exploded with all the wonderful flavors. Ruth could cook up a mean lasagna. I chewed, my eyes on Marcus's jacket, wondering what that vial was.

I swallowed and said, "You better pay up for whatever my aunt gave you. I don't care if you're the chief. She doesn't work for free."

Marcus's eyes widened, and for a moment he looked shocked. He made to answer me, but Dolores got there first.

"So, Tessa, did you finish those book covers you were working on?" Dolores smiled at me, but I could see it was forced. Nice way to change the subject. "My niece is an artist. Did you know that, Marcus?"

The chief shook his head but said nothing. Good. I didn't like the sound of his voice anyway. Better keep it shut. Or my fork might find its way to lodge in his throat.

The silence stretched.

"Here you go, Tessa," said Ruth, stepping into the silence before it got awkward, and placed a tall glass of water next to my plate.

"Thank you." I took another bite of the lasagna, my eyes still on Marcus. I was waiting for him to pull out his wallet, but he just stood there, hands in his pockets. Maybe he paid her before I got there. Either way, I would make sure he wasn't stiffing my aunts. And I *was* going to find out what that vial of blue liquid was. You could count on it.

"You like it?" Ruth asked, her smiling face so innocent sometimes, she looked like a young girl. She was the most free-spirited of the sisters, and I wouldn't want it any other way. She wouldn't be Ruth if she wasn't.

"It's amazing. Really. And that sauce? What's in it?"

Ruth's smile widened to her ears. "Ah. It's my secret." She spun around and went back to the kitchen, humming a tune that sounded a lot like Deck the Halls.

Heels clicked on the hardwood floors. "What smells so good in here?" asked Beverly as she entered the kitchen, her perfect face smiling and beautiful. She was graceful in her sophisticated blue dress. "Oh. It's me," she laughed, winning a scowl from Dolores.

Beverly sashayed her way to the kitchen table, sat, and began applying powder to her nose and forehead.

I flicked my eyes back on the chief, wondering why he was still here if he'd paid Ruth for whatever concoction was in that vial.

"Well, I should go," said Marcus, having read my mind. "Thanks again, Ruth. You're a godsend."

Ruth turned around, beaming. If there was a contest in Hollow Cove for the most radiant smile of the year, this would be it. "Oh, nonsense," she made a gesture with her hand, her cheeks a little pinker than before. "I'm here to help."

Marcus cleared his throat. "Ladies," he said as he started for the kitchen's back door. "I'll show myself out."

"And not a moment too soon," I muttered under my breath, which turned out to be louder than I'd expected as Marcus whipped his head in my general direction. *Whoops*.

"Just a minute, Marcus," said Dolores, her gaze over me again. A faint smile curled up on the corners of her mouth.

Hmm. Why didn't I like her smile?

"Marcus, could you give my niece a ride?"

That's why.

I choked on the piece of lasagna in my mouth. Cauldron be damned. "What? No? I'm not riding with him." I hesitated. "Why would

69

I need to ride with him?" Yes, that sounded a little childish, but the guy had basically expressed that he hated my guts to the entire town, the entire universe.

Dolores put one hand on her hip and gave me a pointed look. "Because you have a new case today, and Ruth and I have a meeting with the town mayor so we need the car."

I looked at Marcus to see his face had gone two shades darker. "He was just leaving. He has places to be. I'm sure he's too busy."

Marcus rubbed the back of his neck. "Yeah. I need to get back to the office."

Dolores put her other hand on her hip, her face pinched. "Are you refusing to give my niece a ride?"

The chief looked taken aback. "Ah…"

"Hmmm?" pressed my aunt Dolores.

Marcus blinked a few times. "No. It's just… that's not it… I guess I could," he added finally.

Dolores clapped her hands together once. "Excellent."

I stood up, heat rushing to my face, and I was very aware I was probably the color of molten lava. Hell, that's exactly how I felt. "No, *not* excellent." I pointed at Marcus. "There's no way in hell I'm going to ride in a car—with *him*. I despise his ass, and I don't care that he hears it. No. Way. You'll have to kill me first." A little overkill, but I couldn't stop myself.

Dolores turned on me. "Are you finished?"

No. "Yes."

"Good," said Dolores. "Marcus has agreed to drive you."

I gritted my teeth, wanting to scream. I gave my aunts my word to join the Merlin Group but asking me to ride with a man who despised me as much as I despised him was too much. Even for me. I was emotionally drained and didn't need this right now. What I needed was a tall glass of wine and to binge-watch something on Netflix.

I averted my eyes, and they settled on a silent witch. "Beverly? Can't you work this case?"

Beverly pulled out a lipstick from her purse and smeared it over her full lips. "Can't, darling. I have a date."

"Can't you cancel it?"

Beverly looked at me like I'd just soiled her best dress. "Is the world on fire?"

"No."

Beverly slipped her lipstick into her purse. "Charles is taking me to Chez Maurice. Do you know how hard it is to get a decent table? I can't wait to show him my new dress." She laughed and adjusted the spaghetti straps of her light blue dress that accentuated her eyes. "Besides, Dolores and Ruth are taking the car.

And I haven't ridden on my broom in ages." She gave me a wink.

My face was blank. I didn't find her particularly amusing at the moment. I never understood why my aunts only owned one car, an old gray, 2000 Volvo v70 station wagon.

I wanted to combust into flames right there in the kitchen. This was not happening. They knew I loathed the man. We all knew the feeling was mutual. How could they do this to me?

Ruth came and patted my head like I was a Golden Retriever who'd just performed a trick for her. "You'll do fine. Don't you worry. You've got this."

I shook my head, refusing to look at Marcus but noticing he hadn't moved. "What's this new case, anyway? Does it have something to do with what happened to Avi?"

Ruth smiled. "No idea."

"What? But you just said—"

"Here it comes," said Ruth. "It's on its way right now." She moved away, nodding. "Any minute now. Here we go…"

"What?" This was weird, even for them.

There was a sudden ting, and the toaster ejected a white piece of paper like a cue card. Ruth stuck out her hand and snatched the card in midair. "It says it right here. Requests the help of The Merlin Group."

I had to refrain from my mouth opening in surprise.

"See for yourself." Ruth handed me the card. I took it and read.

Notification alert.
Attention: Merlin Group. Services required.
Problem: Unlawful pixies.
Location: Hot Mess Witch, Beauty Salon.
Hollow Cove, Maine, USA.

I shook my head, rereading the card over and over again, hoping this was a bad dream. "This is not happening."

"It's happening." Dolores eyed me for a moment and then nodded in something like approval. "Put your big girl pants on and get to it."

I dropped my hand with the card still holding it. Guess that settled it, huh?

I was in hell.

The muscles around Marcus's jaw tightened. "I'll be in the car," was all he said as he left through the back door.

The door slammed, and I bared my teeth and hissed like a cat.

I was going mad.

I stood there, wanting to strangle him. Emotions pressed against my head and my heart as I started to shake again. I could feel the pressure inside me, ready to flick back beneath a tide of raging anger.

73

Just breathe, Tessa. You can handle this pompous bastard.

I moved toward the back door and grabbed my black cotton jacket from the wooden peg rack. I slipped it on and pulled the strap of my black leather messenger bag over my head.

"Here, you'll need this." Dolores handed me a large red leather-bound book.

I grabbed it. A star was etched into the leather, right smack in the middle. "*The Witch's Handbook, Volume Three*," I read.

She raised a knowing brow. "Never leave home without it."

I flipped it open to the first page and peered down at the handwritten notation. *Amelia loves Sean* was written on the right top corner, encased within a heart.

It had belonged to my mother once. Guess it was mine now.

"And these." Ruth handed me a handful of chalk. "You'll need those too."

I stared at the chalk sticks, five of them, all new.

I looked up to find the three witches watching me steadily and expectantly. But there was also a hint of mischief flashing behind their eyes. Almost like… like they were testing me.

I dropped the chalk and the book in my messenger bag, closed the flap, and frowned all the way out the back door.

CHAPTER

7

It was the worst six-minute-and-thirty-three-second car ride of my life.

I sat in the front passenger seat, pushed up against the door as much as I could without actually feeling the pain of the door handle poking against my side. Marcus's burgundy Jeep Grand Cherokee was supposed to be a comfortable ride with all the luxury of an expensive four-by-four. Yet I was only aware of an eerie feeling like my insides being rearranged in my belly and swirling up into my throat with an added uncomfortable silence, accented by the whoosh of igniting gas. Freaking fantastic.

We didn't speak. We didn't as much as glance in each other's direction. I even tried to hold my breath, not wanting to share the same air with this guy. But when my lungs burned after a minute, I let go. Yeah, not smart.

My anger sizzled inside me. I could barely think as my fury clawed its way up to the forefront of my mind and took over. What made it worse was the bastard had the nerve to keep breathing hard through his nose, like he was irritated and angry that I was soiling his expensive jeep with my dirty ass.

Marcus swung the car at the curb of Charms Avenue, his white knuckles and red neck telling me his blood pressure was probably as high as mine.

"Out," growled the chief, staring at the street in front of him.

He didn't have to tell me twice.

I was barely clear of the jeep when it started moving forward. I stumbled, catching myself with my hands as I nearly went sprawling. The pavement burned the skin on my palms.

I straightened, seeing Marcus reaching over to shut my door as the jeep pulled out from the curb and took on speed down the road.

"You're welcome!" I shouted after him, realizing only the moment the words were out of my mouth that *he* had given me the lift.

"Jerk off."

After I pulled my hair back into a messy po-nytail, I adjusted the strap on my bag and turned around.

A pink, two-story Victorian house with white trim and moldings stared back at me. Above the front porch was a large, flashing ne-on pink sign written in bold letters: HOT MESS WITCH, BEAUTY SALON. And then below that was written: Where magic transforms the ordinary to extraordinary!

Marcus was a douche, but at least he'd dropped me off at the right place. He could have made me walk. *I* would have made *him* walk.

Screams erupted from inside the salon in startled panic, drawing my gaze up. Shadows moved past the windows on the first floor, and I ducked as a black shoe crashed through a front window to land at my feet.

"This is going to suck." I sighed, knowing I wasn't mentally prepared for whatever was happening. "Follow the screaming," I told my-self. I climbed up the steps, marched up to the front door and stepped inside—

Right into a war zone.

Miniature humans the size of my hand with multicolored wings that looked like they be-longed on butterflies darted through the salon, leaving trails of brilliant dust in their wake as though the shop's sprinkler system was raining glitter.

Five pixies had a woman pinned against the far wall next to a row of shelves filled with bottles of shampoo, conditioner, and an assortment of hair products. The woman's eyes widened; her face rippled from what looked human to the tawny-colored face of a deer. It seemed as though she couldn't control her inner beast under the stress of getting her eyes poked by pixies. She was shifting back and forth like a cartoon character.

Two other women—one with light hair crammed onto purple rollers and the other with dark hair—were hiding behind a long counter to my right, their faces cut and bleeding from multiple wounds.

The hum of wings reached me, and I ducked as a throng of pixies flew at me like a swarm of giant wasps. Only wasps didn't carry miniature swords. These pixies did.

A pixie hovered in the air, right below a crystal chandelier. He blew a blast on his trumpet and shouted, "Kill the giant beasts before they eat us! Kill them all! Kill the enemy!"

"Oh. My. God."

Pixies charged, exploding in clouds of pinks, blues, yellows, and orange sparkles as they dived around the salon, their eyes wide with manic glee. From what I remembered about pixies growing up, they were territorial and would attack if you threatened their homes. But this was not their home. Pixies didn't attack people for no reason. They attacked when they felt threatened. But what did this salon have to do with them?

A large woman spun on the spot at the other end. Martha swung a broom at a pixie, missed, and nearly tripped on her own legs. The pixie—I couldn't tell male from female at the speed they were zipping—rose and shot toward Martha again in a cloud of red sparkles and glinting knives.

She caught sight of me, her eyes round. "Don't just stand there! *Do* something!" she wailed and swatted at the pixie. "They're attacking my clients! They're ruining my salon! My business!"

"But," I began, "aren't you a witch?" I knew it was the wrong thing to say by the deepened scowl on her face and the ugly twist of her mouth.

"I do beauty potions and spells," the large witch hissed. "I can spell you a new haircut or a French manicure that will last you for a year. I don't do hard magic!"

Damn it. I didn't know any spells or how to deal with a mass of what looked like crazy-killer-pixies. Heart pounding, I rummaged through my bag and pulled out *The Witch's Handbook*.

"Pixies Gone Wild," said a voice next to me, making me jump. "I've seen this movie, though the females were *a lot* bigger—but the wings... the wings were an awesome touch."

"Ronin?" I said, seeing the leggy guy next to me. Damn that vampire stealth, I never heard him come in. "You here for a haircut?"

Ronin smiled at me. "I saw you come in, so I followed you."

"A half-vampire stalker. Nice," I breathed. And then, "Duck!" I fell to the ground on my knees, pulling Ronin down with me, and cried out in pain as what felt like twenty needles pierced my scalp and sliced at my ears. My eyes watered at the pain. I reached up and swiped with my free hand, hitting something solid—a pixie—and some pain stopped. I rubbed the top of my head with my hand, and my fingers came back wet with blood.

"The little shits. I'm bleeding. I'm freaking bleeding!"

Ronin turned his head toward me, the gold in his eyes shimmering. "I thought pixies were supposed to be on our side."

"That's what I thought too," I hissed, wondering why my aunts thought I could handle this alone. You'd have to be out of your mind mad to handle a mass of pixies this size. "Down!" I cried as another onslaught of mad pixies shot at us, swiping their tiny silver swords. I hissed as another volley of searing pain hit my scalp. "Urgh. I'm going to kill them!"

"What did you do to them?" shouted Ronin with his hands on his head, like that would help anything.

"Me?" I frowned at him. "Nothing. I'm here to stop this madness."

"Then get to work!" howled Martha.

I looked up at the desperation in her voice and let out a little moan.

Martha was floating in the air, and not by her magic.

Eight pixies latched on to her dress, pulling her toward an open window. Once she was out, they could fly her to Canada for all I knew. I couldn't let that happen.

"Oh. Shit."

Ronin laughed. "That's a good look on her. Floating Martha. I should get a picture—" he rummaged inside his jacket pocket.

"I heard that!" shrilled the sizeable witch. "You better help her get me down, Ronin. Or I swear, I will tell the entire town how you come in once a week for a manicure!"

I looked at the young vampire beside me who just shrugged and flashed me a smile. "The ladies like clean nails."

Oh boy.

Okay. Time to focus.

"Do something!" shrilled Martha.

"I'm trying!" I shouted as I flipped open the book with my hands trembling and the words blurring on the pages. I didn't know why the pixies were acting this way, but I couldn't worry about that now. As I flipped through the pages, the book fell open where a yellow Post-it was stuck on the top of a page. The title read *Sleeping Spells for the Witch in Need*.

"Thank you, Ruth," I breathed, knowing my aunt had put that there on purpose.

"A sleeping spell?" Ronin's head was next to mine as his eyes moved along the inscriptions. "You think it's going to work?"

"Yes." If my aunt thought it would, I was certain of it. She wouldn't have marked that page if it wouldn't. Right. Now came the hard part.

I would have to perform my first real spell (the thing with Marcus didn't count) in the middle of a pixie battle. Excellent. No pressure. None.

"Hurry up!" cried Martha, as her head slammed against the wall. She reached out and grabbed a doorframe, holding on for dear life.

"I know!" I placed the book on the floor and skimmed the spell. Following the instructions, I grabbed a chalk and drew a circle on the floor about twelve inches in diameter. Next, I wrote the word PIXIE in the center of the circle.

"You have nice penmanship," muttered Ronin, still way too close. "I like the way you draw your p—"

"Shhh." I glared at him. "You can't speak. I need to concentrate. Just… keep an eye out and let me know if more pixies come this way… and I don't know… do some of your vampire mojo."

Ronin laughed. "You want me to scare them with my handsome good looks?"

"Just keep them off of me, okay?"

"Aye aye, captain," said Ronin, grinning.

I pulled my eyes away and read the next instructions—the invocation phrases. I needed to say the words. I could do that.

Here goes. With my heart thrashing, I took a deep breath and tapped into my core, my will, where I knew some magical energy was generated by living beings—our life force itself. I felt a tug on my aura as it answered.

I cleared my throat and said, "By this spell, you shall sleep, hidden from day, in the night so deep. Those who waken from this sleep return at once to slumber deep."

As soon as the last word left me, I looked up.

The pixies swarmed around us, their steel blades cutting through the women's clothes as though it were cardboard. From all directions, in a whirling cloud of pixie dust, the pixies struck.

"Damn," I said, a chill running through me. The spell hadn't worked.

Oops.

CHAPTER

8

Ronin raised a clenched fist. "I'm all for witch empowerment and all. But… was that what you intended to happen?"

"Of course not!"

Ducking, I pulled the book on my lap and read the spell again. My face fell. Crap. I'd forgotten a crucial part.

"Hurry!" cried Martha. I looked up to see her clinging to a window frame with her bottom half and her legs hanging on the other side of the open window.

My pulse fast, I tossed the book to the side, tapped into my will again, and slammed my palm down inside the circle over the word PIXIE as I shouted, "By this spell, you shall sleep, hidden from day, in the night so deep. Those who waken from this sleep return at once to slumber deep!"

The wood floor seemed to vibrate below my hand, as if its stored life force were running through me, connecting me to the earth and stones beneath it.

My breath came in a quick heave as a jolt of power spun from me, overflowing in my core to my aura. Magic roared. A gasp slipped from my mouth, and energy from the circle flooded me. The rush was intoxicating, and then the energy exploded into existence.

In a rush, magic raced out of me and into the shop in an invisible kinetic force.

I was hurled back and landed on my ass.

I heard a sudden collective intake of tiny breaths, and then the pixies fell from the air, like wasps sprayed with insecticide, and landed on the floor in soft plops, unconscious.

I stared, blinking for a moment and trying to see if any of the pixies stirred. The pixies didn't move again.

"You did it." Ronin got to his feet with a strange smile on his face—half goofy, half impressed.

I didn't know whether I should be insulted that he hadn't believed I *could* do it or proud that I actually *had*. Hell, I was proud it worked. And the feeling of power coursing through me felt… well, I felt freaking awesome.

A wave of dizziness hit, and I took a moment to steady myself as the magic took its payment. The spell took more of my energy than when I'd spelled Marcus's ass, but it had been worth it.

I'd done it. My first case. And I'd done it all on my own.

A smile grew over me. You'd have to slap the smile off of my face because it wasn't going anywhere for now.

"A little help here!" shouted Martha, hanging over the windowsill.

"I got her," said Ronin. He strolled over to Martha and pulled her to her feet as though she weighed nothing.

The women behind the counter rushed out the door. She was followed by the other shifter lady who stopped and kicked one of the unconscious pixies, the one with the trumpet, as she scurried out the door, her arms wrapped around herself.

Martha's business would definitely suffer for this.

Still smiling, I looked at the ground littered with tiny pixies, most of them snoring and some even twitching in their sleep. My elated feeling didn't last long. The pixies' behavior didn't settle well with me.

I turned to see Martha patting herself down, like she was making sure she still had all her very large parts. "Martha, do you have any idea why the pixies reacted like this?"

"No." Martha's face was covered with tiny red cuts. "Why do you think I contacted the Merlin Group? To discuss Ruth's box-dyed hair job? No. The little creeps just came through the open window and started attacking us." The witch looked at her shop, and a deflated expression shifted on her face at the damage the pixies had done. "If I were to guess, I'd say it was almost as though they're under a spell or something."

Right. That would make sense. But why? And who would benefit from something like this?

"Will they wake up?" asked Martha as she picked her way around the sleeping pixies and grabbed an empty cardboard box on the floor.

"Yes." I had no idea. When in doubt, go for the positive.

I watched as Martha picked up two sleeping pixies by their feet, holding them away from her like she was picking up dead rats, and dropped them inside the box none too gently.

"There's more outside," said Ronin staring out the window. "A crapload."

Damn. I didn't like the sound of that.

Leaving Martha to pick up the pixies inside her shop, I snatched up my book, slipped it in my bag, and followed Ronin outside.

My mouth fell open as I hit the bottom of the front porch steps. A dozen or more pixies were snoozing in the grass at the front of her shop, but that's not why my jaw dislocated. The *trail* of sleeping pixies started from the shop, spread across the street, and disappeared into the now-darkened town. The sun had swiftly vanished, and the lengthening shadows triggered the streetlights.

"What is this?" I asked as I started forward, careful not to step on any of the dozing pixies.

Ronin shook his head. "Beats me. I've never seen this before or that many. It's like the entire pixie clan of Hollow Cove came out to play tonight."

Yeah. But why? "Come on. Let's follow the trail." I wasn't exactly sure why I asked him to come with me. But he was here, and seeing as he was half-vampire, he might be useful.

Together, we picked our way across the street and down two more blocks. The wan light of streetlamps cast long shadows, adding to my unease.

We reached Shifter Lane and passed the local café joint, Witchy Beans Café, and a few other shops that were closing for the night. A few townspeople had spotted some sleeping pixies and were pointing at them. A glare from a small, pudgy man with large brown eyes caught my attention.

Hands on his hips, Gilbert stood in front of his shop, Gilbert's Grocer & Gifts. His face pulled into a scowl as he mumbled something I couldn't hear. If he could do magic, he was probably cursing me because of what Dolores had done. Great. Another person who hated me by association. Love this town.

An excited buzz of voices rose up as more townspeople began circulating, either on their way home from work or from doing their shopping. They all took a moment to inspect the sleeping pixies.

The same little girl I'd noticed the night Avi's remains were discovered stood across the street with her gaze fixated on me. She stared at me for a long moment without blinking as an expression I couldn't quite identify flickered across her face.

We hit the town square and moved toward the large gazebo sitting in the middle surrounded by a small park with benches and a few fruit trees. Lit only with the few streetlamps, the square was empty. A large water fountain gleamed in the light from the streetlamps, and water trickled from the top of a statue that resembled a laughing witch with a pointed hat, her arms out and legs splayed like she was dancing.

"Holy crap." I stood ten feet from the fountain because I couldn't get any closer if I didn't want to step on more pixies. There were about a hundred here, all piled on top of each other, at the foot of the fountain, and sprawled across the grass.

"Looks like you found the source," commented Ronin.

My unease tripled. How was it possible that my spell reached all the way here? But I didn't have time to worry about that. I'd look into it later.

I grimaced and covered my nose. "Damn. What's that smell? Like a mixture of bad eggs and rotten cabbages."

Ronin leaned toward the fountain and pulled back gagging. "It's coming from the water."

"It smells like the town's sewer."

"You think the water is cursed?" Ronin eyed the fountain like he was about to kick it.

"Maybe. But why would the pixies all come out at the same time for a drink? Especially when it smells like the town's toilets? What about this water *made* them drink it?" It made no sense. A lot didn't make sense. If the water *was* cursed, who cursed it and why? Why pixies?

Whispers of dread crawled into my mind. "First there's the dead werewolf Avi, and now this? Can't be a coincidence."

Ronin's brows reached his hairline. "You think they're connected?"

"It's a possibility. Two strange and unexplained things happening in this town in two days. Something's up. And I'm going to find out what."

"A witch with a plan," said Ronin, and his face shifted with a sly delight. "I like that."

We were so enthralled with the pixies and the stinky water that by the time I heard the sound behind us, it was already too late.

CHAPTER
9

From the shadows outside the light came a low hiss. With a surge of cold energy, cold magic, and a shimmering blur, a great serpent coalesced from the shadows.

"Cauldron help us." My skin erupted in goosebumps and I took a step back.

At first, I thought it was a snake, a boa constrictor by its sheer size, that had probably eaten all its brothers and sisters, possibly its parents too. But then it sprouted four limbs with dark fur, ending in sharp claws like the legs of a grizzly bear. The beast was the size of a pony with a mouth full of yellow teeth and flaming amber eyes.

"That is one *ugly* bastard," laughed Ronin.

"No shit." I wasn't fully versed in Demons 101, but I made a mental note to read up on them as soon as I got home—if I survived. I had no real training and no idea which demon this was. Was it a lesser demon or a greater demon?

The demon took a jerky step forward, like it was testing its new legs. Its head was swinging from side to side, low to the ground, and its gray forked tongue darted out from its large mouth as it smelled the pixies on the ground. It let out a strange, wet, bloodthirsty screech, as though it was thrilled at its newly found feast of sleeping pixies.

One demon slipping through the wards was bad. Two, well, two was a gigantic problem of magnanimous proportions.

A small gasp escaped me as the snake-bear demon snatched up two pixies and tore into them like it was munching on potato chips before grabbing another three.

"Now that's disturbing," commented Ronin.

Pixies could be a real menace sometimes, but they didn't deserve to be eaten like this, especially while unconscious and unable to defend themselves. If we didn't do something quickly, the demon would eat *all* of them in a few minutes.

My heart beat loudly and a sweat broke out all over my body. "We've got to do something."

"Yeah," agreed Ronin. "Like run. I'm very good at running. And *a lot* of other things, but right now, running would be good."

My mind told me to run, but my legs seemed to be cemented into the ground. "No. We can't leave them to die like this. It's wrong." Strange how the longer I stayed in this town, the more I sounded like my aunts and like a true member of the Merlin Group.

"It's survival," answered the vampire. "Don't look at me like that. I didn't make the demon eat the pixies."

I braced myself for what I was about to ask. "Do you have Marcus's number?" The thought of seeing the chief again brought bile up in my throat. Still, I figured this demon was way out of my league. The chief should deal with demons.

Ronin gave me a look. "You want to call the dude who's got a burr up his ass? Now?"

"Yes."

"You feelin' all right?"

"Look," I said, my nerves and anger mixing to make me feel dizzy. "I've never dealt with a demon before. Have you?"

Ronin's eyes were wide. "What do I look like? Van Helsing? I'm soooo much better looking."

I didn't have time to explain that Van Helsing was a fictional character who hunted vampires. "Do you have his number!"

Ronin blinked and said, "Dial 911-hollow."

My brows rose in surprise, but I quickly drew my phone from my bag and dialed, hating how fast my heart was beating—and not because of the demon.

"This is the chief," said the voice on the other end of the line after two rings. The heavy background noise of an engine rumbling told me he was in his jeep. At least he was mobile, so he could get here sooner.

"There's a demon in the town square," I blurted loudly, and the snake-bear demon's amber eyes fell on me. I swallowed hard, holding on to my veggie lasagna and willing it to stay put in my belly.

A pause. "Who is this?" His voice sounded irritated.

Damn him. I really didn't have time for this. Ronin cut me a look, making me wonder if his list of vampire abilities included acute hearing.

"Does it matter?" My voice rising. "There. Is. A. Demon. In. The. Town. Square," I repeated, enunciating each word.

The snake-bear demon stepped forward, a pair of pixie legs disappearing into its mouth. Its eyes never left me as it tilted its head in a way I didn't like. I felt like it was contemplating whether to ditch the pixies and come after me.

The demon hacked and a green ball shot from its mouth to land on the ground a few feet away from us. It hit the ground and promptly flattened in a puddle of noxious-smelling goop that looked like the digested parts of a few pixies.

"Okay, *gross.*" Now I was going to puke.

"Is this Tessa?" asked Marcus, a note of casual disdain to his voice.

My queasiness vanished. This guy really knew how to push my buttons. "Just get here. Now!" I hung up and dropped my phone in my bag. No point in hearing his reply. I did my part. If he didn't show up, he'd have the town to deal with later.

"Tess! Watch out!" cried Ronin as he leaped sideways.

I barely had a chance to look up as the giant snake-bear demon came at me like a raging bull. My night was just getting better.

So, what do you do when a large demon from the Netherworld is charging at you, its eyes gleaming with hunger?

You get off your ass and you run. That's what you do.

Ronin beat me to it. His long legs propelled him a lot faster than mine did and with an unreal grace, like his supernatural vampire speed on high. Plus, I had my bag to lug along, making it more difficult, not to mention awkward, to run. Adrenaline pumping, I ran as fast as I could, pushing my thighs to their limits with just one thought in my head.

How do you kill a demon? I had no freaking clue.

"Get back!" I shouted, waving my arms around as I, unfortunately, ran toward the crowd of curious townspeople. I came barreling down the street as the crowd scattered like frightened mice with a cat on the prowl.

Ronin was a good fifty feet ahead of me, that lanky bastard.

The sound of nails tearing up the pavement sounded behind me followed by a low hissing so close, it was almost like cold fingers at the nape of my neck. The damn thing was going to eat me.

I threw myself behind a park bench, just as I felt claws ripping the back of my jacket. I fell to the ground and rolled, coming up on my knees and whirling around.

The snake-bear demon opened its maw and let out a sound that was part roar, part hiss, and scary as hell.

"You're an ugly SOB. Aren't you?"

The demon hurled itself at me with a bellow, rearing up on its hindmost legs. It plunged at me, jaws gaping.

I wasn't about to let it eat me.

I kicked out with my legs and struck the creature's jaws with a crunching impact as my boot made contact. The demon stumbled back, giving me those few precious seconds to get my butt off the ground.

I pushed myself up, pirouetted like a dancer (don't ask), and started running again. I ran in fear without knowing where I was going. I just wanted to live. Living was good.

Plus, I did not want to die, eaten by an ugly snake-bear demon.

Just when I realized I'd lost sight of Ronin, searing pain assaulted my back, as though someone had just slammed knives into my skin.

I cried out and pitched forward on the hard pavement, tearing up my jeans, the flesh from my knees, and my palms as I tried to brace for impact. Didn't work.

My book slipped from inside my bag and landed before me.

I braced for the feeling of claws tearing into my flesh and razor-sharp teeth biting my skin. But it didn't come.

"Take that. And that. You want some more? Here you go. Boom! That's how you do it!"

I spun around. Ronin had a broom in his hand, and he was smacking the demon with it.

The guy was nuts. But he'd also probably saved my life.

Ronin rushed up behind the demon, and it turned to follow him, its huge jaws snapping in rage. In a burst of vamp speed, Ronin darted back, staying just ahead of the thing's jaws as he swung the broom like he would a baseball bat.

Ronin flashed me a confident smile. "See that? I've got him." He turned and hit the demon across the head with the broom again. "This way, you stinky bastard. You want a piece of me? Do ya? Do ya?"

Grimacing, I stood and grabbed my spell book while I still could. My back was still flaming with what I could only assume were deep gashes made by the demon's sharp claws.

Ronin bounced and danced around the demon, hitting it at every turn and laughing like a crazed person. "I could beat you with my eyes closed." He swung again—

And then the demon caught the broom in one of its front paws and yanked it out of Ronin's grasp, as though Ronin wasn't even holding it.

"Oh, shit," he breathed.

The demon picked up the broom in its mouth, clamped down hard with its powerful jaws and snapped the broom in half like it was a toothpick.

Ronin stepped back and caught up to me. "If you've got something in that book of tricks that can kill a demon, do it now."

Breathing hard, I held my spell book close to my chest and flipped through the pages to look for a spell, which was almost impossible to do while looking up every other second to see if the giant snake-bear demon was about to take a chunk out of my soft flesh.

The demon took a last bite of the broom and then its glowing amber eyes fixated on us.

Crap. Crap. Crap.

"Hurry up," said Ronin, jogging on the spot and looking ready to bolt again. "It's looking at us… it's *still* looking at us."

My heart slammed against my ribs. "I'm going as fast as I can. But it would go faster if I knew where to look." Damn it. I needed more training. "Where the hell is the chief?" Marcus should have been here by now. That he wasn't told me he didn't take me or my call seriously.

It also told me he wasn't coming.

My adrenaline masked some of the pain in my back. If I lived through the night, tomorrow would hurt like a bitch.

"It's too late for him," warned Ronin. "It's coming."

My pulse skyrocketed at the tension in Ronin's voice, and I looked up from the book.

The demon pushed off the ground and came at us in a blur of scales, dark fur, and claws. Fury flashed in the demon's eyes. It was either really pissed or really hungry. Possibly both. We would not survive this.

I had a small freak-out moment. I think I even peed a little.

Damn it. "I need a spell to kill a demon!" I shouted and started backing away, still holding the spell book in front of me like a shield.

A flutter of energy spindled around me and the book opened on its own, like invisible hands flipped the pages, searching for something. After a second, the pages stilled, and the book fell open. I stared at the page titled How to Vanquish a Demon.

"Nice."

Ronin eyed the book and shook his head. "Witches." He stepped away from me and said, "I'll keep it busy while you do your spell."

I stared at the vampire. "What? Are you crazy? How are you going to manage that? You've lost your broom."

Ronin's eyes dilated and flashed to black. He raised his hands as talons sprouted from his fingertips, and he gave me a finger wave.

I pursed my lips. "That was unexpected." I watched, half amazed, half nervous as the half-vampire flew at the demon, his sharp talons extended.

The demon was too focused on me to notice the vampire until he was on him.

The demon let out a shrieking sound of pain as Ronin ripped into its left eye with his talons, pulling out its eye. Black blood gushed through the hole that once held a red eye.

I wanted to keep watching, but I still had a job to do.

Reading down the list of different spells to kill a demon, I opted for the easiest, the fastest, and the one that didn't require any additional ingredients that I didn't have in my possession at the moment.

I found it. "Bingo."

Chalk in hand, I dropped to my knees and drew a circle—more of an oval really—large enough for a person to step into—me. Not all witches needed to do this step, but seeing as I was inexperienced, I thought it best to protect my ass first and then move on with the spell.

Another loud shriek pulled my attention back on the demon. The snake-bear demon's face was trickling in black blood. Both eyes had been torn out, and the demon flailed around wildly, striking blindly with heavy sweeps of its arms.

Working fast, I finished drawing the Circle of Solomon, the magical circle of protection against demons, with all the added Latin names and symbols.

I stared down at my handiwork and cringed. "A five-year-old could have done better." I doubted it would work, but I didn't have time to draw up another one.

Pulling my eyes away from the worst protection circle in the history of witches, I steadied myself and drew in my will. Focusing on the incoming energy soaring through me and continuing to build, I stepped inside the circle.

My skin prickled, energy rolling all over my body like tiny needle pricks. I wasn't sure if that was normal or not. Oh well.

Next came the invocation words, the big boys that would hopefully destroy the demon. I looked at the page again, found the words I needed to recite, and took another breath.

A sharp cry of pain pulled my attention back up.

The demon's snake tail caught Ronin in the chest. He flew at the nearest electrical post, half spinning in the air, and hit hard. He slid to the ground and didn't move.

"Ronin!" I shouted. Killing the only friend (if I could even call Ronin that after the few hours we'd spent together) I had in this town, was a big no-no.

My breath hissed in through my nose and I stiffened, almost falling as my anger shifted.

My sudden scream had gotten the demon's attention. It couldn't see, but it had heard me.

Nice going, Tessa.

Like a bull, the demon pushed off with its back legs and shot toward my voice and me standing in the circle.

Oh. Shit.

A second moment of panic. My mind had gone blank. Fear could do that to a person. Blinking, I stared at the page with the spell, the sound of claws tearing up the pavement loud in my ears and making it hard to concentrate.

I opened my mouth and cried, "By my will and the powers of the elements—"

The force of a bus knocked me off my circle, and I landed hard on the ground. I wasn't sure how I knew what to do, but I just did, as my arms came up and I held on to the demon's head, keeping it from tearing my jugular.

The creature reeked like it had been spawned in the Netherworld's bowels, but I hung on. If I let go, I was dead.

The demon screamed and thrashed its head, its jaws snapping an inch from my face as strings of yellow spit fell on my face right before its gray tongue slapped me. I gritted my teeth, grabbing the demon's head with both hands. I might as well have been trying to push over a car with my pinkies.

My eyes watered, and my arms shook under the weight of the beast. I didn't have the supernatural strength of a werewolf or a vampire, nor did I have the fighting skills of a warrior or a hunter. All I had were my wits.

And a spell I had somehow memorized.

Don't ask me how. I had no idea. But I could see the words clearly in my mind as though I were staring at them on the page.

With the last of my breath, I wheezed, "By my will and the powers of the elements, obliterate demon!"

Energy coursed through me at my will, and a spark leaped up from my core to the tips of my fingers. Magic boomed, and I felt the power hit the demon with a jolt like a sledgehammer.

The pressure on my chest disappeared as the snake-bear demon fell back. I could breathe again. I took giant gulps of lovely, lovely air and sat up.

The demon staggered, wreathed in a corona of blinding energy. The night was lit like it was midafternoon, and I had to shield my eyes against it. When I could see again, the demon's body was extending and collapsing, its limbs shrinking and elongating, as though it didn't know whether to be a serpent or a bear.

The demon struggled and screamed, its limbs and tail thrashing and flailing. Its body rippled and grew as though it had swallowed a pool of water.

And then it exploded in a burst of black demon blood and guts.

I had the good sense to close my mouth and eyes, but I still got hit with it.

I jerked back as the mess of sloppy innards fell on me like a pot of hot soup. But it wasn't soup. And I won't even begin to describe what it smelled like.

"I'll never get the smell out of my hair." I scooped what I could from my eyes and blinked. When I could see again, a shape leered over me.

Marcus stood over me, a smile on his stupid handsome face. "Looks like I got here just in time."

I spat on the ground. "Bite me."

CHAPTER

10

"**O**rder! I will have order!" shouted Gilbert as he slammed his gavel on the desk and scowled at the crowd, his face an ugly red. The expression made him into a mass of wrinkles. He sat behind a long table with Martha and Marcus sitting on either side of him.

The Hollow Cove Community Center was packed with two hundred bustling residents. It looked like the entire town had crammed in. Most of them were standing along the back and side walls because there weren't enough chairs for everyone.

"He looks constipated," commented Ronin next to me as he popped a gummy bear into his mouth from the bag on his lap.

"There is that," I said. The vampire looked fine apart from a small purple bruise on his forehead that seemed to get smaller every time I glanced at it. Vampire mojo crap, no doubt. My back still throbbed from where the demon had clawed it, but it was a lot better after Ruth had applied a healing ointment.

The vampire had saved my keister. If I hadn't been sure we were friends before, *that* had done it.

I let out a sigh and looked around. Fear was the winning emotion on the faces of all the townspeople, and they seemed to harbor the nervous energy of spooked kittens. I didn't blame them. Something was happening to their town, and it wasn't good.

After we'd defeated the demon, I'd stayed and helped Martha and a few others pick up the still unconscious pixies out of the streets and lay them carefully on a spot on the grass where they wouldn't get trampled. We were careful not to tear or damage their delicate wings. When I was done, I'd rushed back to Davenport House and took a shower the moment Ruth had finished with her ointment and most of the wounds had scarred over. It had been a quick, two-minute shower since my aunt Dolores had practically dragged me out, naked and wet, howling that we were going to miss the town meeting if I didn't hurry.

"I don't care if I have to drag you naked my-self!" she'd told me. Right. Like that was going to happen. The witch was mad.

A pretty blonde in the aisle next to us kept throwing smiles over her shoulder to Ronin, whose own smug smile kept getting wider and wider, almost to his ears.

"If you keep smiling like that, you won't feel your face anymore," I laughed.

Ronin kept his eyes on the blonde as he said, "What can I say? I'm the delectable flavor of the hour. The ladies love a strong, muscled he-ro." I couldn't help notice how his tone had deepened.

News of his battle with the demon had spread like a bushfire in the town, awarding him much attention from the opposite sex. Like right now.

I spotted the same girl I'd seen earlier to-night. Though this time she was glowering at Gilbert like she wanted to spit in his face. I liked this little girl.

"Who's the little girl?"

"Oh, her? That's Sadie. She's a witch, like you. Both parents were killed by demons three weeks ago. Martha offered to take her in. Poor kid. She looks pretty messed up. She hasn't said a word since her parents died. They think she witnessed the whole thing."

My heart clenched at his words, and I felt a deep sadness for Sadie. I didn't think a person could ever get over something like that. "Damn."

"Damn is right. When you think about it, this entire town is made up of cast-offs and orphans. It's a haven for rejected paranormals, those who don't have a pack or a community. Most of us are here because our own community shunned us."

Ronin's smile faded, and I could see a history of pain behind his eyes. I contemplated asking him about his past, but now wasn't the best time.

"Exciting, isn't it?" Ronin offered me the bag of gummy bears as his smile returned.

I grabbed a handful. "Not sure giving Gilbert a gavel was such a good idea. Look at him. There's a manic glee in his eyes," I said, as Gilbert pounded his gavel like he was hammering a nail.

Ronin laughed, easing my nerves a little. "Maybe they shouldn't have voted him mayor."

I choked on my gummy bears. "He's..." I coughed. "...the mayor?"

"Has been for the last five years," said Ronin between chews. "Love these meetings. Wait till he and Martha argue about the proper mowing height of grass." His white teeth flashed. "We've got great seats."

"Keep talking, Ronin," growled my aunt Dolores on my left side, next to Beverly and then Ruth, "and I'll give your seat to Brendan."

Ronin flashed her a smile, one I suspected he used on the ladies. "Yes, ma'am."

I felt eyes on me and darted my gaze back to the front. Marcus was watching me across the table, his gray eyes narrowed. His lips were pressed tightly, his expression irate as if this was my fault. Whatever *this* was.

My heart sped up, and I had to strain to keep from shifting in my seat. A rush of fluster ran through me, and I loathed that he had that effect on me. The guy was a jackass. If he thought he was intimidating me with his glare, or his fine looks, he didn't know me. I crossed my arms over my chest and glared right back until he looked away. *I win.*

Ronin leaned forward and whispered in my ear. "Man. Why does the dude hate you so much? It's like you murdered his puppy or something."

I wanted to know too. It couldn't just be that he thought my mother was a "waste of space." There had to be more to it than that. "No idea. Maybe he's jealous I defeated the demon, and he missed out on the party."

Marcus's eyes snapped back at me, his brow cocked in question, and my breath caught. Crap. Did he just hear that? Could his hearing be that good? Sure it could. He was paranormal like the rest of us. I just didn't know which kind. I made a mental note to watch what I was saying around the chief.

Gilbert slammed his gavel, making me flinch as the sound echoed around us. "Order! This meeting is now in session." He waited for silence. "Good." He let go of the gavel and interlaced his fingers on the desk. "Now. The first order of business." He looked at Marcus before he continued. "The chief has requested an emergency town meeting after the debacle of the pixie incident and the demon in the town square."

"My kids play in that square," said a man in the row in front of me as he stood up. I hadn't noticed how large he was until now, as though a rhinoceros was his close cousin. Maybe it was. "This town is supposed to be safe. You told me it was safe. It's why I brought my family here. You said we'd be protected."

"Calm down, Clive," said Marcus, his jaw clenching. "The town is safe. I promise."

Clive pointed a finger toward the exit. "Tell that to the demon that's plastered all over the ground."

Ronin whistled excitedly. "The crowd's going wild. Excellent. If all goes well, we might get a mob." He tossed a few more gummy bears into his mouth.

I leaned over to my Aunt Dolores. "I thought they cleaned it up?"

"They did," answered my aunt, "but not before the whole town got a good look."

Great.

Gilbert smacked his gavel. "Sit down, Clive, or I'll have you escorted out. You'll have your chance at the question round after we're done here."

Clive's wife pulled on his arm until the sizeable man sat down with his arms crossed over his chest, breathing heavily.

Gilbert cleared his throat. "Now, I was saying before I was *rudely* interrupted… after much debate with the town councilors, we have put it to a vote." He swallowed and waited to get everyone's attention back on him again. "The town has called in the Unseen."

There was a general murmur of shock and agitation from the gathered townspeople in the community center. Before I could ask Dolores who the hell the Unseen were, she shot to her feet like a girl in her twenties.

"You cannot be serious!" she cried with a voice just as youthful and strong.

Gilbert gave Dolores a pointed look. "They have agreed to aid in surveying our town until we can figure out what is happening."

Dolores raised her hands. "The wards were tampered with. That's what's happening."

The little man made a noise in his throat. "Yes. Wards that the *Merlin Group* specifically said were *unbreakable*."

"I never said that," she countered. "I said it would take a great amount of magic to break them."

"In any case," continued Gilbert as he dismissed her with a wave of his hand, which I knew he would regret later. I had a feeling this was payback for Dolores slapping him. "Your wards *failed*," continued Gilbert. "You were sworn to protect us—and *failed*. And we've already lost one member of our community—"

"Eight pixies were killed," interrupted Martha.

Gilbert shot her a glare and then turned to face the room. "Nine. We've lost nine members of our community. We won't lose another."

"You cannot let those goons into our town," cried Dolores.

Gilbert flashed her a little smile. "The decision's already been made, Dolores. The Unseen arrive tomorrow."

"You stupid little man," hissed Dolores, and I felt waves of power rolling off of her. Oh. Dear.

Gilbert's face went tomato red. "Why you… you…"

Marcus put a hand on the smaller man's arm, but he was looking at my aunt. "I know you're upset, Dolores."

Dolores laughed bitterly. "Upset? I'm livid," spat my aunt.

"But you see that we have the town's best interest at heart." Marcus moved his gaze around the room. "Right now, we don't have the necessary… people… we need to police the town. I don't have the men, and well, you don't have the magic."

I gave a tiny gasp. What the hell did he just say to my aunt?

"He's so dead," Ronin whispered excitedly. "Oh, man. He's dead."

I had to agree. What the hell was he trying to do? Dig himself an early grave? He was beautiful but clearly had a brain like a stone.

Gilbert gave Dolores an icy smile. "Marcus is right. The Merlin Group is not what it used to be. Sorry, but how are three old witches supposed to protect us?" He sneered, a victory smile on its way.

Beverly shot to her feet. "Who you calling old, you miserably *tiny*, little man."

Ruth joined her. "Yeah. She's only fifty-two."

Beverly gasped, her eyes round. "Ruth!"

Ruth gave her a wide-eyed shrug. "What?"

Dolores squeezed her way through the row of seats and reached the front desk, all the eyes of the room homed in on her. Her face was a mask of deep frowns and wrinkles. I'd never seen her so angry.

With her signature hand on her hip, she used her free hand to point at me.

115

Oh. No.

"We've got Tessa now," said Dolores. "A Davenport witch. And a powerful one."

Gilbert threw back his head and laughed like a gremlin. I was going to punch that little owl.

"Tessa?" he said. "She's inexperienced. She can't help us. You'd get more help from Martha and her beauty spells."

Martha leaned in close. "Watch it, Gilbert. Or I'll spell you a perm."

The little man grimaced. "I'm just telling it like is it."

"Tessa proved herself tonight." Dolores's voice rose. "If it weren't for her, the demon would have probably eaten all the pixies and then moved on to bigger and better meals."

"Ha!" Gilbert laughed. "If your niece is a powerful witch, then *I'm* the president of the United States."

My face flamed. I wasn't sure whether to get the hell out or stay and play tetherball with Gilbert's face.

Ronin spat out some gummy bears and shot to his feet. "Dude. You need to stop double-dipping in your crazy sauce. And you need to seriously reconsider that shirt—"

"Ronin, sit down!" cried Gilbert. He leaned forward and pointed a pudgy finger at him. "You owe me twenty dollars for that broom you broke."

Ronin's jaw fell. "What? Are you serious? The demon broke it. Bill the Netherworld. I saved this town with that broom. So, the way I see it, you owe me."

Gilbert leaned back in his chair. "You broke it. You buy it." He hit his gavel on the desk as though that was final.

Ronin let out a few curses and fell back in his chair. "I hate him. I really hate that guy."

"Totally understandable," I muttered. "He *is* wearing an ugly shirt."

I shifted in my seat, my temper reaching a dangerously explosive level. Though Ronin had been unconscious toward the end, I had risked my life. Maybe it had been stupid to fight the demon on my own, but it was the only thing I could think of. I just never thought it would come back and bite me in the ass like this.

But I stayed because I wanted to know who the hell these Unseen characters were. I was a curious beast.

"The Unseen can't be trusted." Dolores turned to Marcus. Her posture was stiff with anger. "Please. You know I'm right. Don't do this, Marcus. I beg you."

Marcus looked straight at her, and even from a distance, I could see he was struggling with something internally. "My hands are tied, Dolores. I have no choice. The town's in trouble, and it's my job to make sure it's protected."

"It's our job too," said Dolores, though I didn't think anyone heard her.

"The Unseen will patrol Hollow Cove starting tomorrow," said the chief. "I need to keep everyone safe."

"And the Merlin Group?" asked Beverly, her voice beautiful and clear, though with an underlying tone of fear. "What happens to us?"

Marcus's eyes focused on me. "The Merlin Group… is off the job."

CHAPTER

11

Even after popping two Tylenol, sleep didn't come easily. My body ached from my fight with the demon, and though Ruth had prepared a healing elixir for me that would help me sleep, I was still sore. Magic didn't always make the pain go away.

And it did nothing to snuff out my burning anger. My pillow became my enemy all night long. More like it was Marcus's face as I kept punching it, trying to get comfortable for hours. But I'd dozed off sometime in the night, only to be woken a few hours later with my heart thrashing and my body covered in sweat.

It went on like that all night long.

As the hours went by, my anger lessened as despair crept over me at the looks of misery on my aunts' faces at the meeting last night. My aunts were out of a job.

The Merlin Group was over.

No one uttered a word on the ride back home. Either my aunts were in shock, their feelings of betrayal running too deeply, or they were too hurt to speak for fear that they might break down. They probably didn't want me to see them like that. I know I wouldn't either.

I'd been dying to ask them about the Unseen. But one dark look from Dolores as I shut the front door of Davenport House a bit too forcefully told me that if I didn't want to end up like burnt toast, I'd better keep my mouth shut.

Yes, I was angry. Angry for my aunts but also angry that I thought I'd finally found my true calling, where I truly belonged—and that was working for the Merlin Group.

I would polish my own magical skills and learn as much as I could to be as proficient as my aunts. I wanted to prove to myself that I wasn't my mother, and I wouldn't abandon them. I was better than that.

And then just like that, the Merlin Group was no more.

Hell no. I would not lie here all morning and wallow in self-pity. That wasn't me. I got shit done. I would get the Merlin Group back on its feet if it was the last thing I did.

And what better way to help my aunts, to help relieve some of the stress, than to make them a special dinner tonight. They could relax while I tried to cook. Yeah. That would be an adventure.

I leaped out of bed feeling energized. I had a mission. After a quick shower, I went downstairs to the kitchen where my aunts were already assembled. The united feeling of gloom was almost palpable.

That would change.

"Can I borrow the car?" I asked as I grabbed a carrot muffin off the kitchen island.

Dolores took a sip of her coffee at the kitchen table. "Why do you need the car at nine in the morning?"

"It's a surprise." I broke off the muffin's top and shoved it in my mouth.

Ruth clapped her hands together. "Oh. I *love* surprises."

Beverly choked on her coffee. "You love everything. It's not natural."

"Don't you start," snapped Dolores, her magic crackling in the surrounding air.

Beverly raised a perfectly groomed brow, her magic rising in a challenge that had my skin riddling in goosebumps. "Don't you tempt me."

This was not going as well as I had imagined. "Who are the Unseen?" I blurted, wanting to change the subject. Their eyes all snapped to me, and I swallowed. "Well?"

Dolores looked down at her coffee mug. "The Unseen are mercenaries. Hired killers."

"Really?" Now that was a surprise. I was really intrigued now.

"Dreadful lot," muttered Ruth as she made a face. "Unlawful. Scary. Ugly. They're no better than demons."

Beverly wiped her brow with her fingers. "We've had the pleasure of working with them in the past. I don't care to work with them again."

"You won't," said Dolores, her fingers around her mug turning white. "The town made sure of that. The town made sure we never work again."

My heart beat loudly in the silence. My once strong, able aunts looked defeated and angry. Ruth clutched her arms around herself, a sad look in her eyes.

This was wrong. All wrong.

"Are they witches?" I asked.

"Some are, yes." Dolores met my gaze. "They're a mix of paranormal thugs. Cutthroats that only care about the size of their wallets. The worst of the worst, if you ask me."

"And the town thought hiring this group was a good idea?" Were they smoking crack?

My aunts had been replaced by these thugs? That didn't sound right. How could the town council agree to this?

Dolores sighed. "They do. They did." She took a wary sip of her coffee. "I'm sorry, Tessa. We made you come all this way for nothing. The Merlin Group is finished."

I frowned. "Don't. This isn't over."

The three women went silent again, and I knew I wasn't going to get much else out of them. Grabbing the car keys from the small wooden bowl in the middle of the table, I walked out the front door with my bag wrapped around my shoulder and got in the old Volvo. The car roared to life as I turned the ignition and pulled out of the long driveway. I didn't have far to go. There was only one grocery store in Hollow Cove. But I didn't want to have to walk back with all those bags. After a two-minute drive, I pulled the Volvo to the curb on Shifter Lane and stepped out.

Someone called my name, and I turned to see Ronin across the street, leaning on the side of a gleaming black car and flanked by two pretty women. He waved, and I waved back, smiling. Looked like he was working early.

Most of the lore about vampires was crap. Even if Ronin had been a full-fledged vampire, sunlight would not affect him, and neither would a cross. Vampires had human blood flowing in their veins. And unlike demons, it protected them from the sun.

My eyes drifted past him to a bland, gray brick building. The sign read HOLLOW COVE SECURITY AGENCY. My chest tightened in anger. This was Marcus's office. The way he'd just dismissed the Merlin Group had me wanting to throw a brick through his stupid window.

I turned around before I did something stupid—like throw a brick through his window. Gilbert's Grocer & Gifts stood before me. I had a moment of second-guessing myself, but then I took a breath, pulled open the front glass door and walked in.

And walked right into Gilbert.

"Hey, watch it," I growled, stepping back, or rather *bouncing* back from his protruding belly.

"Me?" Gilbert made a face. "I don't like your tone, young lady. I'm not the one who's not looking where she's going. Head in the clouds, just like your aunts."

A growl escaped my lips. "Don't talk about my aunts, Gilly."

"It's *Gilbert*."

"Okay, Gilly."

Gilbert's face darkened into an angry red. "What are *you* doing here? Shouldn't you be back on a bus to New York City?"

I smiled, though my mood was souring by the second. "Shopping for worms. Looks like

I'm in the right place." Ignoring his outrage, I moved past him and grabbed a shopping cart. I wasn't here to argue with that old fool. I was here to get what I needed, and then I was going to get out.

Fuming, I grabbed my phone and went through my list of items. There were ten aisles in the entire store, not huge, but at least it wouldn't take me too long to grab everything.

I pushed the cart down the first aisle and grabbed some milk and two cartons of eggs. Whispers reached me, and I spotted Martha in the canned goods aisle next to mine.

"… don't know how they can afford to live now that the council has cut them off," Martha was saying to a short, dangerously thin woman I didn't recognize. "At their age, they'll never find work again. Believe me. Who wants to hire old, battered witches when you can find much younger, more beautiful ones?"

"I know," answered the woman, her eyes wide. "Tragic."

"It's worse than tragic, hon. It's a catastrophe. You should let me do your roots. Gray doesn't suit you, darling."

I rolled my eyes and spun the cart the other way. I was in no mood to talk to Martha, who'd apparently been part of the vote to get the Unseen to replace my aunts.

Head down, I rolled the cart through the store, grabbing everything on my list in under five minutes.

Thrilled with my new shopping skills, I pushed the cart back toward the front to the cashier, only to find myself sandwiched between Martha and that woman she was speaking with.

"Tessa!" said Martha. Her blue eyeshadow matched her blue blouse. "Tell me. How are you aunts doing? The poor things. Such a sad, sad day for the community."

I placed my milk, eggs, four tomatoes, and cheese on the conveyor belt. "You don't look sad." I reached down in my cart and grabbed a box of organic corn flakes and three cans of organic red beans.

"I know you're upset, hon," said Martha as she grabbed her single grocery bag, standing way too close so I could see her purple lipstick was applied way too perfectly to have been anything but magical. "But this is no one's fault. Unfortunately, we women age. And with it, so does our power."

I wanted to smack that fake smile off her face. I shook my head as I emptied the rest of my cart. "You're wrong." I watched the cashier—a young teenager with overly drawn eyebrows and lips that looked like a duck's bill— scan the items. I took a calming breath, and after she was done, I gave her my credit card.

"Your aunts are practically *ancient*, hon," Martha prattled on. "It was time for them to retire. No harm done. It leaves room for the next generation to rise."

"No harm done?" I seethed, my voice rising dangerously, as I snatched up my card from the cashier. The poor girl looked frightened as she bagged my items. "I should have let the pixies destroy your salon." There I said it.

Martha drew in a breath, her eyes wide. I didn't think the witch was accustomed to people talking to her like that. Tough. The cashier froze with the egg carton in her hands. "I don't know why you're so angry with me," said Martha, her tone taking on an edge. "If you want to be angry with someone, be angry with Marcus."

I stilled. "Marcus? Why?" My hands started to shake, and my hair lifted in an unfelt breeze. The cashier rushed to grab another bag.

"It was *his* idea," expressed the witch. "*And*, he had the final vote. He could have voted against it, but he didn't. He voted to have your aunts *removed*."

A surge of energy coursed through me—

The eggs in my carton exploded, showering the cashier and Martha in yellow yolk. *Whoops.*

"You idiot! Look what you did to my new blouse!" shrilled Martha, seemingly at a loss

for what happened. I knew I had just made another enemy, but I didn't care.

Pissed, I grabbed my bags, left the eggs, and
stormed out.

CHAPTER

12

Your brain does funny things when you're mad. Like things you wouldn't normally do on any other given day when your emotions are stable and not high on anger. As it was, my emotions were not stable in the least. They had been on a giant roller coaster since I stepped into this town.

And the beast's name was Marcus.

I didn't even realize I was crossing the street with my bags still in my hands. I barely felt the weight of them as I hit the sidewalk, making a beeline for the gray stone building with the large stupid letters—HOLLOW COVE SECU-RITY AGENCY.

A shape ran up to me. "You don't want to do this, Tess," said Ronin, his voice strained and a little nervous.

Blood thumped against my temples. "Yeah. I do," I said with an added deranged giggle.

"You're not thinking straight. Just wait a second. Will you? Let's talk about this."

"There's nothing to talk about. I thought about it all night long," I said, through gritted teeth. "I know what I'm doing." Not really. But my legs had a mind of their own. I could see shapes through the double glass doors. Good.

Ronin jumped in my way and planted himself in front of the doors. His long arms stretched out on either side. "I know why you're pissed. I'd be mad too if Marcus had sacked my aunts." He shrugged. "Not really. My aunts are dead, but I get it. I really do."

My sense of betrayal rose higher, cementing my anger. "Out of my way, Ronin."

"Or what? You're going to turn me into a toad?"

"No. But I might roast you."

Ronin swallowed. "How about we go somewhere and talk? Talking is good. Women love to talk. Right? And I'm an *excellent* listener. I'm the pillow talk prince. I even do the encouraging nod and the widening of the eyes on the important bits."

"I don't want to talk." I want to break Marcus's face with my fist.

Ronin looked over his shoulder and then back at me. "If you go in there, it's not going to solve anything."

I was shaking so hard I felt I might fall apart. "Maybe not. But it will make me feel *so* damn good."

Ronin stiffened. "He can hurt you, you know."

My thoughts drifted to last night at the meeting, when Marcus told the entire town that the Merlin Group was off the job. He might as well have killed my aunts right there and then. He took their entire lives away in the three seconds it took him to utter those words.

"We're past that," I ground out. "He's already hurt my family. There's not much more he can do to me."

Ronin shifted nervously. "You can't just go in there."

"Watch me. Now move." I shoved Ronin with my arm and moved past him. Slipping the fingers of my right hand through the bag loop, I grabbed the cold metal handle and yanked the door open. I marched in, grocery bags and all.

I rushed down a hallway into a lobby, not caring about taking in any of the details except that everything was covered in beige. The hurried steps behind me said Ronin was following me. As I passed a few closed doors, the sporadic conversation and clatter of keyboards hit me, so did the smell of freshly brewed coffee.

A desk sat at the end of the lobby where it opened up into a larger space, and a woman with short white hair was seated behind it. She wore a white pressed shirt and a pointed look, making the wrinkles around her face sharper.

I could see other doors that led to more offices and four more desks. Two men I recognized from the crime scene on my very first night in Hollow Cove were looking at something on one of the computers.

"Can I help you?" asked the older woman. She cocked a brow at the sight of me. Her tone was belligerent, as though sitting in that chair in this building gave her some misplaced authority.

"Hi, Grace." Ronin stood next to me. "You look lovely today. Those are lovely pearls."

Grace narrowed her eyes at me, ignoring Ronin. "I know who you are. What do you want?"

Ribbons of anger tightened in my gut. "Is the chief in?"

Her eyes flicked to the door to her right. It was all I needed.

And then I was moving.

"Hey! You can't go in there!" she shouted. "You need to make an appointment!"

I made for the door, my heart pounding like a machinegun. Stenciled on the window was the name MARCUS DURAND with the words CHIEF OFFICER written under it.

Okay, so I might have gotten arrested for what I was about to do, but it would have been worth it.

I didn't know what I would say to him. I figured I'd just wing it and see what happened.

Working my fingers through the bag's loops, I turned the door handle and kicked the door in.

"You son of a bitch," I seethed. The door smashed into the wall with a loud crash.

Marcus looked up from his desk. "Tessa?"

I planted myself in front of him as my fury fed whatever innate power I had inside. It stirred from my feet to my head, swirling up to settle in my belly. I was shaking with it. The strength flowed through me, carrying a pleasant slurry of tingles with it, and it felt good.

I knew my hair was floating around me. I probably looked mad and ready for the loony bin, but I didn't care. I wasn't leaving until I'd given this pompous bastard a piece of my mind.

"How could you do that to my aunts?" I shouted, and I felt some spit flying out. Great. I was a rabid witch.

"Hey! Watch it!" cried Ronin as two thick brutes came crashing in. They saw me and made to move toward me, but with one flick of Marcus's hand, they halted.

My anger broke like a fever. "You took away their lives. It's all they've ever known. All their lives they've been watching over this town to keep everyone safe. And you just took that away in one stupid town meeting. Who the hell do you think you are?"

Marcus's expression darkened. "The chief."

My pulse raced. "A bastard is more like it," I said and saw the two men stiffen. "You had no right to do what you did. Tossing them away like they were garbage." The image of their faces, beaten and frightened flashed in my mind's eye and intensified my rage until it was nearly palpable.

Before I could control it, a spark of my magic left me. I wasn't sure where it came from. It just was. The papers on Marcus's desk floated up and so did his small garbage pail and his coffee mug. He didn't look surprised. His face was carefully blank, which only made me angrier.

Marcus leaned forward and put his elbows on his desk. "You need to calm down."

"It was *your* idea. Wasn't it? To call in the Unseen?" I wanted to hear him say it.

He shifted in his chair. "It was. Yes."

"Just like it was *your* idea to cast away my aunts."

A small noise escaped him and his eyes widened in mock concern. "I didn't cast them away."

134

"Dude, you sorta did," commented Ronin, nodding his head slowly.

Marcus glared at my only friend in this town. "I made an informed decision in a difficult time. The council voted."

My eyebrows rose and a wry smile came over me. "But you pushed it. Didn't you?"

Marcus settled back, a thoughtful expression smoothing his handsome features, and his posture confident, strong. "My community is scared. My people are frightened. I have a death still unsolved, and our wards are failing and letting demons in."

"That *Tess* killed," said Ronin. "Just FYI if anyone's still wondering." He looked at the two goons. "You might want to write that down."

Marcus's face became angry and his posture stiff. "I'm responsible for every single soul in this town. It's *my* job to keep them safe. I had to do something." He folded his hands on his desk. "I won't let more die. I stand by my decision. It was the right call."

Sweat broke out on the small of my back. "You do realize it was their only source of income," I ground out, imagining his head popping off like a dandelion. It was a good visual. "Did you ask yourself how three older witches, without any retirement savings, would support themselves? Did you think they could magically make money appear and put food on their tables? How do you suppose they would live the rest of their lives? Because, let me tell you, witches live *very* long lives."

Marcus's face flashed in alarm and his eyes dropped. He looked taken aback for the first time since I stepped into his office. "But…" said Marcus carefully, "the Merlin Group has members all over the world. I thought they worked on other jobs—"

"They don't, you pompous asshat!" I growled, sounding like an enraged lioness. I was losing my cool—no, I had lost it the moment I walked in. "It's not like they're living in luxury either. They have one car that's older than me. Their clothes are from the eighties, for cauldron's sake."

"They totally are," agreed Ronin. "Boy George wants his dresses back."

Marcus's gaze flicked to mine and then away. He was hunched with discomfort. "I did what was best for this town. I never meant—"

"If you hate witches so much, why do you ask for their help?" I asked.

Anger returned to his features, and his jaw clenched. The deep fury in his eyes scared the crap out of me, but we were way past that. "You don't know what you're talking about," he growled, sounding like a beast. Perhaps he was a werewolf or a werebear.

"I do." I leaned forward. "I know Ruth gave you some sort of tonic. Probably some healing elixir or something like that. Right?" His eyes widened a millimeter, and I took that as a yes. "Because that's what she does. It's where her magic shines. In healing magic."

"I have nothing but respect for your aunts."

"Bullshit. I don't know what Ruth gave you, but it's obvious it's something important to you. Your health or someone else's. A girlfriend? Your parents? I don't really care. But I know she worked on it for you. Probably spent hours, just to get it right, because that's who she is. She *cares*. And you thank her by stabbing her in the back."

Marcus's mouth fell open. His eyes widened even farther. His lips parted, and he sat there, seemingly unable to even blink. "I did what I had to for the town—"

"No." I shook my head. "You did it because you could. Because you had the power to do it. But having power doesn't give you the right to abuse it."

"Hear! Hear!" cheered Ronin. I was starting to like him.

"You hate my mother," I accused, my voice trembling. I couldn't help it. "You hate me. You hate my aunts." I narrowed my eyes. "Be careful, Chiefy. There might not be a lot of witches here in Hollow Cove, but there are covens everywhere around the world. And once they hear about how you've mistreated their members… because I *will* tell them… you'll wish you'd never been born."

Marcus shifted in his seat. "Are you finished?"

I looked down at him. "Yeah. I am." And with that, I whirled around and stormed out of his office, grocery bags and all, and never looked back.

And when I heard him swear as his hot coffee mug fell into his lap, I smiled.

CHAPTER

13

Ten hours later, I was still shaking from my ordeal with Marcus. I'd mashed up the tofu imagining it was his face. Now it looked more like a purée than the chunks I was going for. It was no secret that my cooking abilities were as good as my rocket science skills. But damn it, I *was* going to make my aunts dinner—tofu avocado tacos—even if they had to drink it through a straw.

The only thing that eased my temper was reading through *The Witch's Handbook*. It lay open on the kitchen island away from the mess of ingredients and bowls scattered over the counter. I had a quarter left to read in the book, and I was determined to have read it at least once by the end of the day.

I glanced at the page. *A Witch's Guide to Power Words.*

This was by far my favorite subject. I'd been reading the same six pages over and over for the last two hours, letting the information sink in, savoring it, and committing it to memory.

Power words were a witch's sword, her grenades—weapons used to command and to destroy. They were considered battle magic or defense magic. Badass witches used them when facing an enemy.

And I would become one of them.

I'd always known there was power in certain words. It had been a recurring subject with my aunts over the years though I'd never actually witnessed any of them use a power word. And when they spoke of power words, it was always said in hushed tones, as though they feared the words. Which only increased my curiosity a thousand-fold.

The more I read, the more excited I got, especially when I read the part where power words and elemental magic went hand in hand. You could use power words with the elements. Though I'd never imagined I could pull on the energy of the elements and throw a couple of power words in the mix to create the atomic bomb of magic. Now *that* was hardcore magic.

So far, I'd memorized four essential power words: Accendo, to ignite fire; Ventum, to call up wind; Protego, to conjure a sphere-shaped shield of protection (because I would need it); and Fulgur, to conjure a bolt of lightning.

One in particular I'd saved for Marcus later (involving his groin).

Yet, like all magic, power words came with a price. No surprise there. The tiny asterisk at the bottom of the page noted: *The use of any power word will cause excruciating pain to the witch invoking it. The more dangerous the power word, the worse the pain will be. Some witches have died using a power word. Tread carefully.*

Power words were dangerous because they were raw magic. They needed to be wielded with great precision, and using them took a chunk of power that left the conjurer near exhaustion. When using power words, there were no second chances. If you messed up, got tongue-tied, and said the word wrong, you died. Yup. Plain and simple, which explained why so few among witches used them. For one, they hurt because magic claimed a piece of you, even if you did it right. And if you didn't, well, it didn't really matter since you'd be dead.

Power words were used as a last resort, when all else failed. And yet, something inside me stirred as I kept reading about them. It was like they called to me. They *wanted* me to use them.

The kitchen's back door swung open making me flinch.

"… I told you it was a waste of time," Dolores was saying as she hung her purse on one of the wooden pegs. Ruth walked in behind her. "That chief won't listen to reason. Just like his father, that one—" Dolores's eyes widened when she spotted me. "Tessa? Are you working on a science project?"

"What?" I looked around the kitchen, over the mess of flour, splattered tofu and beans on the counter, at the cookbooks that were speckled with tomato sauce. "Okay. It does look like a science project."

Ruth giggled. "I think you failed. You've got avocado in your hair."

"I do?" I reached up and pulled a clump of avocado out of my hair. "Great."

"What are you trying to do here?" Dolores walked around the kitchen staring at the four steaming pots on the stovetop. Her face looked puzzled, and I could see she was trying hard not to laugh.

The back door opened again, and Beverly strolled through, pulling a man behind her. "Attaboy, Henry," she said and yanked the doe-eyed Henry into the kitchen.

"Your date?" I asked, staring at the middle-aged man with gray hair and thick glasses. His navy suit looked like it had seen a few generations.

"Cauldrons, no." Beverly let go of Henry's hand. "Henry thought it was a good idea to *expose* himself to the high school girl volleyball team. Didn't you, Henry?"

Henry nodded, his eyes distant and weary like he was sleepwalking.

I frowned. "I don't recognize him. Is he from Hollow Cove?"

"No." Beverly walked over to the basement door and pulled it open. "Let's go, Henry." She yanked him forward. "Attaboy. In you go. That's right. There's a good boy." With a shove, she pushed him through, slammed the door and locked it behind him.

There was no surprise yelp this time. Just the familiar sounds of grunts of pain as someone fell down the stairs and a final groan as he hit the floor.

Once again, Davenport House shook and rattled like we were hit by a 5.0 earthquake on the Richter scale. The lights flickered on and off. The walls moved, and I swear it looked like the house was expanding, like it had just swallowed poor Henry and was making room in its belly. With a last rumble, the house settled.

Okay. This was getting weird. "What's going on here? That's two strange men you've locked in the basement. Is there something I need to know?" Were my aunts vigilante serial killers? Were they venturing outside the town in the search of victims? And if so, victims for what? What the hell was down there, anyway? And why did I get the impression I'd never see those men again?

It was almost as though… as though Davenport House had eaten them.

Beverly adjusted her bright pink dress and took in the sight of the kitchen. "I haven't seen the kitchen in this state since Amelia tried to make Sean that three-month anniversary dinner." The three sisters laughed, their eyes lost in some shared, distant memory.

My heart gave a tug at the mention of my parents. "I know you're just trying to change the subject." I looked around at my aunts, noting that not one would make eye contact with me.

"Looks like you've inherited her culinary skills," laughed Beverly, though her face held traces of sadness.

"You could never teach Amelia anything," commented Dolores as she eyed one of the simmering pots on the stove, angling her body like she was contemplating whether she should grab the pot and dump it.

"Her head was always in the clouds," added Ruth, looking up at the ceiling as though she could see the sky through layers of drywall, subfloor, and roof shingles.

"Not in the clouds," said Beverly. "She was thinking of Sean. It was always about *Sean*. Her world revolved around him. You could never get her to settle down and try to learn spells or anything to do with magic."

Dolores sighed heavily through her nose. "If it didn't involve Sean, she wasn't interested."

So true. And that also included me.

I'd come to terms with my mother's lack of parenting skills over the years, her ignoring me as she worshiped the ground my dad walked on. She wasn't perfect by any means, but she was my mother. It's not like I could trade her in for another.

"Oh, I know what this is!" shrilled Beverly, her green eyes sparkling with delight. "You're cooking for a man. Aren't you?"

"You know what they say?" offered Ruth, her smile lighting up her face. "The way to a man's heart is through his stomach."

"No, it isn't," laughed Beverly. "Everyone knows the way to a man's heart is how well you perform in the bedroom."

"Spoken like a true tramp," muttered Dolores, winning a glare from Beverly.

Yikes. This was getting ugly.

I wiped my forehead with the back of my hand. "Actually, this is for you." My face grew warm from embarrassment. "Well," I straightened. "This was my way of saying thank you for letting me stay with you for a while. I wanted to do something nice. You weren't supposed to be back for another hour." My shoulders sagged. "It was supposed to be a surprise."

Dolores met my gaze, her eyebrows high on her forehead. "Oh, it is a surprise," she laughed. "We have no idea what *this* is. What are you trying to make or are we supposed to guess?"

"Tofu avocado tacos," I said. "I wanted to make dinner for you guys. Guess I should stick to making book covers, huh?"

"Nonsense." Ruth came over and gave me a shoulder hug. "That was very generous and kind of you to want to do this, Tessa."

"It was?" Dolores lifted the top of one of the pots and took a sniff, her face twisting. "More like trying to poison us." She howled in laughter.

Ruth laughed. Beverly laughed. I laughed. It was better than crying.

"Should I throw this out, then?" Hands on my hips, I looked around. Jeez. It looked like a food fight, or that the kitchen had thrown up.

"Nonsense. We never throw away food. I think I can fix this." Ruth pulled out an apron and tied it around her middle. "You should keep studying, Tessa. I can manage."

I thought about protesting, but I knew Ruth could probably salvage my cooking.

"You went to see Marcus? Why?" I wiped my hands on my jeans, wondering if he'd called my aunts after my little temper tantrum. What a baby. That's what he was. A giant, handsome baby, who needed a good ol' spanking. I wouldn't mind spanking his nice behind.

"To try and talk some sense into that thick skull of his." Dolores pulled up a chair and sat at the kitchen table, looking like she'd want nothing better than to throw Marcus in the basement with the other men. "Bringing the Unseen in our town won't solve anything."

"More like scare everyone," said Beverly as a glimmer of annoyance crossed her pretty face.

I nodded. "The demon. The wards. Do you have any idea who's behind this?"

"Not yet," answered Dolores.

"Did he mention me by any chance?" I regretted the words as soon as they spewed out of my mouth. *What the hell was I thinking?*

Dolores cut me a look. "No. Why?"

"No reason." I popped a cherry tomato into my mouth so she couldn't make me say anything else. Until I ate the tiny tomato.

"We're not going to give up," said Dolores still eyeing me, her dark eyes calculating like she was trying to read my mind. "The town might not pay us anymore, but it doesn't change who and what we are. We swore an oath to protect our town. And we will. With or without their money or their help."

"I was hoping you'd say that." I was really looking forward to testing my newly acquired power words. A couple would work wonders on Marcus's face.

Dolores tapped the table with her finger. "The town needs us, more than ever. We won't let them down."

"What about the Unseen?" I asked, my flash of excitement growing. "What are we going to do about them?"

The kitchen back door crashed open.

"Quick! Hide!" cried Ronin, his face flushed from what I suspected was running over here.

I searched his face. "Is this a weird town thing where we all join in a game of hide and seek?" I'd always known Hollow Cove was a little out there when it came to the town festivals. I wouldn't be surprised if this was one of their regular activities.

Ronin shook his head. "The Unseen. They're coming."

Dolores let out an exasperated breath. "We know they're coming, boy. You were there at the town meeting. This shouldn't come as a surprise. You seem a bit slow for a vampire."

"No." He shut the door behind him and locked it. "They're coming *here*. Like—right now."

"Here?" I jumped forward, my heart thrashing in my chest like a jackhammer. "What are you talking about? Why would they want to come here?"

The vampire flicked a nervous gaze over us and then said, "They want Davenport House."

CHAPTER
14

You know that moment of shock where it feels like everything is at a standstill while you're trying to process what you just heard because it just can't be true? Well, it was happening.

My aunts and I stood still in the kitchen, staring at Ronin as though it was the first time we'd laid eyes on him. Silence soaked in, but I could almost hear my aunts formulating deadly plans in their heads.

Dolores straightened her back, pulling herself to her full height. "Ladies," she said, and turned on her heel out of the kitchen, moving quickly down the hallway toward the front door.

Ruth raced to join her, not bothering to take off her apron. Beverly's heels clicked on the hardwood floor as she hurried behind her sisters.

A wicked smile formed on my lips as I looked at Ronin. "Showtime," I said and ran to catch up to my aunts.

"Why don't I like the sound of that!" said Ronin running behind me.

My pulse thrashed at the thought of seeing my aunts do some serious magic. Yes, they might be a little gray-haired, their reflexes a little slow, but these witches were in their prime. They had years of knowledge and magical wisdom. Knowledge was power.

Dolores was the first at the door. It swung open on its own, as though an invisible butler had opened it for her.

I was nearly jumping out of my skin with excitement.

Dolores stepped on to the front porch with Ruth and Beverly on either side of her, a united front.

When I neared the doorway, a wave of energy hit me, like I'd stepped into a pool of cold water. My skin prickled from its strength. Power touched my skin like the flowing of a wild river—a strong, powerful, current. Their lips were moving, and their hands gesturing. My aunts' clothes and hair lifted and moved in an invisible breeze. The hair on the back of my neck pricked at the sudden rise of power, a crapload of it.

They were witches, and their strength lay in their magic.

I stepped onto the porch and moved around them so I could get a clear view of the action because there would be lots of it. When I had a clear view, my breath caught.

Below the front porch, standing on the flagstone path, was a cluster of five figures.

Dressed all in black, the only thing that stood out was the golden masks that hid their faces. They stood with a casual and predatory edge, the way a person stands when they know they have the upper hand in a battle.

The masks were a creepy touch. Though their faces were hidden behind them, they were shadowed but confident. Without the masks, I didn't see what the fuss was about. Okay, two out of five looked like they were professional wrestlers, but the others weren't so large. I was sure the last one on the left was female.

My breath came slowly, and I rocked forward on my boots, feeling the stir of adrenaline.

Ronin bumped into my side. "You'd think they were at a costume party," he commented as he positioned himself next to me.

"Is there something I can help you with?" Dolores's voice cut through the silence like a sledgehammer pounding on rock.

The largest of the Unseen, male no doubt, with a mass of long, wild red hair, broke from the rest and took a step forward. "We want your house," said the Unseen, his voice thick and heavy like his body. "There's no inn or hotel in this place. Your house is the largest here, and it has enough rooms for all of us. It's the best house in your crappy little town. And we'll take it."

"At least he's direct," I mumbled.

"And stupid," said Ronin.

"How did you know they were coming here?" I asked, keeping my eyes on the Unseen.

"I overheard them," answered Ronin.

I raised a brow. "You were spying on them."

The vampire flashed a smile. "It's one of my many talents."

"Davenport House is not for sale," continued Dolores. "Best be on your way."

The beefy Unseen's shoulders rolled in laughter, and the others joined in, sounding like the cackles of wild hyenas. "We're not here to buy it, old witch. We're here to *take* it. The Unseen take what we want."

My blood raced. My body was both hot and cold from the nerve of this giant SOB. "You're even more stupid than you look in your faerie masks if you think you can take this house," I growled.

Blue eyes flashed behind his gold mask as the same Unseen's attention snapped to me. "What's this? A little witch with little threats? You think you can scare me with your little voice?"

"Maybe not," I said, my voice strong and bold, "but I can still kick your ass."

At that, all the Unseen threw back their heads in laughter. Okay, that didn't help my ego. But I didn't care about my ego. I cared about this house. It was the only home I had, and no way were they taking it. Not without a fight.

The large Unseen tilted his head, and a red beard peeked beneath the mask. I heard him sniff the air. "Smells like you're cooking something. I'm hungry. Haven't had a good home-cooked meal in ages." His eyes moved along my aunts. "I don't want to have to kill three old ladies and a little mouse of a woman, but I will. The Unseen take what we want."

My lips parted. "Did he just call me a mouse?"

Ronin snorted. "He did."

There was a murmur of consensus among the Unseen and a snicker from the one I pegged as a woman. I would kick her ass first.

"Seeing as I'm in a very good mood to-night," said the bearded Unseen. "I'm going to give you the chance to walk away." He lifted his arms and gestured like we were too daft to understand the meaning in his words.

"You'll be dead by the time you step onto this porch," challenged Dolores. "Davenport House belongs to the Davenport witches. It will not be soiled by the likes of the Unseen."

The big Unseen chuckled. "The house belongs to the one who can take it from you. That's me"—he gestured behind him— "and that's them."

Beverly moved forward. "How dare you speak to us like this? Don't you know who we are?"

The Unseen snickered. "No. And I don't care. But you… on the other hand… are much older than I usually like my women… but I might make an exception. You have a pretty face. It won't take long. That's a promise."

A volley of curses flew from Beverly's mouth and she ended them with a spit on the floor, which only made the large Unseen laugh harder. Bastard.

Ruth braved herself forward. "Who do you think you are? You can't barge in here with pitchforks and torches!"

The Unseen looked over his shoulder at his cronies. "We don't have pitchforks or torches."

"You know what I mean," said Ruth, her cheeks bright pink. "This is private property. You're trespassing."

The Unseen took another step forward. "Oh my goodness!" He made a show of stomping his boot. "Look. I'm trespassin' again. What are you going to do about it?"

"Listen here, Ginger," I seethed and moved down the first step. "You've got balls coming here. I'll give you that. But only the stupid would challenge the Davenport witches."

Ronin let out a chuckle. "You can't cure stupid."

"Tessa, watch yourself," said Ruth. "These guys don't play by the rules."

"Good."

"They'll kill you."

No one was killing me tonight. "They can try."

I focused my will and pulled on the raw energy of the surrounding elements. It answered. I felt it in the rain clouds that covered the night sky and felt it in the moving winds, in the earth, and in the roots of the ancient trees that surrounded our property. The energy of the elements interacted, moving as they waited for my command.

The same Unseen pulled a long gleaming sword from under his jacket. "I don't think I like your tone, little mouse," he said his voice making my skin crawl. "Pity that I'll have to cut that pretty face of yours."

"How about you take off the mask first," I said, pulling on the energy of elements around me. A lot of energy waited to be used, up there, where the forces of ancient nature brawled and tumbled. Only a fool would tap into such power. That fool was me.

"Only a coward hides behind a mask," I continued. "Is that what you are? A coward?"

The big Unseen shifted on his feet. I couldn't see his face, but his body hardened in anger. He pounced, moving faster than I thought a man his size could move, his gleaming sword coming at me.

Words spilled from Dolores's mouth. But I was faster.

"Accendo!" I shouted. A ball of fire sprouted from my palm and I sent it hurtling at the Unseen.

It flew straight over his head.

Whoops.

The Unseen spun around. Latin spewed out of his mouth, and a sphere of blue energy rose and caught my fireball, extinguishing it with a simple *pop*.

Crap. The red-bearded Unseen was a witch. Damn, I did not see that coming.

"Um. That was a serious airball, Tess," expressed Ronin. "You might want to work on your aim."

If I wasn't occupied in a one-on-one witch duel with the Unseen, I would have punched Ronin in the face.

The beefy Unseen turned his ugly golden mask toward me. "My turn." Was the only warning I got as he and his cronies sprinted toward us—

A gust of kinetic force blew from my aunts' outstretched hands, hitting the five Unseen and sending them sprawling back to roll over our front lawn like tumbleweeds in an old Western movie. Impressive.

"Oh, darn. There go my rose bushes," said Ruth, scorn ringing in her tone. "Now I'm really, really mad."

"Be glad the thorns pierced their *little* parts," smiled Beverly. And the three sisters snickered. Was there something about the roses I didn't know?

The Unseen howled as they leaped from the ground, running their hands all over their bodies frantically—under their shirts and pants like they were trying to get rid of an itch that wouldn't go away.

Ruth saw me watching and said, "Poison roses."

"Ah."

"What's going on here?"

I looked past the Unseen to see Marcus marching up the flagstone path. His face was screwed up in anger, the light from the porch reflecting in his gray eyes. I was truly amazed that he looked that good when he was angry. Pretty people—so annoying.

"These old bags put a spell on us!" shrieked a female voice as she stood up, her arms a blur as she scratched her neck, her arms, and her chest, giving everyone a glimpse of her red bra and her thighs all at once.

"I knew it!" I raised my fist in the air, which at the time, I thought had been a good idea. But I lowered it at the scowl on Marcus's face.

"You really know how to get on the guy's bad side," whispered Ronin. "I love it."

Curses and hisses flew from the mouths of the Unseen as they got to their feet, their bodies twitching and fidgeting. It was an awesome sight.

"Ants in your pants?" smirked Ronin. "The hives that come with it are out-of-this-world disgusting. You're going to love 'em."

The red-bearded Unseen approached Marcus, his mask in his hand giving everyone a good look at his face, which was marred with nasty-looking rashes. Thick, red eyebrows were high on his forehead, and thin lines creased around his eyes and mouth, making him look to be in his mid-forties. But if this guy was a witch, he could be a lot older than that.

"We were just having an amicable discussion," began the redhead, scratching his neck with his thick hand. "When these bags of bones"—he gestured with his mask at me and my aunts—"drew the first blow."

Marcus looked up at the porch. "Is this true?"

Dolores let out a puff of air. "Only because these nitwits threatened to take our house!"

"Yeah!" agreed Ruth, and she stomped her foot like a little girl, getting a nod of approval from Beverly.

"Take your house?" Marcus turned his attention back on the Unseen with the beard. "Emmet? Did you try to take Davenport House? Please tell me you didn't."

The Unseen called Emmet shrugged. "Of course I did. I happen to like this house." He raised his chin. "It calls to me."

Marcus smacked his forehead. "Why me."

"I can help you with that." Pulse throbbing, I stepped down the front porch and walked up right in Marcus's face. "Because you hired them. That's why." *You big, stupid, stupid, man.*

Marcus's jaw clenched. "I'm not having this conversation again with you. The Unseen are here to stay."

"Not in our house, they're not," I said.

Marcus looked at Emmet. "What gave you the idea you could just take this house from its owners?"

Emmet smiled, his teeth white and gleaming in the soft light of the porch. "The Unseen take what we want. And we want that house."

"Well, you can't have it," said Marcus, raising his hand and cutting Emmet's protest short. "You'll have to find other lodgings for now."

"Where?" Emmet growled. "There's no other lodging in this crappy little town. No hotel. Motel. Nothin'."

"You can sleep in the park for all I care," said Marcus. "Your sleeping arrangements weren't in the contract. They're not my concern."

I cocked a brow. I was surprised the chief even cared enough to be on our side for our house since he'd been quick to remove the Merlin Group from paid employment.

Emmet narrowed his eyes. "This isn't over —"

"Help! Help me! There are demons on the loose! Loose!"

I turned to the sound of the terrified howl and let out a laugh.

"They ate Mrs. Bright! Ate her!" said a man in his fifties running across the lawn of Davenport House. Which wasn't unusual on its own, considering this eccentric town. But what made me smile was the fact that he was buck naked—and wet.

His hair was wet, either with sweat from running across town, or he'd just run out of his shower.

"That's Earl Johnson," said Ruth, her lips parted in shock. "What in the cauldron's name is he doing?"

"Taking a midnight naked stroll." I laughed, and so did Ronin. He was a great audience.

"Nothing wrong with showing a little skin," said Beverly, smiling, her eyes fixated on the naked, but scared-out-of-his-mind man.

Dolores was silent, her eyes focused on the Unseen. She wasn't even looking at the naked man.

"Earl!" Marcus shouted. "Where? Where are the demons?"

Earl Johnson kept running. He should have been on the Olympic team the way he was running barefoot with everything flailing and swinging—and I *mean* everything.

Emmet whistled and four of the Unseen shot after the naked man. After a moment, he crossed his arms over his large chest and stared at my aunts, his expression hard, now that we could see his face.

"Emmet," warned Marcus. He shifted on his feet as though he was contemplating whether he should grab the big guy and pull him away by force. "Leave the ladies alone."

The big man shrugged. "There's no law that says I can't stay here all night and watch the house."

"The town's paying you to protect it," pressed Marcus.

"Didn't I just send four of my Unseen? Yes. Yes, I did."

I looked up and met my aunts' stares, my pulse thrashing. "You guys good?"

Dolores looked down at me. "I'm not leaving this porch until the filth is removed from our front lawn."

"Me either," said Ruth.

"You go on ahead, dear," encouraged Beverly. "We've got this covered."

I made to move.

"You don't work for the Merlin Group anymore," said Marcus stepping in my way.

Wow. He was really asking for it. I gave him a bitter smile. "I never stopped working for them."

And I wasn't about to ask Marcus for permission either. I was still part of the Merlin Group, even if the town wasn't paying us.

Besides, I'd been meaning to hurt something all day. Now, this was my chance.

I waited, daring Marcus to say something, but he pulled his eyes away from me. Good choice.

"Where are we going, boss?" asked Ronin, his tall, lanky body appearing next to me.

I smiled, feeling a little wicked and excited. "Follow the naked," I answered and sprinted across the lawn after Earl.

CHAPTER

15

When I said *I* went sprinting across the front lawn, it was more of a decent jog, really. Ronin really did all the sprinting with his vampire speed.

"That's cheating!" I'd howled after him, owning that I wasn't known for my sprinting abilities, nor running long distances.

Ronin let out a laugh as he put on a burst of speed, his legs blurs of black to where I didn't even think his feet actually made contact with the ground. Now he was just showing off. The bastard was probably gliding. But it made me smile—something I hadn't done a lot lately.

I ran past Martha's salon, Hot Mess Witch. The witch stood on the front porch smoking a cigarette as she eyed the commotion. A quick glance in her direction told me her salon was empty. Guess the pixie attack had been really bad for business.

My lungs burned and so did my thighs. I could still make out Earl—or rather, his pale butt gleaming in the moonlight—with the four Unseen right on his tail. The man had some serious running skills.

But I knew I couldn't run like this forever. And I didn't want to. If I knew a spell that would sprout me some wings, I would definitely do it. But I didn't know of any. In my haste, I'd forgotten my loyal *Witch's Handbook* in the kitchen. I'd memorized a few power words. I just hoped it would be enough.

Earl's butt was still visible as I ran past Gilbert's grocery store. The lights were on. The shop was still open, and if he stepped out now, I might have to run him over.

Earl's shrilling cries sounded over the thumping of my boots. "Where the hell is he going?" I panted.

And then it hit me.

I staggered to a slow jog because if I stopped short, I'd pitch myself forward on the pavement.

Ronin stopped ahead of me and spun around, like his uber vampire senses had told him I had stopped. Either that or he heard me.

"You can't keep up?" The vampire smiled as he strutted my way. "I can carry you if you want. You don't look that heavy."

I would not have that conversation. "I'll tell you why I stopped. By the time we catch up to naked Earl, the demons might have eaten someone else already."

"Your point being?" said Ronin.

I pinched the cramp in my side with my right hand. "If I was Earl, and had just seen a demon that made me run out of my shower, where would I be running to?"

"In the opposite direction of the demon."

"Exactly. I'd be running the hell away and as far as I could. He's dragging us *away* from where it happened. So, we need to go the *other* way," I said, my heart thumping. "Where does Mrs. Bright live?"

Ronin flashed me a wicked smile and pushed off on the balls of his feet, racing past me and back down the road from where we'd come.

"Like I said!" I shouted at him. "Not fair. You're *so* at the bottom of my friends list."

I doubled back and ran up the same street again. The sounds of naked Earl died out behind me until I could only hear my own laboring breaths and my loud thumping boots.

Thank the cauldron we didn't have to go too far.

Ronin leaned against the wall of a sizeable, gray stone building with his arms crossed over his chest, looking pleased with himself. The words HOLLOW COVE LIBRARY were stenciled above two massive wooden doors.

"You sure we're in the right place?" I asked, a little skeptical.

"Nah, I thought we could do a little night reading," said the vampire, a cheeky smile on his face.

I gave him a pointed look and glanced around. I spotted a small apartment above the library. Odd place to live, but when I swung my gaze across from the library, I saw the lit second-floor bathroom window where rolls of steam were still spilling out and the bottom front door was standing wide open. I knew this was Earl's place. He'd looked out his window, saw something, and decided it would be a good idea to run out naked in the streets. Weird guy. Weirder town.

I pulled my eyes back to the library. As I moved toward the front steps of the building, droplets of dark maroon spotted the concrete mixed in with some strands of blonde hair. Yikes.

"Looks like Mrs. Bright was grabbed out here and then pulled inside," I commented, following the trail of blood like a hound and seeing it disappear through the double doors.

"Look at you... getting your Sherlock on. It's sexy," commented Ronin.

"Man, you're aggravating tonight."

Ronin shrugged. "I aim to please," he answered, a wicked smile on his stupid face.

Scowling, I pushed open the doors to the library and slipped inside. I was met with darkness.

And something else.

Even though my senses weren't as attuned as a well-versed witch to demon energies and the vibrations of magic, I still felt an icy transition of energy as soon as I stepped through the entrance—a shift in the air, a cold pulsing, the throb of magic. It was similar to that which I felt from the snake-bear demon I vanquished but different.

All witches were born with an innate ability to sense all things supernatural and magical though their level of keenness depended on the witch in question and their inner strength. I was still getting used to all these sensations and feelings again, the differing energies from shifters, vampires, and all other half-breeds. But now, all these energies were intensified, and I didn't know why.

I blinked, waiting for my eyes to adjust to the darkness until I could see. The lobby was lit only by the fading red emergency lights hanging above the doorways. I tried to peer around but saw nothing other than dim shapes and outlines of what might have been a few chairs and a desk.

When shapes came into view, I walked inside the entrance lobby and found the main light panel. I flicked them up and down. "Great. The power's out."

"Looks like it's just the library," commented Ronin. "The lights are on everywhere else."

Alarm washed through me. "I might be a little rusty with my demonology, but I don't remember demons taking their time to cut off the power of some building. They're always too busy feasting on innards of some mortal."

The darkness created deep shadows around Ronin's face, making him appear older. "So, who cut the power if not them?" he asked, worry coating his tone.

"Well, it wasn't Mrs. Bright." I squinted in the darkness. I stood for a moment, listening and sending out my senses in search of demon energies. "Maybe we're not dealing with just demons."

Ronin shifted his weight. "Who then? The Boogeyman?"

"Let's find out." I moved past the lobby. With no light, it would be impossible to follow the blood trail. So, I opted for the next best thing—my gut.

If I were a demon, I would want to eat my prey somewhere quiet where I wouldn't be interrupted. And that somewhere was straight through the lobby to the actual library.

"Don't you have some witch light?" whispered Ronin. "I saw you use one on the first night we met. Remember? I was the hot guy next to the dead guy."

Damn. I knew I should have brought the book. There might have been a spell in there to cast some light. "It wasn't mine. The witch orb was my aunt's," I answered feeling like a fool. "Casting a light right now isn't such a great idea. We don't want to attract the demon's attention." It was a half-lie, but Ronin didn't need to know that.

I made a promise to myself that next time I wouldn't leave without that book. Not until I knew it by heart, cover to cover.

The scent of sulfur—the stench of demons—caught in my throat as we passed the lobby and front desk.

Ronin moved next to me, a stapler in his hand, holding it up like it was a deadly weapon.

I halted. "You plan on stapling the demon's eyes shut with that?"

"What?" Ronin shrugged. "It's a weapon if you know how to use it." He held the stapler like a gun and squeezed. I heard a few staples fall, though I couldn't see them.

My pulse raced as we moved inside the library, meeting shadows but not much else. A coffered ceiling disappeared into the darkness, and windows lined the exterior walls, giving us just enough light from the streetlights to be able to make out shapes.

The library was huge, considering the size of the town—about the size of a gymnasium. I strained my ears for any sudden noise and hurried through the library, past the rows of reading desks and leather-cushioned chairs that were positioned in the middle of the large space and surrounded by countless rows of bookcases. Each shelf was crammed with old books in leather bindings, their volumes neatly aligned with the spines showing a dizzying variety of subjects.

I smelled the blood before I saw the body. And when I say blood, I mean a hell of a lot of it.

On the ground next to one of the reading desks was a slop of ghoulish entrails and torn pieces of fabric that could have once been a pair of pants or a shirt with pale white bones gleaming on top of it all. It was like the meat had been picked clean from the bones because I was staring at a complete skeleton.

The skeleton of poor Mrs. Bright.

Bile rose fast in the back of my throat as I took in the scene. Blood was scattered all over in thick droplets and splashed in spurts against the desk. The scarlet footprints of something huge headed toward the back of the library.

Ronin stood next to me. "Where's the body?"

"You're looking at it." I knew whatever demon had done this—because I was certain it had been a demon attack—had devoured poor Mrs. Bright, leaving only her bones as evidence.

"Damn." Ronin whistled. "It was a hungry bastard."

"Hungry still," I said, whipping my head around and searching the shadows as my eyes fell back on those bloody footprints. "It feasted on her and liked how she tasted, which means it's going to go for more. It's not going to stop. Come on."

Tiptoeing around the blood, I followed the footprints as best as I could in the semi-darkness, my heart thrashing hard against my chest. I weaved a power word in my mind, keeping it there, ready in case I needed it. The scent of sulfur was strong, and I blinked the water from my eyes.

The air suddenly sizzled and cackled with energy.

I froze.

Ronin crashed into me. "What is it?" he whispered. "Why'd you stop?"

"Magic." Magic was here. And lots of it.

Ronin stepped away. "That's good, right? We like magic. Magic is our friend."

I shook my head. "Not all the time. Stay alert," I said as I ventured carefully toward the wash of magic.

I came upon three reading desks pushed to the sides, leaving a large open space.

And in the center of the space were the remains of a large, summoning circle, its three rings of symbols carefully wrought in white chalk upon the wooden floor with burning candles interspersed among the symbols.

"A magic circle." Ronin knelt next to a still-burning candle.

"Not just any magic circle. A *summoning* circle," I told him, my eyes on the bloodstained floor a few feet from the circle. "Someone summoned that demon."

He looked up at me. "Why the hell would someone be stupid enough to do that?"

"Good question." I followed the bloody footprints and my chest went tight.

"What? There's more?" came Ronin's voice behind me.

Carved into the wood floor a few feet away from the summoning circle was a triangle within a circle. This wasn't a summoning circle. This was a ward. I was sure of it. Not that I was adept in wards, but I could still recognize one when I saw it. A part of me knew this was

one of the wards put here by my aunts to protect the town.

But that's not what had icy pricks crawl up
my neck.

It was the fact that this one was dead.

CHAPTER

16

"**A**re you going to tell me what I'm staring at or do I have to guess?" Ronin gazed at me, the stapler still gripped firmly in his hand.

I sighed. "A ward—one of my aunts'."

"So, why do you look like you just took a cold shower?"

I met his gaze. "Because it's been lifted." At his puzzled expression, I added, "Someone *destroyed* it."

Ronin's mouth fell open. "The same someone who summoned the demon, I presume?"

"Pretty sure. Yeah."

I edged closer to the ward. I felt none of the familiar pulsing magic of a protection ward, but I felt *something*. The cold remnants of foreign forces that had attacked the ward, like someone took a sledgehammer to the ward on the floor, rippled through my senses like a prickling, pulsating sensation—faint but still there.

Creating wards took some serious magic. Not all witches could create them, let alone such complex ones with so much power they protected an entire town.

And it took even more magic to destroy one.

Crap. This was worse than I thought. This wasn't just a case of random demons slipping through the Veil and eating a few mortals. This was *planned*. Careful, flawless planning was required to pull off something like that. I was dealing with someone powerful and schooled in the arts of magic, possibly more powerful than my aunts.

Ronin fiddled with his stapler. "Any ideas why this crazy-ass person would want to do this?"

"Wards protect or keep certain things away from a specific place." I sighed. "The only reason you lift a ward is for the reverse." I looked at Ronin. "Whoever did this wants to kill everyone in this town, or something along those lines."

Ronin screwed up his face. "That makes no sense. We're nobodies. We're the half-breed community's rejects and castaways. Why would they want to kill us? Most of the time they pretend we don't even exist."

My muscles stiffened in tension. "Can you think of anyone who would want to harm you? Kill you, even? Or anyone here? If Hollow Cove is made up of castaways and loners, someone here may be hiding from this very person trying to kill them."

Ronin's face was tight in anger, and I could tell he was hiding something. "Maybe. But to kill everyone? That's crazy."

I shook my head, a feeling of unease washing over me. "Not really. You have no idea how *crazy* people can get." My eyes moved over the summoning circle. "That's the demon's name. In the center there, written in Latin. If I knew how to summon and control demons, with its name, I could have sent it back to the Netherworld." I was getting a little ahead of myself, but somehow I felt as though I could, if given the chance and the means.

Ronin dipped his head, his brow furrowed. "I'm not a witch or anything. But… isn't that Dark witch magic? I thought you were a White witch. You know… dandelions and mushrooms, dancing naked under the full moon? Did I mention naked?"

"Dandelions and mushrooms?" I stared at his cheeky grin. "Magic is neither White nor Dark. Magic is magic. Someone years ago made two separate covens, a Dark and a

White. But we're all just magical practitioners. It's all about stringing things together, pouring your power into them to make something happen." I've always known this, or rather, felt it to be true. Maybe not all witches thought about their magic this way, but I did. If we could do both, why the hell not. Right?

One thing was for sure, I would up my knowledge of demons tonight. If more demons were going to show up—and I was sure they would—I needed to know what I was dealing with. But mostly, to save my ass.

"Well, the demon's long gone," I said after a moment. "Let me blow out the candles first. You know. Fire hazard. We *are* in a library."

"Ah, yes," said Ronin grinning. "The scholastic achievement of others. Wouldn't want those to burn."

I rolled my eyes and made for the nearest candle.

Behind me, something like the sound of nails scratching the wood floors drew close. Then I heard a swift, rushing sound of something large moving toward us.

I stiffened, and all the muscles in my body went taut.

"What the hell was that?" came Ronin's low voice.

I turned my head slowly, gathering in my will as I looked to where I'd heard the sound and tapping into the surrounding elements. A power word sat on the edge of my lips—the only one I could remember in my moment of panic.

I listened. Again, I heard the scuffling sound of nails on the hardwood. Then there was a quiet sound, a thump of something large taking a step.

"Maybe it's just a dog," whispered Ronin hopefully, the whites of his eyes showing in the dimness.

"It's not a dog." Unless the dog weighed five hundred pounds.

I could hear the sound of breathing in the room somewhere behind us in the shadows of one of the bookcases. The room dropped into dead silence. No moving. No breathing. Nothing. I waited, tense and ready to run as fear iced through me.

From behind a bookcase stepped a creature of nightmares.

It stood ten feet high if not more with a set of glowing red eyes perched in the middle of an abnormally large head. Ram's horns curled around its head and its gaping mouth was full of shark teeth. Its twisted and corrupted body sported way too many arms and too many legs to make it anything I was familiar with. The already enormous demon began to swell, growing in mass as its skin thickened and an extra set of limbs swelled out from its sides. It moved, undulating darkness and shadow moving with it, as it shifted from its solid form back to a liquid shadow. And it was blocking our exit.

"You're a shadow demon," I muttered, terrified and amazed at the same time.

"Uh, Tess," Ronin blurted. "I'm glad you two are getting acquainted but—we need to get the hell out of here. Right now."

"Right."

We vaulted into motion.

We ran over the summoning circle and across the library toward the back of the building, praying we'd come across a back exit. Ronin, once again propelled by his vampire speed, was way ahead of me, which totally annoyed me. I put on a burst of speed, trying to catch up.

A flashing red sign above a hallway that disappeared into more shadows read EXIT. Well, at least we were running in the right direction.

My left leg jerked, and something yanked me back.

Not something. The shadow demon.

I flew across the library floor like a rag doll, screaming all the way of course, and smashed, back first, into one of the bookcases. *Ouch.*

My breath escaped me as I fell to my knees, blinking the pretty little stars that danced in my vision, only to be ruined by the vision of a giant, twisting shadow that was heading my way.

Letting my instincts drive me, I pulled on the elements and hurled all my will into the power word and bellowed, "Accendo!"

A ball of fire sprouted from my open palm and shot forward. It was beautiful as it soared through the air, lighting the library in hues of golds and orange. I smiled to see my aim was spot on. Yay for me.

The shadow demon shifted so its body was just a mist of black cloud as its solidity vanished.

And my pretty ball of fire went right through it, exploding in a shower of ambers and flames against the wall behind it.

"Oh shit." Not what I was expecting. It was more clever than I'd first thought.

Ronin was next to me in a flash, his arms around me as he helped me up. "Okay, so the big, bad demon has a few tricks up its ass. At least your aim was good this time."

"Thanks for the pep talk." I stood on shaky legs, my back throbbing.

The shadow demon shifted, revealing its solid body once more. I knew what that meant.

"I've got this." Ronin arched back, lifted his right leg and twisted his body. In a blur, the vampire pitched the stapler like he would have a baseball. The stapler flew straight and true.

It hit the shadow demon in the face, and then it fell with an echoing clang on the floor.

Ronin looked at me and shrugged. "What? It seemed like a good idea at the time."

The shadow demon roared and came at us like a twisted, humongous centipede-fish-dragon.

"Great, now you pissed it off," I muttered.

Its massive maw opened, waiting to devour us like it did Mrs. Bright.

I don't think so.

I planted myself and said, "Vinti... uh... Volent? No, that's not it... Ventu!" I let out a nervous giggle. Crap. That wasn't it either.

"What the hell are you waiting for?" cried Ronin, a bewildered expression on his face. "This isn't funny! Do something! I'm too pretty to die!"

"You remember the power word for wind?" I asked Ronin, shaking out my hands, as though somehow that would help get my magic juices flowing again.

He looked at me like I'd just insulted his manhood, his eyes wild. "Why the hell would *I* know that? You're the witch."

"Worth a try." Damn it. I couldn't remember. It was hard not to panic in a situation like this—when the big, bad, ugly demon was about to eat me.

The ground shook beneath my feet as the giant shadow demon barreled toward us.

"You better witch something fast," yelled Ronin. "Can't you just pull out your wand and blast it?"

"Ventu…" I was not going to be eaten by the overgrown slug. "Ventur," I tried again, seeing Ronin backing away, which was what I should have been doing too.

"Tess! Let's go," I heard Ronin shout, his voice farther away from me. "Let the Unseen deal with this. I've got a date tomorrow that I would really like to be present for."

Something in me clicked. If I let the Unseen handle the demon, maybe I didn't deserve to be part of the Merlin Group. I had to defeat this ugly sonofabitch. I had to show everyone that I could handle myself when facing imminent death. But mostly, I had to prove it to myself.

With a new rush of determination or pure stupidity, I steadied myself, the stink of sulfur and rotten flesh almost making me gag.

I can do this. "Ventem…" I tried again.

The shadow demon howled as its red eyes flashed with hunger. It was so close now, the stench of carrion burned my nose. If I wanted, I could reach out and touch it.

I was dead…

A word flashed in my brain.

"Ventum!" I shouted, barely getting the word out in time. But I did.

183

A rush of power overflowed my aura. And then I let it go.

A blast of wind shot through my outstretched hand with the force of a hurricane.

The shadow demon, having either recognized the power word or just the magic, shifted into its shadow self.

It was a stupid demon.

The wind hit the cloud of black mist and shadow and propelled it across the room, smashing into the wall. The demon shifted back to its solid form, black blood seeping from multiple breaks in the skin. My bad.

I limped toward it, putting on speed as I went and drawing forth all the power I could muster.

It turned its head at me, hatred flashing in its red eyes. The shadow demon began to shift back into its shadow form.

But I was faster.

A surge of energy poured out of me. "Accendo!" I shouted and hurled my ball of fire straight at it.

It hit the shadow demon and exploded on impact. Shrieks of alien agony rose in the air toward a breaking point. The fire rose high above the demon, enveloping it like a great big bonfire.

I took a step back, feeling the heat against my face.

The stink of burning flesh rose as the shadow demon thrashed in a demonic frenzy. And then it fell, writhing on the floor until the fire was out and all that remained of the demon was a pile of gray ash.

Ronin swore, appearing next to me. "Damn, girl. Now *that's* a barbecued demon."

A gasp slipped from me as I felt like I was being poured out of myself. A wave of dizziness swam up, and I had to take a breath to steady myself. That last power word had taken a huge chunk out of my energy. I didn't think I could do more magic until I had a rest and maybe something to eat, possibly Ruth's homemade brownies.

"We need to tell my aunts about this," I said, swaying on my feet with a cold sweat breaking all over my skin.

Ronin reached out and grabbed my arm, steadying me. "You okay? You look a little pale, and that's saying a lot coming from a half-vampire."

"I'm fine." I shrugged it off. "I just need to eat something." Movement caught my eye.

A tall, slender figure in a black robe, black cape, and black hood appeared from behind a veil of black mist, standing at the mouth of the hallway that led down to the exit.

"Who's that?" asked Ronin.

I glowered. "The one who summoned that demon," I answered, knowing it to be true. I was going to fry that SOB. This bastard was mine.

I yanked my arm free from Ronin's grip and staggered forward like a drunk.

"Tess, wait!" cried Ronin.

But I was running on the last of my adrenaline, anger fueling my thighs as I rushed forward. It was stupid, I knew, especially when I was drained of my magic. But I still had the use of my fists, or better yet, a big ol' kick to the balls. Because, when in doubt—go for balls.

The robed figure spun and rushed down the hallway.

I was right behind it.

"Why are you running? I just want to talk!" I panted. Yeah right. I was *way* past a chitchat.

It hurt to run. I'd admit it. I felt weak, like my legs were about to give out at any second. Shoving all that out of my thoughts, I forced myself to breathe steadily and gather whatever strength I had left for this final push.

The robed figure wasn't as fast as me, which was really surprising. The only explanation was that using his power on the ward had drained him. That would work.

I was nearly there, just a few more seconds, and that SOB was mine.

The figure ran straight ahead and then took an abrupt turn to the right at the end of the hallway.

I was right behind him. I reached the end of the corridor and pulled right—

A whimper caught my attention to my left.

I staggered at the sight of a small head with blonde hair. Next came the tiny body cradled on the floor in a fetal position. Her head came up at the sound of me, her nose and lip bloody and her face wet with tears. Sadie.

I had a split-second thought about going after the mysterious robed figure, but the little girl's whimper tore at my heart.

My maternal instincts were a strong force of their own. Nothing else mattered as I rushed over to her, fell to my knees, and pulled her up on my lap, cradling her. She let out another whimper as she turned around, her little arms wrapping around my neck and her tiny body shivering as she held on tightly.

I almost burst into tears as I held her tighter. That little girl had seen something terrible. And someone, that robed figure, had tried to kill her for it. But I got to her first.

I am going to kill that SOB. I swear it.

Things that attacked little girls deserved to die.

"It's okay," I soothed, rubbing her back as I stood up with her in my arms. "I gotcha." She weighed practically nothing, just skin and bones. "It's over now. You're safe."

Ronin stepped into my line of sight, his face pulled in worry and deep anger. He kept shaking his head.

And when I looked back down the corridor, the figure was gone.

CHAPTER
17

I shoved a fifth piece of Ruth's famous chocolate brownie in my mouth, my taste buds exploding like fireworks as I did my best not to moan. Funny how chocolate made everything better. And hers did some serious magic to ease the pain in my joints, get rid of my nausea, and boost me with new energy and renewed strength. I wasn't back to my normal, pre-power-word self, but I felt a lot better.

"What's in these?" I asked Ruth, who was standing across from me at the kitchen table. "They're super good. My taste buds are having a party in my mouth."

Ruth beamed. "I can't give away all my secrets." She laughed as she went back to a simmering pot on the stove. The smell of rose-water wafted to my nose.

It was eleven at night by the time Ronin and I got back to Davenport House, having left Sadie with a frantic Martha. It took longer to calm the older witch than the little girl, and only when I agreed to have highlights put in my hair did Martha finally stop crying and throwing a fit.

I threw my gaze around the kitchen. My aunts had been quiet after I'd told them about the demon in the library. And when I got to the part with the ward, energy had buzzed in the air, wisps of their hair floating about them like they were in some hair commercial. The three witches looked like they were about to blow.

Something was happening in this town. And I was about to find out what.

"Did you call Marcus?" asked Dolores as she paced around the kitchen. "He should know about the library and what happened there."

Ronin choked on his beer, leaning back in his chair, and I shot him a hard look.

The thought of speaking to that hateful man made me want to throw my brownie across the kitchen. No way was I going waste a brownie on that guy, though.

I grimaced. "I don't work for him. I don't have to tell him anything."

Dolores spun and faced me. "Maybe not. But as part of this family, you have an obligation to inform the chief of any crimes committed in this town. He has to clean up the mess. Has to alert Mrs. Bright's family. That's why the town elected him as chief. You might not get along, but he is very good at his job."

Ronin wiped his mouth with the back of his hand, his chair balanced on two legs. "Let the Unseen take care of it. It's what this town's paying *them* for, right? You gonna eat that brownie?"

I pushed the plate of brownies over to Ronin. "You're lucky I like you. I don't share Ruth's brownies with just anyone. Vampire."

Ronin laughed. "Thanks, witch." He leaned forward, his chair miraculously still balancing on two legs, and snatched up the brownie before I changed my mind.

Dolores's eyes bore into mine, the corners pinched. "Tessa," she commanded. "You need to call him. Right now."

"Fine." I reached for my phone and texted Marcus. Skipping the part of the robed figure we saw and just sticking to the essentials. He'd get the picture once he got there. I read the text over twice, checking for typos though I didn't know why I cared, and pressed the send icon.

"There. Done." Dropping my phone, I picked up another brownie. I could practically feel the weight gain as I swallowed another large piece. I smiled. *Bring it on, weight. I just don't care anymore.*

"How did you get the Unseen to leave?" asked Ronin as he took the last swig of his beer. "Red-beard seemed pretty determined to get the house."

It was a question I'd wanted to ask as well.

Dolores straightened. "With persistence," she began, and then she dipped her head. "And a good ol' smackdown."

I laughed, imagining Dolores holding that redhead in an armlock. "That red-bearded one was pretty special."

"Specially stupid," commented Ronin.

"What was his name again? Emmet? And a witch too."

"Witch or not, the man was vile," said Beverly as she shifted in her chair. She patted her hair and tucked a strand behind her ear. "Wild, that one. No manners. A big ugly beast. He's more of a caveman than a delicate witch. With those big, hairy arms and hard, muscled chest and thick thighs…" Beverly fanned herself with her hand. "Is it getting hot in here?"

Ronin laughed. "Think they'll try to take the house again?"

"They can try." Dolores smiled wickedly, her eyes churning with some unspoken spell. "And we'll be waiting."

That I wanted to see.

The room fell into silence except for Ruth humming to herself as she stirred her simmering pot, only breaking now and then to sprinkle in some herbs.

"That poor child." Beverly stared down at her cup of tea, looking a little disheveled, her perfect hair not so perfect. "She's probably scared to death. She might never recover, you know. Some children never recover from their childhood traumas."

"I'll say," commented Dolores, "the child won't speak. She's terrified. After what happened to her parents... and now this? What was she doing there anyway?"

I'd been wondering that too.

"Sadie is always hiding and pulling disappearing acts on Martha since she came to live in Hollow Cove," said Ronin. "She can't sit still. She's a runner. It's her instinct to flee from danger. Guess she never recovered from that. She was probably in the library hiding when this happened. Saw everything too."

"And that SOB wanted to kill her." A bell sounded from my phone, telling me that Marcus, because no one else would be texting me now, had answered. I ignored it.

"Aren't you going to see what he wrote, darling?" asked Beverly, leaning forward in her chair.

"No."

Beverly cocked a brow and reached over the table to snatch up my phone. Her lips quirked into a smile that I didn't like.

My eyes narrowed. "What? What is it?"

Beverly's eyes met mine. "I'm not sure I should tell you but… he's declaring his amour for you."

"What?" I leaned over the table and grabbed my phone from her, making Ronin burst out in laughter, my face flaming. I was going to smack him.

I looked down at the phone.

Marcus: *Thanks. Sorry about the Unseen at your house earlier. It won't happen again.*

I stared at the text, my stomach doing some spins and somersaults I was not happy about. Why did he care? He was probably embarrassed. No, he didn't want Ruth to stop making whatever tonics she was brewing for him. He wanted me to "share" what he'd written. I wouldn't have, but Beverly had seen it.

The damn witch was still smiling at me.

I dropped my phone again and sat down. "I want you guys to be straight with me. You want me on your team, so you need to start talking."

"Is that so?" Dolores stared at me. "Are we your subjects now, oh master?"

Okay. It came out a little harder than I had intended. "That ward in the library was destroyed tonight." I cast my gaze to each aunt. "It wasn't the only one. Am I right?" When no one spoke, I kept going. "That first night I was here, when the body of Avi was discovered,

194

you all went somewhere. You went to check on the wards. And you never said you actually *fixed* them. You just said everything was fine, but it wasn't. Was it?" I took a breath and asked the question I'd been dying to ask. "How many wards have been destroyed?"

Dolores sighed through her nose. "Three."

"That's three wards destroyed by that same sonofabitch," I said, my heart pounding as I connected the dots. "The pixies were drugged on purpose. They were a distraction while they worked on the ward. Yes, it's all making sense now. And demons were summoned for added protection. At first, I thought it was just a random someone with a grudge. I know that's not it."

"You do?" said Beverly.

"Can't be random. It's too planned out. It has purpose."

"Yeah," said Ronin. "To kill us all."

I shook my head. "No. I'm not buying that. Who would benefit from removing everyone from this town? Like you said, we're just a bunch of has-beens and losers and the old."

"Watch where you're going with that," snapped Beverly, staring at me like I'd told her that her lipstick didn't match her skin tone.

"Maybe it's humans." Ruth turned around. "It wouldn't be the first time the human population discovered us and wished us dead. Look what they did in Salem. Someone says you're possessed by the devil—and the next thing you know you're hanging by a noose."

"It's not them." I wasn't sure, of course, but humans didn't fit in this equation. "To destroy these wards you need serious magic. Right?"

"That's right," Dolores answered, bobbing her head.

"How many of these wards are around town?"

Dolores came to stand next to me. "Five. With three gone, that leaves two."

"Two is not enough to protect a town of this size. Right?" I took their silence as a yes. "Can you put them back?"

The three sisters were silent again, and I knew they were hiding something. "What is it?"

Eyes worried, Dolores looked at me. "Whoever destroyed them put a spell on them too. The spell keeps us from reaching the wards, like a layer of magic is holding us back. So, until we can figure out what spell they put and break it, I'm afraid we can't."

Dread was a tight ball in my gut as something occurred to me. I looked over to my right to the framed picture of the aerial view of Hollow Cove hanging on the kitchen wall.

I shot to my feet, grabbed the picture, and moved to the small desk stacked with bills to get a black marker. Then I settled back in at the kitchen table.

"What are we looking for?" asked Ronin, his head practically on my shoulder as he peered down at the picture, the scent of his cologne filling my nostrils.

I stared at the picture, feeling I was onto something. "Where was the first ward destroyed?"

Dolores moved to my other side and placed her finger on the picture. "Here, carved into that big oak tree on Potions Avenue."

I drew a small black dot where she'd showed with her finger. "Was the other one in the town square somewhere?"

"At the base of the water fountain," answered Dolores.

I made another small dot above the picture of the fountain. Then I made another dot when I spotted the library. I looked up at my aunts, twirling the marker between my fingers. "Where are the other two?"

Dolores tapped her finger on the frame again. "Here, on the corner of Jack O'Lantern Avenue and the last one on Hollow Cove Bridge."

I put two additional dots where she'd pointed. My pulse quickened as I stared at the five dots. Next, I grabbed a small ruler from the same desk and connected the dots. Don't ask me how I knew how to connect them. I just knew, like my inner witch had taken control of the ruler and marker.

I took a breath and leaned back, staring at the picture.

Ronin shifted next to me. "Holy shit—ow," he said, after Beverly smacked his head.

"Watch your language, boy," she admonished, looking a little too pleased to have done it.

Ronin was right. Holy shit with a capital S.

"It's a star. The wards make a star?" I stared at my aunts. "This isn't a coincidence. You put those wards there for a reason. And that star... a five-pointed star... it's a pentagram." We all knew pentagrams were used for protection.

Dolores nodded, a proud smile on her face. "We did. The pentagram is for another layer of protection within the wards."

I looked back down at the star, all the wards placed strategically, all with a purpose to protect the town, but also to protect something else. "So, what's in the middle?" I asked and tapped my finger on the picture. "What's here?"

Dolores's brow etched in worry, and her dark eyes seemed to darken even more. The three witches stiffened, sending my instincts flaming. I'd figured out something important.

I wasn't sure she would answer. "That's Mad Cat Park," said Dolores after a long moment. Her eyes met mine, and she added, "It's the convergence of the ley lines. Where they intersect. Where their power is abundant and everlasting."

"Ley lines. Right." I wasn't an expert in ley line magic, but I knew they were used as conduits of magical power.

Dolores took a deep breath. "Hollow Cove was built over a grid of ley lines, a web of some of the most powerful ley lines in this country. It feeds the town with magic. It's in the very soil, in the trees, and the surrounding buildings. Everywhere."

"How many of them?" asked Ronin, reading my mind.

"Five," answered Dolores.

"Five?" I knew one was powerful, but five? Five was like a nuclear plant of ley lines.

"That's right." Dolores took a breath. "One runs right here, under this very house."

I looked down at the floor. Don't laugh. "Explains a lot."

"That's why Hollow Cove is so special," continued Dolores as though I hadn't interrupted her. "Why it's the only place like this in the world and why it's so attractive to others. Those who would take control of this town hold the power. Take the town, gain immeasurable power."

I was willing to bet the ley lines were the reason my magic felt so uber-powerful in this town, as though it was magnified a hundred times. Having had a taste, I could see why others would want a piece.

My heart started to pound faster. Here came the big question, and somehow I knew they already had the answer. "So, who would benefit from all this power? Who's behind the destruction of the wards?"

"The Church of Midnight," blurted Ruth, a wooden spoon in her shaking hand, looking like she was about to hit something.

Ronin gave a small laugh. "Sounds like a group of little ol' ladies playing bingo in some church's basement."

I stared at Ruth. "The Church of Midnight? Never heard of it. Who are they?"

Ruth looked at her sisters before she answered me. "A circle of powerful sorcerers and sorceresses."

There was a sudden smash of glass hitting the floor.

I looked over to see Ronin's face—pale, wide-eyed and frightened.

"Ronin?"

The vampire stilled, a turmoil of emotions playing over his face. He looked... he looked scared to death.

I reached out with my hand to touch his shoulder. "Ronin? What's the matter?"

And then just like that, he shot to his feet, spun around and ran out the kitchen's back door with that supernatural speed, without a second glance or even a goodbye.

"Looks like Ronin's heard of your Church of Midnight." And just the name terrified him.

"What's gotten into him?" asked Ruth, looking puzzled.

"He didn't like the beer," snapped Dolores.

I stared at the back door as it pulled itself shut with a click. "Don't worry. I'll find him later." Ronin was my only friend in this town. He'd stuck out his neck for me and that meant a great deal. I would help him, any way I could.

"I'll pick this up." Ruth came around me with a duster and broom in her hand that weren't there a moment ago.

I felt the tension in the kitchen shift from anger to fear. Whatever this Church of Midnight was could only be bad news. Dread twisted in my gut at my next question.

My gaze rolled over the three witches. "What happens if these sorcerers destroy all the wards and get ahold of the ley lines?"

Dolores's expression darkened, anger bubbling until her face twisted into an ugly mask. "Then they will take Hollow Cove and kill everyone in it."

Yeah. Of course, they would.

CHAPTER
18

Sleep was becoming more of a luxury since I came to Hollow Cove. Forget my usual wonderful eight hours of sleep. I'd be lucky if I got four.

I stood in front of the mirror on the dresser, looking at my thinning and haggard face. This was not the youthful face of a twenty-nine-year-old. Right now, I looked like I'd aged ten years. Damn.

"I look like the walking dead," I told the mirror. The bags under my eyes were beginning to look like someone had punched me in the face.

After a quick shower, I applied some concealer under my eyes to brighten them up a bit, pinched my cheeks, because I didn't have time to apply any blush, and headed downstairs.

The scent of carrot muffins wafted to my nose as I hit the bottom of the stairs. My stomach roared—literally roared—when I entered the kitchen. So, I obliged it and grabbed a freshly baked carrot muffin to settle the beast.

The kitchen was empty. I leaned over and peeked out the window that looked out into the side driveway, seeing the old Volvo station wagon. If the car was here, my aunts were here somewhere. Davenport House was a sprawling farmhouse, so they could be anywhere.

"I'm going out to look for Ronin," I called out as I headed down the hallway.

I'd gone out to look for him late last night, but after an hour of not finding him, I'd gone back home. I figured he was probably in the arms of some hot babe, pouring out his vampire feelings.

Still, there was a reason he'd left like that, at the mere mention of that circle of sorcerers. And I would find out.

When I'd returned, my aunts and I had stayed up for hours, discussing what measures to put into place to best protect the town from this foreign attack. For now, we'd decided that protecting the last two wards was our best option.

I was to protect one while Dolores protected the other. Beverly and Ruth were charged with removing whatever spell or curse the sorcerers had put on the other three wards. If they could break them, the wards would be active again.

It was a solid plan, and I'd gone to bed feeling marginally better. But then I couldn't sleep so I'd gone up two floors to the library and read everything I could on sorcerers.

Most of it was the same. Sorcerers and sorceresses were led by a High priestess or High priest. They worshipped Nyx, the goddess of night. And, like witches, they practiced magic and could draw their power from the elements and ley lines.

It was obvious they were powerful enough to break my aunts' wards.

I pulled on my boots, grabbed my bag with my ever-faithful *The Witch's Handbook*, slid the strap over my shoulder, and opened the front door—

And crashed into Marcus.

If there was an emotion worse than awkward, I was feeling it.

"You?" I managed to get out. Not quite as articulate as I had envisioned myself to be when I'd pictured myself standing before Marcus again. I blamed the carrot muffin and lack of sleep.

Marcus stood in the doorway, a strange expression on his face. His brows lifted in surprise at my comment or me, I couldn't tell. A loose black T-shirt that did nothing to hide the ripples of muscle underneath was tucked in nicely to a pair of dark jeans. Was his chest larger than I'd remembered? I pulled my eyes away from his chest before I broke the "three-second rule" of allowed staring time—before it became stalkerish. I just made up that rule.

He didn't even move out of the way. He just stood there, watching me.

I raised the strap of my bag over my shoulder. "You should apologize to my aunts after what you pulled with the Unseen," I said, thinking that was why he was here.

Marcus lowered his eyes looking uncomfortable. "That was a mistake, them coming here. But I stand by my decision for bringing them in. The town needs them."

"Like we need ticks and mosquitoes." I scowled at him because punching him in the face seemed a little too reckless for so early in the morning. "Well, isn't that dandy? Out of my way, Marky."

I made to move forward, but the damn chief didn't budge.

I gave him a quick mirthless smile. "Are you going to move out of my way, or do I have to grab a broom and fly over you?" Not that I could. I'd never seen a witch fly on a broom. I thought that was mostly on TV.

Marcus's gray eye bore into mine, and I didn't like how they were making heat rush from the tips of my toes to my head. His jaw clenched, and his lips opened and closed like he was fighting for what he wanted to say. He was uncomfortable. Interesting. And I liked it.

"Thank you for… taking care of that demon in the library," he said finally, those damn fine eyes meeting mine again.

Crap. I might have been drooling. "If that's your way of apologizing for being such a dick, you suck at it."

Marcus hesitated, anger thick in his pinched brows. "I'm trying to do the right thing here. Why are you being so difficult?"

"Me? *I'm* being difficult?" I was practically shouting. "You're the one who's been biting my head off since I got here—for no apparent reason, other than your hatred for my mother. News flash, Marky. I'm. Not. Her."

The chief's eyes widened even farther. His lips parted, seemingly unable to even blink.

"Nothing to say?" I snarked. "Really?"

Marcus said nothing, the glint in his eyes going right to my core.

Fuming, I stepped around Marcus and down the porch steps. I'd gone down the path to the sidewalk before realizing I had no idea where Ronin lived. I could have asked Marcus. I shot a glance over my shoulder to see him still on the porch, watching me walk away. Creep. I could not figure this guy out. But right now, he wasn't important. What was important was to find Ronin. I wasn't about to lose my only friend.

I'd barely walked down the block when Martha came bustling up the sidewalk, her eyes wide and on me, all happiness and light on her feet for such a large woman.

"Oh, my darling, Tessa," squealed the woman as she came in for a hug. I stepped out of her way, but the woman was fast. She grabbed my arms and pulled me into her extraordinary large chest. "Thank you! Thank you for saving my Sadie."

"No problem," I wheezed and yanked myself back out of the woman's iron grip.

Martha's eyes brimmed with tears. "I know I'm not the child's mother, but I've grown so attached to her. We've bonded. I don't know what I'd do now if I lost her."

The witch wasn't my favorite person, but she had a big heart to take in an orphan half-breed. That said a lot about a person.

"How is she doing?"

Martha never stopped smiling. "Better. She ate a little this morning. Now she's disappeared again. She's like a werewolf cub that one. Always running."

I smiled. "She'll be back. I wouldn't worry."

"Oh, I know that, dear." Martha's eyes flashed, and she clapped her hands together, making me jump. "Well, I gotta run, hon. I have Mrs. Van Nutt coming in for a perm and there's Sophie Stark—she's a werewolf, not blessed in the looks department, if you know what I mean—so she'll need the makeover of the century for her hot date tonight. Ta-ta!"

I watched as Martha crossed the street. I felt a little relief that her business hadn't been spoiled by the pixie invasion.

"Martha!" I yelled, and the witch turned around when she reached the other side.

"Yes, hon? Did you want to book an appointment?" she asked, her face hopeful.

I shook my head. "No, thank you." At the slight disappointment on the woman's features, I added. "Do you know where Ronin lives or where I can find him?"

"Upstairs from Gilbert's grocery store." Martha waved at me and was off marching toward her shop.

Huh. I'd never even noticed there was an apartment up there.

I made it to Gilbert's grocery store in less than three minutes. What can I say? I'm a fast walker. I stood in front of the shop, glancing past the large glass windows and looking for another entrance. I didn't want to have to go in there, especially not now that Gilbert had spotted me. He walked to the window. His face pinched in a grimace, making his eyes into tiny slits and causing his mouth to disappear into a thin line.

I let out a breath and turned—

And bumped into Ronin.

"Weird. That's twice today," I said, stepping back.

"What's twice today?" asked Ronin.

"Never mind." I looked at the tall vampire. "I came looking for you. Martha says you live here, but I can't see a side entrance."

Ronin jabbed his hands in his front pockets. "You have to go through the alley here. The entrance to my apartment is at the back. Why were you looking for me?"

He'd lost some of his flare, his cunning, his smiling face. I could tell he was still bothered by what had happened yesterday.

"You want to go for a walk?" I didn't want to have this conversation here while Gilbert was still giving me the "evil eye" on the other side of the glass.

Ronin lifted his shoulders. "Sure."

We walked in silence for a moment. Ronin's gait was stiff, and I knew he knew what I was about to ask. We strolled over to the town square.

"Here." I gestured with my hand to the nearest bench. "Let's sit." I plopped myself first and waited for Ronin to sit next to me. He wouldn't make eye contact. My heart tugged at the visible pain on his face.

"You told me Hollow Cove is made up of rejects and those who'd been exiled by their communities," I started. Nope. Still not looking at me.

Ronin hunched his shoulders, staring at his slick pair of black sneakers.

I laughed. "It's a strange town, I'll admit. But there's a real sense of family here. It's special. And the people of Hollow Cove protect their own. And that's what I want to do. Protect those who matter."

"Sure," muttered Ronin.

"I'm going to have to beat it out of you. Aren't I?"

Ronin looked at me. "What?"

"Look. You're my only friend in this town, apart from my aunts, and I don't enjoy seeing you like this. I want to help you if I can."

Ronin looked away. "You can't."

"Look, Ronin," I shifted on the bench. "I know this is none of my business, but seeing as we fought—not one but *two* demons—I thought that made us friends. And friends help each other out. Can you at least tell me why you ran off like that last night? What are these sorcerers to you?"

It was a long while before Ronin answered. He exhaled and looked out toward the street. "Sorcerers killed my family. No. That's not exactly right. Sorcerers *abducted* and put my much younger two half-brothers and half-sister into slavery, torturing them for years before they were killed."

I felt the blood leave my face and end up in a pool around my feet somewhere. "I'm so sorry, Ronin."

"They killed my father and stepmother first. They only wanted the younger vampires. The older the vampire, the harder to break."

"Why?"

"They wanted an army of vampires to control, to kill for them."

"And did they?"

A dark cast covered Ronin's face. "The only reason I wasn't killed, because they wouldn't want a half-vampire, was because I was in LA, partying with some humans. When I heard from a friend what had happened, I came home to Chicago. But I was too late."

"So what happened?"

His expression grew distant and pensive. "I looked for them for five years. My mom died in childbirth, so they were my only family left. I searched everywhere for these bastard sorcerers. There were rumors of this church down in New Orleans, a group of sorcerers that had vampires working for them. I went. And when I found them…" Ronin's face hardened until I barely recognized him. "They were beasts—my brothers and sister. I didn't even recognize them. Their bodies were twisted, corrupted. There was nothing left of them. They were gone. And in their place were monsters. They looked like demons, Tess."

211

I swallowed hard. "That's sick. I'm so sorry."

Ronin shook his head. "They turned on me. My own family tried to kill me. I barely got out of there alive. I ran away and never looked back."

"Could you not report it to your Head vampire? I'm sure you guys have one in Chicago."

Ronin gave out a bitter laugh. "Please. Why would they want to help me? A half-human vampire vegetarian who doesn't drink blood? They hate me. To them, I don't exist."

My stomach did a neat little rollover. "And so you came here."

"And so I came here."

I couldn't even imagine what that must have been like, to witness your family turned into creatures, into *things*, and then have them turn on you. Ronin had been through hell. It made sense now why he'd taken off like that. I would have done the same.

"Well," I sighed. "It's payback time."

Ronin stared at me. "What are you talking about?"

I flashed him my teeth. "Revenge, baby. That's what I'm talking about. Maybe these are not the same sorcerers who murdered your parents and manipulated your siblings, but hey, that's all I got."

Ronin raised a skeptical brow, and a tiny smile curled the edges of his lips. "You're speaking in riddles again, Obi-Wan."

"I need you for a job tonight, you big dumbass," I teased.

Ronin watched me, his eyes narrowed in suspicion. "You do? Why?"

"Because, bloodsucker," I said, though I knew technically he wasn't. "Tonight, you and I are going to keep watch on one of the wards. And when those sorcerers show up… we're going to smoke 'em."

CHAPTER
19

I must have walked this bridge hundreds of times as a kid, and not once did I notice the ward carved into one of the large wooden planks.

It sort of made sense when I thought about it. Hollow Cove Bridge was the only access into Hollow Cove, apart from flying in, if you had wings, or rowing your way here from the mainland. A ward right at the entrance was smart and essential. It might have stopped a demon from wandering in, but now with the three other wards down, the remaining two were weak, and I had the horrible feeling the bridge was a free pass for the wandering and hungry demon.

I was really hoping Ruth's and Beverly's magic mojo would fix that. Sorcerers used similar magic to witches. It shouldn't have been that hard to remove whatever spell they put on the wards. Right?

I pulled my phone from my bag. The clock said it was five past midnight and so far, no sorcerers. No demons. Nada.

"Maybe they're off tonight," said Ronin, sitting above the bridge's handrail. "Maybe they're too busy worshiping Satan."

I dropped my phone in my bag. "They don't worship a fallen angel. They worship Nyx, the goddess of night."

The vampire snorted. "Yeah. Because that's better."

I stood over the plank staring down at the ward, my eyes tracing the runes and sigils inside and around the triangle within a circle. A warm pulsing came from it, rhythmic, like the beating of a heart, as currents of power moved and dispersed. It was the opposite of what I'd felt from the ward in the library.

Satisfied the ward was sealed and strong, I moved over to the railing and climbed up next to Ronin. "Thanks for coming." I dug my heels into the bottom rail and balanced myself. I knew coming here would be hard for him, probably excruciating for the vampire. And even so, he'd come.

The vampire rolled his shoulders. "Karen broke our date tonight. She didn't like it when I called her Katie by accident. Karen… Katie… they're practically the same. I don't know why she got all angry. So, I'm all yours, baby."

I laughed. "Maybe you'll wish she hadn't if nothing happens."

"Nah. Don't worry about it. It's Lucy tomorrow night. Can't get that one mixed up. And then there's Stephanie the night after that."

I turned to look at his face. Seeing how handsome he was, no doubt many women would agree. "How many women are you dating?" I couldn't imagine dating more than one guy at a time. One was enough, thank you very much.

Ronin raked his fingers through his hair. "Depends on the week. This week it was three—two now that Karen canceled."

"You're insane," I laughed, shaking my head. "Only an insane vampire would date more than one woman at a time."

"What about you? How long has it been since John dumped you? You should be dating by now. Get back in the saddle. Ride that pony, baby—"

"Okay. Thanks for the visuals." Heat spiraled through me and I whirled on him, pointing a finger. "Who told you that?"

Ronin raised his hands in surrender. "Please don't shoot. It was Martha. Your aunts told her."

I lowered my finger. "Sorry. I don't know why it still bothers me. Guess it's a pride thing. And it really hasn't been that long. I'm not ready for anything right now. I need to take care of me."

Ronin was silent. "What do you think of Marcus?"

If I had any food in my mouth, it would have gone spewing across the bridge.

My eyes widened, and I turned to him again. "Marcus? Are you serious? The guy would send me off packing if he could. He hates me, remember? You saw the way he looks at me."

"Which is why I'm saying this," continued Ronin. "He *is* looking at you. A lot."

I pressed my lips together in anger. "I know he's looking. He's imagining ways to remove my ass from here. Possibly in a body bag."

Ronin shook his head. "No. That's not what I'm getting from him at all."

Body tense, I stared at the vampire. "What are you talking about?" Maybe vampires had some special intuitive skill at sensing people's feelings and moods. Even then, why should I care what Marcus thought of me? He'd gone too far with what he said about my mother. I could never forget or forgive him. Some things you just didn't cross, especially dealing with a stranger. Which was exactly who I was to him on the night we met.

"Yes, the guy was a total jackass that first night," Ronin began. "He shouldn't have said those things about your mom."

"No. He shouldn't."

"But… he's a dude… you're a girl." He raised his brows at me suggestively.

"And you're about to get your ass kicked if you don't drop the subject."

"Fine." Ronin gripped the railing with his hands. "He might have suffered from a giant brain fart when you two met. But he's looking at you differently. That's all I'm going to say."

My jaw tightened as emotions swung from one extreme to the next. Adrenaline coursed to settle deep. My thoughts moved upon both how alluring and how darkly terrifying it would be to date Marcus. Yes, he pissed me off more times than not, and he knew how to press all my buttons. And yet… something about him made him very attractive. I'd be a fool if I didn't admit that part of Marcus's allure was the mix of the dark handsome stranger with a little bad boy. Yeah, I was stupid, and that kind of thinking had gotten me into trouble in the past.

I shook my head of all thoughts and focused on the job at hand. Even if I wasn't going to get paid for it, it needed to be done.

Ronin whistled low and my head snapped up.

"It's the masked police," he said loudly. "Praise the Gods. We are saved."

I scowled as two of the Unseen hit the bridge on the north end and started for us. Their golden masks reflected the yellow from the few lights on the bridge, casting weird shadows and making it seem like their masks were shifting with expressions. The smallest of the pair, with a thin frame, I recognized as the only female of the Unseen faction. The other, dressed in all black, with a cape billowing behind his big frame, and the tuffs of red beard beneath his mask, was none other than their leader, Emmet.

I smiled. This was going to be fun.

"I was hoping for a little action," I muttered, not caring to hide the grin on my face.

"Me too." Ronin leaped off the railing and landed on the bridge without making a sound. "Wrong kind of action, though."

My grin widened, and I jumped off and landed next to him. I searched behind them, half expecting to see Marcus. He wasn't there, and I was a little disappointed.

I moved quickly to stand in front of the ward, shielding it with my body. I didn't know these Unseen, and I didn't trust them.

Emmet planted his larger-than-life body right in front of me. "What's a witchling and a vampire bastard doing near my mark. Are you lost?" he said, making his partner laugh.

I gave them my best smile as I looked to the ground and then back up at Emmet. "Oh, sorry. Did you say you peed here?"

Ronin snorted. "Yeah. He kinda did. That's pretty crude coming from an older, much *larger* gentleman, such as you." He tutted. "Manners."

Emmet lifted his chin. "My mark," he said again, slowly, as though we were simpletons. "Mine."

I rolled my eyes, getting annoyed talking to a mask. "The mask thing is really getting old."

"It's like a cheap version of *Eyes Wide Shut* without all the sex," said Ronin, pushing in behind me.

"I mean. We all saw your face," I added. "Wearing a mask defeats the purpose now that we've *seen* your face. Get it?"

Emmet reached up and removed his mask, surprising the hell out of me—especially when his sidekick followed his example. Turns out, she was Asian, her black hair pulled back into a long braid. A dark scar traced her face from her right eyebrow to her chin. She saw me looking and smiled, like noticing it was a giant compliment. With her golden mask tied to a thin strip of leather, she swung it around her back, wearing it down like you would a hood.

She had paired her black pants with flat boots. A weapons belt equipped with a multitude of blades hung on her hips, just below her leather jacket. Witches didn't carry weapons like that. Their magic was their weapons, their minds their ammunition. When she turned her head slightly, her pointy ears caught the light from the bridge. I only knew two races of half-breeds with ears like that. She was faerie or elf. I just couldn't figure out which.

I opened my mouth to ask what they were doing here, but then, I just couldn't help myself. "What's up with the cape?" I mused, my eyes on Emmet. "Halloween's not for another five months."

Ronin burst out laughing, winning a growl from Emmet that sounded curiously like a werewolf's.

"The Unseen always dress for the occasion," answered the beefy witch, lifting the cape with his arms proudly and making wings.

I didn't want to have to tell him his cape would only get in the way in a fight, and it was a great weapon for his enemy to use against him. But then again, who was I to judge? He was the professional, right?

"What are you doing here?" I asked instead, my gaze darting from Emmet to the female Unseen.

Emmet's light eyes moved on the ground behind me. "To protect the ward you're trying to hide and doing a piss-poor job of, witch-ling."

I cocked my hip. "That's why *we're* here."

Emmet took a step forward, and I had no choice but to look up. He was a big sonofa-bitch, especially for a witch. If it weren't for the small pulsing of magic that rippled from him, he could have easily passed for a werewolf.

"No," said Emmet, his bushy red eyebrows high on his forehead. "That's why *we're* here."

Anger swelled inside me. "Wrong. My aunts put up these wards. The Merlin Group. I'm part of the Merlin Group, which means *this* ward is my responsibility. My *property*."

At that, both Emmet and his sidekick howled in laughter. Emmet wiped his eyes af-ter a moment. Yes, there were actual tears.

"Yeah, laugh it up." I wondered how fast Emmet's hair would burn if I tested it with my newest power word.

Ronin leaned in. "Can't you just spell them or something?" he asked, reading my mind. "The big one smells."

Of course, I could. But unless he struck first, hitting him with my magic would surely land me in one of Marcus's jail cells. Right now, he was the last person I wanted to see.

My aunts would have never told the Unseen where the wards were, which meant the only other person who could have told them was...

"Marcus," I hissed, the certainty of it making my blood pressure rise. "He told you. Didn't he?" Of course, he did. Seeing as he was the chief, he would know where the protection wards were.

Emmet flashed me a false smile. "You should try smiling more. Your pretty face is ruined with all those anger wrinkles and creases. Makes you look like a dude."

"Where is he?" So I could go kick his ass. I couldn't believe he would do this.

"He's with that really tall witch and three of my Unseen," said Emmet. "He wants us to protect the last two wards." He hit his large chest. "We're here to protect this one." He watched me for a moment and then dismissed me with a swipe of his hand. "Why don't you go home, witchling, and let the Unseen do their jobs."

I sucked in a breath through my teeth. His belief that we were both idiots and incompetent was making me see red—and Emmet's dead body at my feet.

"I was here first," I told them, not knowing what else to say. Really lame, but it was the first thing that popped into my head.

"Good one, Tess," murmured Ronin, and I scowled at him.

"Can't we just kill them?" asked the female Unseen, her hands on her weapons. "They're in our way. If we don't neutralize the threat, we don't get the other half of our pay."

"Patience, Kaito," purred Emmet. "You know the rules. You must wait for your opponent to strike first," he said and then added with a smile, "then we can kill them."

I inched forward. "Is that a threat?" I growled back, releasing some pent-up frustration.

Emmet flashed me his pearly whites. "No, witchling. It's a reality."

I was tired of his crap. First with my family home and now this? I didn't think so. I hated bullies. If he wanted a fight, a fight he would get.

Emotions high, I felt my will reach out to the elements around us, and their power answered in a tickling of my skin. My will and power seethed in my gut, in my core, and a pressure behind my eyes.

The big Unseen's eyes narrowed. "What's this? Are you going to try your witchling magic on me again?" he sneered, and I heard Kaito snicker. "Because we all saw how that turned out for you."

I inched forward again until my nose was practically touching his chin. "You're not taking my spot. If I have to spell your big ass myself, I will."

Emmet lost some of his smile. "You think I have a big ass?"

Ronin smacked his forehead. "This is priceless. So glad Karen turned me down. This is so much better."

"What?" I shook my head staring up at the big witch.

Emmet looked over his shoulder at an attempt to glimpse his behind. "I'm big-boned. Not fat. There's a difference."

My jaw fell and I couldn't get it to shut. "I'm not having this conversation with you." I opened my mouth to tell him to get lost, but a warning vibrated through my body.

I felt it, the cloud of cold energies that accompanied creatures not of this world.

Energy flew around us like a wind, lifting strands of my hair from around my face. With a sudden pop of air pressure in my ears, the scent of sulfur rushed around me.

A thread of alarm unrolled as energy sizzled against my skin along with the tingling cold pricks of demon energies. And when a cold sensation filled me, all my warning flags shot up.

I spun around. "Holy crap."

The bridge was teeming with demons.

CHAPTER
20

"**W**ell, you wanted some action," commented Ronin. "You got it."

Tension stiffened my body. "Not exactly what I was thinking."

I'd never seen so many demons all at once. Not unless you counted doing a flip animation through the Demons of the Netherworld Encyclopedia.

It was like someone had opened the gates of Hell and let them through. No, not someone. A sorcerer.

The demons seemed to have been put together with the idea of "anything goes." No two were the same. Some had flat heads, some had pointy heads, some had no heads at all and just looked like giant slobbery worms. I could see patches of clumping fur on wet, rotten bodies while tendrils grew upon the exposed skin of others. Wide-gaping maws full of fishlike teeth sent out horrific sounds with a frenzied edge of madness as they scrambled along the bridge in a wave of massive demon muscle. One let out a howl of fury so loud the water below the bridge vibrated in time with it.

Shoulder to—scratch that, the wiggling giant worms didn't have shoulders—but it was wall to wall.

And they were coming straight for us.

My eyes widened with horror, and I might have peed myself.

"It's a freaking demon smorgasbord," I breathed, my heart pounding in my ears.

"Where the hell did they all come from?" asked Ronin, throwing his gaze around like he expected to see a doorway to the Netherworld somewhere on the bridge.

"You said it. From *hell*." Emmet pushed his cape behind him—if he had worn tights, the cape would have made sense—and took three steps forward before turning. "You. Witchling. Watch the ward," he ordered, as though I was part of his crew. Then he spun around again, just as Kaito pulled out a long sword that looked like a curved katana.

I didn't really care that Emmet thought he was in charge. I would protect the ward, even if he hadn't mentioned it. That was the reason I was here.

But if he called me witchling again, I was going to castrate him.

The familiar scent of sulfur and the pulse of the paranormal was thick and unyielding, sticking to our skin and clothes like an overlay of heavy mist. The demon energies pulsed, thrumming through me and beating like a second heart, alive as though a second awareness beside my own.

And it creeped me out.

Spurts of blue light exploded from Emmet's outstretched hands like a volley of fireworks, illuminating the bridge in hues of white-blue, just as the demons exploded around him in a storm of frenzied roars.

"Next time you ask me to help you out," said Ronin, his voice a little high. "I'm going to say *no*!"

I let out a nervous giggle. I couldn't help it. No way had I imagined we'd face an army of demons. I was expecting just one stupid sorcerer. Guess the stupid one was me.

I watched as Emmet danced around the demons, shooting at them with a series of different blasts of multicolored magic. His cape billowed behind him as demons fell. Some burst into blue flame while others withered on the bridge floor. He looked like a superhero. Maybe that's what he was going for.

Kaito next to him swung her sword at the nearest demons, cutting and slicing as she spun around like a deadly top. The slaughter she left was incredible. She swept like a great broom down the bridge, tearing and shredding flesh while painting the floorboards with what looked like black oil but was really the blood of demons.

Okay. I'll admit it. I was impressed. And I understood now why Marcus had been so adamant about hiring the Unseen. They were good. *Very* good. Still, even though they both fought like champs, a handful of demons slipped through their defenses and came for Ronin and me.

Showtime.

I planted my feet right next to the ward. My heart rate skyrocketed, though my hands were surprisingly steady. With my mouth dry, my body's reaction to the prospect of mortal danger sent waves of sensation up and down my spine. I embraced the fear and waited.

Though death stared me in the face, I wasn't planning on dying today. I had to stay alive to protect the ward. And I would.

My bag was still where I'd dropped it earlier, but I didn't need it. I'd spent hours memorizing all the power words I could find until they were practically imprinted in my brain and were like second nature to me, like breathing.

Come on, you bastards.

"Get ready," I told Ronin, who was jumping from foot to foot like he needed to pee.

"I should be in bed with a sexy redhead," grumbled Ronin as his eyes flashed black. "Not about to get my innards splattered all over the bridge. I kinda like my innards. They're special to me."

"I won't let that happen," I told him, hoping the slight tremor in my voice didn't betray me.

The first demon came.

It had large, thick legs covered in scales, no arms, a head that was three sizes too big, and a mouth that could swallow me whole. Tentacle-like extrusions spread out around it like arms, and bulbous red eyes watched me.

"Get back! Back! You are not welcome here!" Yes. A touch dramatic in any other circumstance, maybe, but when you've got a demon about to eat you, nothing seems too extreme.

"Think it'll listen?" came Ronin's voice next to me.

The demon lunged.

Nope.

I tapped into my will, pulling on the energy of the elements around me as I shouted, "Fulgur!"

A bolt of white-purple lightning shot from my outstretched hand. Shocked at the sight of it, since it was the first time I'd used it, I flinched and sent the bolt of lightning past the tentacle demon who had halted. It landed near Emmet's feet.

The Unseen witch sprang back, glared at me, and then jumped back into the fight.

Whoops.

"You really need to improve on your aim, Tess," commented Ronin, backing away.

"No shit."

The tentacled demon rushed forward, a blur of scales, slime, and teeth. The horrible face gaped at me, its lower jaw protruding, distorted and wrong, like a blob of melting wax.

Let's try this again.

I flung out my hand, and a rush of power soared through me as I bellowed, "Fulgur!"

A white-purple lighting bolt hit the demon in the chest.

Sparks of white-purple light bounced around the demon, entering its body as steam rose with the smell of burnt flesh and hair. The demon let out a loud, wet crackling sound followed by a high-pitched scream. Then the steaming demon toppled, thrashing wildly as more steam rose and more cries followed.

And then the tentacled demon exploded, shattering to pulp, shards of bone, and scales before simply vanishing into a black-blooded spray.

"Nice," commended Ronin. "Remind me not to get on your bad side."

I rocked back, dizzy from the strength of the power word and the tiny bit of me I'd used to conjure it. I had to remember not to use so much of my will. But it was hard to think when I was about to get my brain sucked out by a demon.

"Watch out!" bellowed Ronin, and I saw him pitch sideways from the corner of my eye.

I wasn't so lucky. I'd been stupid. While I was focused on this fallen demon, I left an opening for the others.

Good one, Tessa.

I looked up, but it was already too late.

A demon burst from the shadows, reeking of death, and hungry for blood.

My blood.

"Accendo!"

I flung out my hands, pushing my will as I grabbed hold of the elements. Twin fireballs blasted out of my hands.

The first fireball missed—total airball.

But I nailed the demon with the second.

Take that, sucker!

The demon, a rat-beetle kind of creature the size of a mastiff, wailed as its body was consumed by fire. It howled, ran to the edge of the bridge—and jumped.

"Not so stupid after all," I muttered after hearing a splash. I didn't know if my fire would eventually kill it, but I didn't think I'd see it back soon.

Ronin let out a laugh. "Tess, sometimes you amaze me."

"Sometimes I amaze myself."

"Good." He pointed with a taloned finger to my left. "Here comes another one."

Sure enough, a spider demon that looked like the offspring of some dinosaur spider from long ago scurried our way. Multiple red eyes burned with awareness, hatred, and hunger.

"Itsy bitsy spider." I frowned at the vampire as he took a step away. My pulse continued to thrash. "We're supposed to do this *together*."

"We are." He grinned. "I'm here with you, cheering you on."

I rolled my eyes and faced the newest demon threat.

"Great. It has fangs the size of machetes."

The giant spider had twelve-inch fangs, but it also had a tail—a scorpion's tail, with a stinger the size of my arm.

"Awesome. It has a stinger too."

The spider-scorpion froze, its head lolling from side to side as though it was sizing me up or wondering which part of me to eat first. The smell was hideous, like month-old garbage sitting in the sun mixed in with a tad of dog poop.

I took a step back. I couldn't help it. I liked regular sized spiders, not ones the size of my aunts' Volvo. "Do spiders or scorpions have a weakness?"

"Sorry. I'm no entomologist," answered Ronin with a bewildered expression on his face. "I can talk about cars, women, wine, and women, but I draw the line with bugs. Just shoot it with your fire magic. It did the trick with the other one."

Emmet's frustrated growl pulled my eyes away from the spider-scorpion demon. The big witch was swinging his arms with green electricity shooting out of him like an automatic weapon.

He swung his cape. "Gotcha, you stinkin' bastards. Take that! And that! You wanna go crazy? Come on! Let's go crazy!"

Kaito was not far away, swinging and spinning and slicing her way through what looked like a white demon slug with no eyes or mouth. The two of them had made a difference in the number of demons. I could only count six more—seven if you counted mine.

I had no doubt Emmet and Kaito could take care of those last demons. If I could take care of mine, we were golden.

Once again, I'd spoken too quickly.

I drew in my will, power simmering in my core as I waited for the spider to lunge at me. So, when it opened its maw and spewed out a shoot of black silk, I froze.

I blamed the lack of experience for my brain freeze.

The black silk hit me like a metal sheet. I screamed as its sheer force knocked me off my feet to my back, the weight of the silk pinning me to the floor. I was covered from head to toe by the web of black silk, and I couldn't move.

How did this happen?

"Tess!" Ronin was next to me in a second, his sharp talons slicing and hacking at the black web.

The smell that oozed from the web was violently rotten, like a combination of vomit and feces. And it was touching the skin of my face. I'd have to use bleach when I got home. The sound of scuttling neared me, and my heart thrashed in my chest. I blinked through the web, staring up at the black sky. I couldn't turn my head. I was trapped.

"Hurry," I cried. "It's coming."

"It's not working!" shouted Ronin, his face twisted in fear. "I can't cut through it. It's like metal or something."

Well, this was just great. I did not want to be eaten by a giant spider-scorpion demon. Not on my back like a helpless female.

But I wasn't helpless. I was a Davenport witch, damn it. It was time to put my big girl pants on.

"Get back," I ordered.

"What?"

"Get back," I shouted again and saw Ronin jump back from the corner of my eye.

There was a rush of scuttling, clicking sounds, and an excited high-pitched hiss rose from the demon. It was anticipating its meal—me.

Not going to happen.

I gritted my teeth as I tapped into my will, my power. A surge of fury went coursing through me, filling me from toes to teeth with scarlet rage. Emotions played an important part when one was about to conjure up a power word—like a boost.

Adrenaline pounded through my body as I focused on the sound of the demon approaching. It was hard to hear it over the sounds of battle still raging, but when I heard that familiar scuttle near my boots, I knew the demon was right above me. I let go.

"Inflitus!" I cried and thrust out my will and sending a blast of kinetic force.

The black web lifted off of me and hurtled into the spider-scorpion demon like a freight train, driving it away from me and crashing into the bridge's railing.

I didn't waste any time.

"Thought you could eat me, huh?" I rolled to my feet, my body thrumming with magic, and shouted, "Accendo!"

The demon didn't stand a chance.

The ball of yellow and orange fire hit the demon, consuming it as tall flames reached high above it. The demon shrieked, jerking back. It fell on its back, like a house spider, arms and legs thrashing uselessly as it lay dying.

Then it stilled and never moved again.

I staggered, staring at the smoking ash pile, the only remains of the demon. A headache throbbed in my temples and behind my eyes. That had taken a lot out of me. Emmet and Kaito were headed my way, and I shrugged off the pain with an effort of will. I couldn't afford to show any weakness now, especially not in front of the Unseen.

"You okay, Tess?" came Ronin's voice next to me.

I turned and looked up at the vampire. "I'm great," I lied. "Nothing like killing giant demon spiders to get my magic mojo flowing."

"That's the last of 'em," said Emmet as he closed the distance between us. He flashed me a smile. "I saw what you did. Not bad for a witchling."

I was not expecting that. I bit my tongue at his use of witchling again since the Unseen had just complimented me. Maybe I'd been wrong about him.

Kaito snorted. "She was trapped in the thing's web. That *is* bad."

"I got out of it. Didn't I?" I shot back, not appreciating her tone. "I'm still here. That's saying something."

Kaito pulled out a cloth from her jacket pocket and used it to wipe her sword of the black liquid and some fleshy bits. "I killed nineteen." Her eyes gleamed, her brows raised in challenge. "How many did you kill, witch?"

I opened my mouth to tell her off, but Emmet beat me to it.

"If this is the best they've got to throw at us," began the large Unseen witch, "it'll be the easiest ten grand this month." He smoothed down his cape and tugged at the edges. I bit the inside of my cheek to keep from laughing.

Giggles aside, unease gnawed in my belly. Throwing a pack of demons at us was one thing. But it couldn't be this easy. If you took out the part where I almost died, it had gone pretty well. And yet, I knew it wasn't over. Something else was coming.

"What is it?" asked Ronin, the worry in his tone pulling my eyes to him. He was learning to read me. I wasn't sure if I liked it or not.

I threw my gaze over the bridge, over the piles of ash and spills of black blood and bits of flesh.

"I feel like this was just a test. A test of our strength. To see what we can handle." I shook my head. "This isn't over."

Emmet spread out his arms and gestured at the slop of demon remains. "It *is* over. We won. I believe a large pint of beer has my name on it. What's that pub called?"

"Wicked Witch & Handsome Devil Pub," answered Kaito, matching his smile.

"Yeah. That's the one. Let's go."

Ronin stepped in the big Unseen's way. "You can't just leave."

"Out of my way, vampire, or you'll find your head stuffed up your ass," growled Emmet.

I waved a hand at Ronin. "Let them go. We don't need them."

Emmet narrowed his eyes at me and scratched his beard. "It's over. The demons are dead. You should be glad this is the bulk of their power, witchling."

"Call me that again and it'll be *your* head up *your* ass," I growled.

Emmet smiled. "You want to pick a fight with me?" he laughed.

"No, you brute. I want you to use that big brain of yours in that big head. Think. These are sorcerers we're talking about. They're smart. They don't do things for no reason. They plan ahead. I'm telling you. It's not over."

I knew the sorcerer was here somewhere. The demons had been a gift to keep us busy while they tried to destroy the ward.

Emmet crossed his arms over his chest. "Yeah, well. Where are they? I don't see any sorcerers... *witchling*."

Glowering, I moved to face him—

239

The sound of wings, very large wings, pulled my attention to the sky above us. And I wished I hadn't looked.

A speckled gray and red body covered in a leathery hide landed on the bridge with a thundering crash, the reverberations echoing around the bridge and water below. Its enormous wings tipped with claws beat twice before folding back to its massive chest. Great big muscled legs were armed with talons as big as my forearms. Its large head twisted my way, with red, glittering intelligent eyes. It opened its maw revealing yellow, curved fangs. Its tail flicked back and forth like a cat's.

A dragon.

The demon dragon was the size of a small bus. It was a truly gorgeous beast, and a foolish part of me wished I could ride it.

Silly me because someone was already riding it.

Sitting astride its back was a dark-cloaked figure.

A sorcerer.

CHAPTER
21

"The bitch makes quite the entrance," said Ronin.

My attention snapped to him. "Bitch? You mean that's a *she*? A sorceress?"

"Yeah. She's a she," he answered, studying her with a dark intensity. The sudden flush on his face was like a great, seething tide of absolute fury. His body tensed as though he were preparing to fling himself at her.

I don't know why but I was expecting to see a male. I shouldn't have been surprised Ronin could sense the rider was female. As a half-vampire, he still had all the vampire senses and strengths.

Below her dark cowl were red, glowing eyes. Creepy. But other than that, I couldn't see her face. She looked to be about my height and build, but it was impossible to guess her age.

A bridle ran over the dragon's head, equipped with reins wrapped around the sorceress's hands, and I could see parts of a bit in the dragon's mouth. The corners of the dragon's mouth were wet with dark blood, and so were its teeth.

Well then, at least now I could hate her.

The air crackled and thrummed with sudden power, making the hair on my arms rise. Okay, the bitch had magic, lots of it. But so did we.

Though anger throbbed in my veins, I cocked my hip and flashed her one of my selfie smiles. "You came all this way for nothing. You're not touching that ward," I called out. "There're four of us and just one of you. The odds aren't in your favor."

Emmet cleared his throat and whispered in my ear. "She has a dragon."

"So?"

"Dragons breath fire."

Oh, crap. Right. "Maybe this one doesn't," I whispered back. I raised my voice again. "Final warning. Leave. Leave now."

The sorceress laughed. The dragon demon shifted anxiously, clearly not happy to be here, or maybe it just hated that she had control of it.

She yanked hard on the reins, making the dragon growl in pain.

I really *hated* that sorceress.

Ronin leaned in. "Just so you know… she's not afraid of you. She's not afraid of anyone."

"She should be." Yeah, I was feeling a little brash and foolish. But this sorceress had destroyed three of the wards, and in doing so, she'd had two people killed. She was the enemy. I wasn't about to let her go anywhere near that ward.

But there was still the dragon thing…

The sorceress's red eyes moved to Ronin, and though I couldn't see her face, I could tell she was smiling. The bitch was going down.

"So, what's the plan, witchling?" Emmet stood on my right side with Kaito next to him, her long curved sword gleaming in the light. His voice was a pale shadow of the confidence it had been. He was nervous, and he was making me nervous.

That he asked *me* what the plan was didn't bode well either.

I watched the sorceress still sitting on the dragon. "We take her down." What else was I supposed to say?

"Good plan," answered Emmet, his fingers clasped around the edge of his cape as though somehow that was giving him courage and a little extra power.

Maybe I should get a cape too? I'd look fabulous in a purple cape. Tights and all…

"What's their weakness," I asked the large Unseen witch, my pulse racing. Everyone had a weakness, and that went for sorcerers and sorceresses too.

Emmet shrugged. "No idea."

My mouth fell open. "Haven't you faced a sorceress before?"

"Nope. Never. This would be the first time."

"You guys are supposed to be the experts!" I hissed.

"Demons, half-breeds—that's what we do. Sorceresses and dragons? We don't get paid enough for that. That's not in the contract."

Dread pounded through me as I stared at the Unseen. "So, what? You're just going to leave?"

Emmet fell silent, and I knew I wasn't going to get anything out of him.

"Leave then, you coward," I growled as I turned to the vampire. "Ronin? What can you tell me about them?"

"I already told you everything I know," said the vampire after a moment. "I can't help you with that."

We stood in silence for another moment, and I had a feeling the sorceress was just sizing us up. I was getting really tired of this.

"Do something," urged Ronin.

"Yeah, good idea," agreed Emmet and he gave me a push. "You first."

I frowned at them. Fine. I was a Davenport witch. My job was to protect the town, and so I would. Besides, she was just sitting there, waiting for me to strike first.

Okay then. Here goes nothing.

"Get ready," I murmured as I focused. I called to the elements around me, drawing them in and holding them where I needed. Then I raised my right hand, called up my will, and cried, "Accendo!"

A bright fireball shot forward from my hand, straight and true, and hit the sorceress right in the hip. The fire consuming her was rather beautiful, rolling waves of flame cherry red and sunset orange.

"Hey! I got her!" I cried, shocked. I couldn't believe my luck. The dragon didn't even react. He just stood there while his mistress burned. But I didn't care. I wasn't here for the dragon. Maybe he was glad I'd done it.

"Not bad, witchling." Emmet slapped one of his beefy hands on my back, sending me forward a step, and I resisted the urge to slap him back.

"We should kill the dragon." Kaito took a step forward, her dark eyes on the great beast. "Keep the head as a trophy. It'll look great over my bed."

My smile vanished. "Leave it be, you psychopath. Look at it. I don't think it wants to be here. And it did nothing to us." I don't know why, but I was feeling protective of this dragon.

"It's a demon," pressed Kaito. "I kill demons for a living."

I moved toward her. "Not this one, you're not. Not all demons are evil, just like not all mortals are good. You're here to protect the ward, right? Well, I got the sorceress so you can go home."

"I wouldn't get too excited."

I looked back at Ronin at the note of disappointment in his voice. "What?"

And then I understood.

A low laugh came from the flaming body of the sorceress. Laughing while being burned alive was a bad sign.

The sorceress lifted her arms and clapped once.

The flames died instantly, sucked into an invisible vacuum, as though they were never there.

Crapola.

Here I was going to add sorceress killer on my list of accomplishments.

"That was pathetic," said the sorceress, her voice dripping with sweet venom. "Witches have no real power. Who gifted you with the earth's fire, little witch? Your mommy or your daddy?" she mocked, her shoulders rolling.

"I think it was *your* daddy," I shot back.

"Nice, one," muttered Ronin.

The sorceress dipped her head, and then she lowered her cowl.

I flinched and Emmet cursed next to me. "Yikes," I said, my face pulling into a grimace. "I think you should have kept it on."

The sorceress was bald, her gray-colored skin a stark contrast to her dark robe. But her skin, the color of a month-old corpse, nor her lack of hair anywhere on her head, nor her creepy red eyes made me cringe. It was her face.

Her flattened features gave her a more bestial appearance, with protruding cheekbones and a nose nearly like that of a cat. She sat smiling as her inhuman features shifted and contorted from something bestial back toward something almost human. It probably made it easier to talk. Her ears were pointy like those of an elf or a fae, but I could see scar tissue around the tips. The crazy bitch had cut them herself.

"Nice ears." I couldn't help it. That was all kinds of crazy.

Her face spread into a smile. "You like them?"

"Not really."

The dragon demon shifted below her, but she never lost her smile. "I came to discuss the terms of your surrender, but you brutally attacked me. I can't forgive that."

My body shook from both anger and fear, but my voice came out strong and even. "There are no terms."

The sorceress waved her hand at me dismissively, and I noticed that she didn't have any fingernails. "No," she argued, "because *you* attacked me."

I took a firmer stance, though I was trembling inside. "You attacked first by attacking our wards. And let's not forget the demons. That's a good enough reason to rid ourselves of you." Yes, she was way out of my league. My fire magic didn't even affect her. But I couldn't run away. If I did, she'd destroy the ward and would be that much closer to conquering the ley lines and our town.

The sorceress's face twisted into a savage glee that would have made a human run away screaming. "Well then," she said, leaning forward on her demon steed, "you give me no choice."

"We're going to take you out," I told her, my reflexive smart-ass coming out. Emmet, Kaito, and Ronin were still with me, surprisingly, and I took courage from that. The four of us might stand a chance against Miss Freako over here.

The sorceress folded her hands on her lap, her no-eyebrows high on her forehead. "Oh, really?" She laughed. "Let's see... you think you can beat me, when your magic has no effect on me whatsoever... how very droll."

"I can." Total lie. "I will."

The sorceress licked her lips. "This misplaced bravado—or is it stupidity? Don't know. Don't care. But it runs in your family. That's for sure."

My breath caught. "What?"

She sneered, her face almost serpentine now. "Your aunt thought she could best me too. Thought her White magic could save her." She threw back her head and let out a jackal laugh. She straightened and added, "It didn't. She couldn't. That old bat shouldn't be practicing magic at her age. I did her a favor."

Dolores.

My pulse leaped, fueled by anger and fear and desperation. Dread rushed through my body, and I could barely get the words out. "What did you do to her, you sick bitch?"

Did she kill my aunt? Did that mean the ward Dolores was protecting was destroyed? Was this ward the only one left?

My head pounded with questions, I was dizzy, and my stomach was knotting as I tried to wrap my brain around this new information.

"Don't believe her," spat Ronin. "She's a liar. They all are. She's just trying to throw you

249

off and see you suffer. They love that kind of shit. Pain and suffering *is* what they do best."

"What's this, half-breed?" sneered the sorceress, and she plunged a finger in her ear and wiggled it. "What do you know of The Church of Midnight?" she pulled out her finger from her ear and wiped it on her robe. Lovely.

Ronin turned slowly toward the sorceress. "You make vampires your slaves. You kill them by turning them into monsters, into beasts."

Her red eyes widened. "Vampires *are* beasts. We only give a little nudge to their true nature. I need a new companion. Yes, you will do just fine."

I stepped in front of Ronin. "Over my dead body, freak."

The sorceress's red eyes pinned me. "I was hoping you'd say that." She swung her left leg over, slipped down the dragon's body, and landed expertly on the bridge floor. She moved to the dragon's right side, her fingers twitching as though she was expecting some curse.

"It's time *I* show *you* fire." Her eyes glowed brighter until they were like two red suns. To make matters worse, the dragon's eyes glowed with the same intensity and color.

I knew what was coming, but I refused to shrink away.

"Tess, let's go!" Ronin shot out and grabbed my arm, but I yanked it out of his grip.

"No." I wasn't going anywhere.

The sorceress's face warped into a manic glee as she shouted, "Agnur zat ulrit!"

The dragon demon's head dipped our way.

"Oooh crap."

The large beast took two steps forward. Then it opened its maw, and a shoot of fire came blasting out, like a giant flame torch.

CHAPTER
22

"Incoming!" shouted Emmet as he pitched himself sideways on the bridge, pulling Kaito along with him.

I blinked at the rush of flames coming my way, but I didn't move.

I was either the bravest witch that ever lived—or the stupidest. Probably the latter.

Everything slowed.

Heat flared on my face and I cried at the last second, "Protego!"

A white, semi-transparent half-sphere burst into existence, lifting over my head and back down into the floor.

And not a second too soon.

The dragon demon's fire hit the wall of the protection shield, and I stumbled back, the half-sphere moving with me. My world was lit with yellow and orange, and I couldn't see past the flames. I couldn't even see the dragon. Everything was fire and heat.

I never let go of my will as power thrummed through me and I staggered. A wave of dizziness hit, but I forced it down. Any second now my half-sphere would collapse, and I would burn.

But it didn't.

I should have been dead, a pile of ash. And yet I was alive.

And by miracles of all miracles, the sphere was holding.

"I'm not burnt," came Ronin's voice next to me and I jumped.

"Ronin?" I stared at his face, red and sweaty and alive. His eyes drifted over the inside of my sphere. He'd stayed with me. He was in my protection half-sphere.

"At another time, being inside this… bubble would have seemed cool," he shouted, over the roar of dragon fire. "But with the dragon about to barbecue us—not so cool."

I nodded my head, unable to form words while I was trying to keep my magic flowing, trying to keep us alive. Sweat broke out all over my body, and I could feel it dripping down my back. I gritted my teeth trembling.

Heat thrummed against us, almost singeing the exposed hairs on my head. Greasy black smoke spread over the floor, and it stank. I curled my fingers into fists, straining to keep my focus on the shield and praying I wouldn't let go. Letting go meant instant death.

The dragon pulled back for a second, and I sighed as the scorching heat left. We were still in a sauna-like bubble, but it was bearable.

Through the semi-transparent half-sphere, I saw the sorceress. She stood next to the dragon demon, her lips moving, but I couldn't hear what she was saying.

Her expression was that of surprise that we were still alive. But something else was there.

Ronin's shoulder bumped into mine. "You think it's all fired out?"

As if in answer, there was a deafening roar, and another blast of dragon fire hit my protection shield.

"Not yet." Grimacing, I took a step back and then another as the dragon's fire kept pouring over the shield, pushing us back down the bridge. Each time the fire hit the shield, it bounced back and fell to the sides, like water rolling off a beach ball. And each time a chunk of my energy and my power left with it.

I reached for more power, gathered it in, and hoped it would be enough. I blinked and shook my head, trying to rid myself of the dizziness.

My lungs burned as they struggled to get enough air.

"How long can you keep this up?" Ronin's eyes were wide, his face red like he'd suffered a bad sunburn. Half his left eyebrow was singed.

"Not. Long." I managed to say.

"Okay. Okay." Ronin made a show of his talons, shifting his feet back as he moved with me. As sharp as they were, his talons wouldn't do much to the dragon. Ronin wouldn't even have time to strike the beast before it'd burn him to vampire ash. But I was too exhausted to say anything.

All my will and focus were on keeping this protection half-sphere up. Once it fell, it was all over for us.

The skin on my face and hands burned, and I could feel my hair, eyebrows, and eyelashes singeing. The smell of burnt hair rose all around. Damn. If I was bald after this, I'd be really pissed.

The heat became unbearable, like I'd stuck my head in a hot oven that sucked the air out of my lungs. I could barely breathe. If we didn't die from the dragon's fire, we would suffocate.

The sound of chanting broke over the roar of fire. The sorceress was working her magic on the ward.

Fear caused my control to slip, and some of my power fell.

I cried as a slip of the dragon's fire seeped through my barrier, burning the skin on my face. But I didn't let go. Adrenaline soared, what I had left of it, and I pushed. Pushed all my energy into the power word, the shield.

My will wavered. It wasn't enough.

"Can't. Hold," I groaned, and my body shook with my spent energy. I stumbled and felt strong hands around my arms as Ronin helped me up.

"Then I guess we die together," said my vampire friend.

Behind the half-sphere, the chanting grew louder in a language I didn't recognize.

Steam rolled up the protection shield, and my body was drenched in sweat. My vision blurred. I blinked the wetness from my eyes as the protection shield thinned, like a soap bubble ready to burst.

The dragon's fire was everlasting. It never stopped.

I could make out voices. No shouts. Definitely shouts. Perhaps Emmet and Kaito were trying to fight off the sorceress. Either that, or she was killing them, and this was them wailing in pain.

"It was nice knowing you, Tess," said Ronin as he gripped my arm tighter. "At least we won't die alone."

This wasn't exactly how I'd planned on dying. I'd never planned on dying, not until I was like two-hundred years old.

Ronin's fingers tightened around my arm. My shield wavered. I closed my eyes. I didn't want to see the fire that would kill me. I braced myself for the excruciating pain of burning alive.

The last of my magic left me in a sudden wave, like a water jug abruptly emptied. With a final tug, my half-sphere collapsed.

This is it. I'm dead.

I waited for the fire to hit.

And waited.

And… nothing happened. At least, I thought I wasn't burning.

When cool air brushed my face, I opened one eye. Then both eyes.

The sound hit me first, deafening blasts like I was standing next to a rocket launcher. Then the light, searing, as the bridge shook beneath my feet. The bridge was illuminated with orange, blue, and purple light, the blasts echoing as though someone had set off a fireworks display. I blinked. Not fireworks. Spells.

And they were hitting the dragon and the sorceress.

"Tess. Look!" Ronin let go of me and pointed. Though he didn't have to. I'd seen them.

My aunts.

Ruth and Beverly stood with their backs to us, Latin spilling from their mouths as they hit the sorceress and the dragon with volleys of their magic. Orange fireballs, purple bolts of lightning, and shock waves that shook the bridge like a giant stomping his foot in anger sailed through the night air.

Emmet was there standing with them in a united witch front. I recognized his cape. I couldn't see Kaito anywhere. I didn't especially like her, but I didn't wish her dead.

I staggered, and though the air was hot, a cold sweat broke along my forehead. Blackness crept into the edges of my mind, but I wouldn't let it. Not yet.

I caught a glimpse of the sorceress's face, twisted into a truly bestial snarl as she pulled herself up on the dragon. Her red eyes were bright with anger and frustration, shocking in their depths.

Sparks of magic continued to hit her as the dragon took flight. I fell to my knees, my eyes on the dragon as it pulled higher into the night sky until it was but a speck in the sea of blackness and then was gone.

"Tessa! Oh my God! Tessa!"

I looked up to see a blurred version of Ruth, just as a version of a blurred Beverly appeared next to her.

"Dolores," I breathed, and I fell to my knees just as the darkness took me.

CHAPTER
23

I woke to the sound of something crashing, like a glass smashing against the floor.

I jerked up in my bed, my heart racing as I blinked the drowsiness from my lids and looked around. I was in my room, the heavy drapes drawn, but some light was coming through, which meant it was morning or afternoon.

Had my bed shaken? I thought I felt a tremor?

I didn't even remember getting into bed. All I remembered from last night was passing out after the dragon took off. Then I got some fragments of random images: Ruth practically force-feeding me some disgusting, fertilizer-smelling tonic that tasted exactly like it sounded; Beverly shooting her mouth at something Emmet had said; and Ronin saying something in the likes of "you weigh a lot more than you look," which is something we woman *love* to hear.

I let out a sigh, trying to shake the sleep from me. I didn't feel rested. My body ached like I'd planted a hundred trees on my own with just a shovel. I was tired, and part of me wished I could lie back down and sleep for an entire month, though I knew that was impossible.

I remember waking up throughout the night. Yes, because of my aches and pains, but also because of the nightmare I kept having. I kept dreaming I was being eaten alive by tiny dragons the size of squirrels. Little bastards had sharp teeth too.

I cast my gaze around the room. I'd been certain my bed had shaken. Or was that part of the dream too?

"Maybe I'm losing my mind," I breathed. "Maybe I'm just—"

My bed rattled, and I was lifted off the mattress in a sudden heave, suspended in the air before falling back down.

"What the hell is happening!" I wailed as I shot up again, only to land back on my bed a second time.

While I was playing rodeo with my bed, I noticed my laptop on the vanity trembling. It moved along the top with my books and pens, which moved to the edge and then crashed to the floor.

My bed jerked again, and I reached out and grabbed one of the bedposts for support. "House! What is wrong with you?"

A crack broke through the plaster in the ceiling, spreading along to the other side. Pictures frames fell off the walls only to smash on the wood floors. It wasn't just my room. The entire house was shaking like we'd been hit by an earthquake. Either that, or Davenport House was coming down.

That's when the smell hit. A disgusting mold-like smell mixed with rotten eggs rose and seemed to come from the walls and the ceiling.

One thing was for sure. Earthquakes didn't smell. So, what the hell was this?

I'd had enough. I swung my legs off the bed and stood. I could still feel the tremors under my feet.

And then it stopped. Just stopped.

I straightened and walked over to the dresser. "House. What's going on? Why are you shaking? And what's up with the smell?"

I waited for House to show me something, but all I saw was a grim-faced woman who looked like she'd crawled out of her grave. Me.

"Hello? House?"

Nothing. And in this house, *that* was *not* normal.

Images from last night's demonic debacle on Hollow Cove Bridge loomed with a terrible clarity in my head. The sorceress's creepy face flashed in my mind's eye. Had she finished destroying the ward? Had she done something to Davenport House?

A coldness swept through me as I remembered something else.

Dolores.

My heart fluttered into a sudden, startled panic. The sorceress had done something to her.

Without another second to waste, I dashed out of my room, barefoot and wearing only my undies and a T-shirt. My feet slapped on the hardwood floors as I sprinted down the second-floor hallway, making a beeline for my aunt's room.

The door was open, which made for an easier entrance. I don't think I could have stopped my momentum at this pace. Voices trailed out, and I dashed in.

I skidded to a stop before slamming into Ruth. She and Beverly were both standing next to a large, four-poster bed, resting above a red and cream Persian carpet.

They turned at the sound of my animated entrance, their faces grave and hollow, and their eyes glistening with sorrow.

I moved past them to the bed and froze. A scream died in my throat.

Dolores lay in her bed, her arms resting above a thick, white, and gray striped duvet cover. Her skin was pale, almost translucent. Black swelled and bulging veins marred her face, her arms and hands, and all of her skin that I could see.

I reached out and grabbed her hand. It was stiff and cold as stone. Her chest rose and fell in a steady rhythmic motion. It was the only sign that she was still alive, but barely.

"What happened to her?" I asked, finding my voice with my eyes burning.

"We think it's a curse," answered Ruth, her voice low and filled with sadness.

"A curse that wretched sorceress put on her," added Beverly.

I swallowed, my throat constricting. My eyes rolled over Dolores's face to her grayish lips and sunken cheeks. "Can't you lift the curse?" A tear rolled down my cheek, and I wiped it away. "Isn't that what you do? The Merlin Group? You're supposed to be experts in lifting hexes and curses. Right?"

Ruth inched closer. "This is no ordinary curse, Tessa. It's complex. Dark. It's a curse we've never seen before."

I let go of Dolores's hand and turned, wiping my eyes as more big fat tears decided to make their appearance. "What are you saying?" I snapped. "Are you going to let her die? Is that what you're trying to tell me?"

Ruth stepped back as though I'd slapped her, making my guilt hit hard. "No. Of course not."

Beverly stiffened, her hands on her hips, clearly pissed at me. "Family comes first. Always has. We don't let the members of our family *die*."

I let out a puff of air, feeling like a giant jackass. "I know. I'm sorry. I shouldn't have said that. I just… wasn't expecting to see her like this." Then I took the time to look around the room. Candles rested on the floor, giving off a soft glow, their flames low, like they'd been burning for hours. Witch runes, sigils, and pentagrams were drawn in chalk over the floor and near Dolores's bed. A large chalk-drawn circle with a tree in the middle and five stars drawn around it was marked at the foot of Dolores's bed. The sigil to protect and dispel curses.

The scent of incense and candles was thick, and I knew my aunts had performed many counter hexes and counter curses. Now, when I truly looked at them, I could see the bags under their eyes, the tiredness in their shoulders and posture. They'd been up all night fighting this damn curse.

I felt like a bigger fool. But now wasn't the time to dwell on my screw-up. There'd be lots of time to make up for my mistake later. Now was the time to act.

There was a sudden loud tearing sound, like the sound of metal splitting apart.

"Not again," said Ruth, her eyes round and wide.

"Grab on to something! Quick!" cried Beverly as she and Ruth leaped forward and grabbed hold of one of the bed's wood posts faster than I thought possible.

"What?" I asked, impressed at their agility.

The ground shook with a violent tremor.

I bit my tongue as my body was thrown to the floor. The scent of rot rose again, only thicker this time, and despite the blood in my mouth, I could taste the rot there too. Disgusting.

I screamed as the house shifted and rocked violently and then banked to the right side, sending me sliding down the hardwood in my underwear. The house rocked like we were in a boat during a storm. I was sure of three things next. One, a wall stopped me from sliding farther. Two, that wall, grateful though I was, hit me hard as I crashed into it. And three, a large, heavy bed with three witches followed closely behind.

I hit the wall with my back and rolled to the left as fast as I could.

The air behind me shifted and a loud crash hit the spot where I had been a second ago.

I whirled, seeing the bed and my aunts still all in it, holding on for dear life. It was as though some giant had grabbed hold of Davenport House and was now shaking it madly to discover what secrets were hidden inside.

I barely had time to recover before there was another loud roar of metal and wood splitting, and the house rocked to the left.

Here I go again.

"Make it stop!" I howled, as I slid to the other side of the room this time. I threw out my hands to grab hold of something, anything to keep me from smashing into the wall, but my hands kept slipping on the smooth polished floor.

"We can't!" cried Ruth as the bed came sliding toward me fast. "It's the ley lines."

"It's getting worse!" shouted Beverly.

I hit the wall with a thud. "Ow." I was going to have some nasty bruises tomorrow. The sound of something heavy scraping the floor pulled my eyes up. The large bed was coming at me again.

I pushed myself up and rolled away, waiting to hear the bed smashing against the wall. When it didn't, I looked up.

The bed had stopped right in the middle of the room, my aunts holding to the posts with their legs wrapped around them like strippers. It made me smile.

"Oh, thank goodness, I think it's stopped," said Ruth as she climbed down her post.

Beverly did the same, looking a little disheveled and angry. "For now. Ohhh. I just hate this. Hate this. Hate this."

I got to my feet, my lower back throbbing, and saw nasty scuff marks on my knees. Nice.

"Why would the ley lines do this to Davenport House?" I asked as I neared the bed, not exactly understanding what was happening.

"It's that damn sorceress," hissed Beverly, tugging down the front of her blouse. "She's pulling on the ley lines, see. Davenport House is basically a conduit of magic, of those ley lines. She's taking the magic from the lines, their power, and by doing that…"

"She's killing House?" Damn. That was bad. I liked House.

"Among other things, yes," answered Beverly.

If the sorceress was dabbling in the ley lines, it could only mean she'd removed all five wards.

"She destroyed all the wards. Didn't she?" I asked my aunts.

Ruth's face was red and blotchy. "Yes," she answered, looking defeated.

But we weren't defeated. Not yet.

I reached out and grabbed Dolores's hand again, my fingers wrapped around her wrist. "Her pulse is really weak. How long does she have?" I didn't know if they could tell me, seeing as this was a new dark curse to them, but I needed a timeframe.

Ruth and Beverly didn't answer at first. And when they finally did, Ruth spoke. "Maybe a day, maybe less. It's…" she took a labored breath. "It's getting worse, Tessa. I've been giving her all my best healing tonics to keep the curse from spreading but…"

"But what?"

Beverly looked at me. "Whatever that sorceress is doing, it's making it worse. It's as though our magic diminishes while hers gains in power."

That did not sound good. If we could figure out what kind of curse she put on Dolores, maybe there was a way to reverse it.

My gut tightened. "If you guys were at the bridge, who brought her here? Who found her like this?"

"Marcus," said Ruth, as she dabbed a cold cloth on Dolores's forehead. "He and some Unseen were with her when the sorceress attacked. The Unseen are dead. All three of them. Dolores did what she could to save them but…"

"And that's why she ended up like this." Beverly's red lips trembled. "Always trying to save everyone." Her shaking fingers gripped the duvet. "She put herself in the way and got hit."

"What good did that do?" said Ruth. "They ended up dead anyway."

"And Marcus told you all this?" I wanted to know how was he still breathing while my aunt lay cursed and possibly dying and three of the Unseen were dead?

Ruth's blue eyes met mine. "Go ahead and ask him. He's downstairs."

Anger bloomed in my chest. "You mean, he's *still* here?" I asked with a smile.

"Yes," said Ruth. "But—"

I rushed out of the bedroom. Yes, I was going to face him in my undies and T-shirt and nothing else but my temper. I didn't care.

My smile turned wicked. Marcus was going to get it.

CHAPTER
24

I rushed down the stairs, which I really *don't* recommend when you're not wearing a bra. The girls were bouncing all over the place. I pressed my right arm over my chest to keep them from ripping to my feet and kept going.

I hit the bottom of the stairs. Following the sound of voices led me to the kitchen—well, what was left of it.

My breath came back in a gasp.

Cabinets lay in fragments on the kitchen floor, their contents smashed in pieces next to an assortment of cereal boxes, rice, pasta, canned goods, a couple of bananas, and a few apples. The fridge and stove sat where the kitchen island used to be and the island was tipped over to the side next to the dining room table. The kitchen was the heart of this home. It was where we'd always congregated. Now, it looked like a tornado had hit it. The kitchen was ruined. Even if we managed to kill the sorceress—because that's exactly what I was planning on doing—it would cost a fortune to replace this large kitchen.

I felt eyes on me, and I turned slowly to the left.

Ronin sat on one of the kitchen chairs, backward, his arms folded on the backrest. A strange smile splayed across his face at the sight of me. Emmet and Kaito sat on the floor in the middle of the living room, as though they were afraid to sit on anything that might suddenly attack them. I didn't blame them.

Marcus stood next to the fireplace mantel. I watched as he forced visible tension from his face and posture when he spotted me until he was the casual, confident chief on the surface.

Your ass is mine, I told him with my eyes.

I marched over, picking my way carefully around broken glass, lamps, and the occasional broken flowerpot.

The closer I got the wider his eyes got, as they flicked to my bare feet, moved up my thighs, very slowly, and then lingered a little too long on my breasts. No idea why. There wasn't much to see there at all.

I wasn't embarrassed to be half-naked, nor that I hadn't brushed my teeth or even attempted to brush my hair. Because I only had room for one emotion right now, and that was fury.

When I deemed I was close enough (so I wouldn't brush my breasts up against him) I planted my feet and pointed a finger in Marcus's face. "How could you do this?"

Marcus's mouth fell open in surprise. "Do what?"

I lowered my hand and kept it close to my body so I wouldn't accidentally spell his ass like the last time, enjoyable though it was.

"You were supposed to *protect* her!" I yelled. He was clearly taken aback, and I surged ahead, glad. "Isn't that what the town pays you for? Protection? How could you let that sorceress do that to my aunt?" I knew my face was red, but he deserved to hear it all, and worse.

He edged closer. "I did everything I could—"

"Not enough," I shouted. I could practically feel the steam coiling out of my ears. I was crazy mad. "Why is she cursed and not you, huh? Why are you standing here without a scratch while my aunt lays dying? Explain that to me."

Marcus clenched his jaw, his features tight, but said nothing.

273

Which only made my anger rise tenfold. "What the hell is the matter with you? Say something!"

"How can I take you seriously when you're wearing… that," said Marcus, his voice calm, stifling a smirk.

Oh. He was going down.

I inched closer until I was right up in his face. "I'm wearing this because I got my ass kicked by an evil sorceress's pet dragon, trying to protect the wards in this town. And you… you look like you just stepped off the set of some Hugo Boss commercial."

Ronin snorted. "Kind of annoying, isn't it? Looking so suave and polished. I'm the one who's supposed to look like that. I'm half-vampire. He's… he's a douche with really good hair."

Marcus stiffened as his eyes traveled over me, evaluating. "You fought the dragon?"

"Yeah, that's right," I said, feeling a little sassy. "A fire-breathing dragon. Didn't you see it?" I frowned when he put his hands behind his back to make himself look immovable.

"I did." He pulled his eyes to the floor. "It killed the Unseen. They were shielding Dolores while she protected the ward."

I rolled my eyes over. "You don't even have a scratch on you. You weren't even there. Were you?"

A muscle feathered along Marcus's jaw, his eyes narrowing dangerously. "You calling me a coward?"

I raised a brow. "Maybe I am."

The sound of a chair scraping the floor reached me, and from the corner of my eye, I saw Ronin.

"No one's calling anyone anything," said Ronin, his shoulder brushing up against mine as he tried to stand between us, but I wouldn't budge. Neither did Marcus.

"What in cauldron's name is going on here?" came Beverly's voice.

I turned to see Ruth and Beverly moving toward us. Ruth's face was twisted in worry while her sister's eyes took in my appearance, looking mildly pleased that I dared to stand half-naked to get my point across.

Reluctantly, I took a step back, seeing Ruth looking at me like I was half-mad. Maybe I was.

"Tessa, I know you're upset about what happened to Dolores," said Ruth, her steps a little shaky. I could see the strain of working spells all night on her now. She was exhausted. "But you shouldn't be saying those things to Marcus."

"Why not?"

Ruth's face took on a tight cast. "If it weren't for him, if he hadn't brought her straight here after what happened…"

"She'd be dead," answered Beverly her tone matter-of-fact.

I looked at Marcus, only to find him staring at me too.

A thread of heat coiled in my gut. Stupid body, reacting to his uber hotness.

Okay, so maybe he had saved her life by bringing her here in time for my aunts to work their counter spells. If he was expecting a thanks from me, he'd be waiting a lifetime.

It didn't explain how he'd survived when the Unseen, the unbeatable mercenaries, had been killed. How had he managed to survive? What made him so special?

"Here you go, Marcus. It's the only one that didn't get destroyed by House." Ruth handed Marcus another vial of the same blue liquid I'd seen her give him the other day.

Marcus gave Ruth a sincere smile as he took the vial and pocketed it. "Thank you, Ruth. I don't know what I'd do without you."

My aunt beamed. It took years off her face. "Anything I can do to help."

"Help with what, exactly?" I stood with my hands on my hips, aware only after the fact that it pulled my T-shirt higher on my hips.

I flicked my gaze between Ruth and Marcus, daring them to answer. But they all avoided my gaze. What the hell was going on?

Ignoring the need to grab Marcus and shake the answer out of him, I focused on what really mattered.

House was falling apart. My aunt Dolores was dying. Like hell I'd just stand here and do nothing.

Everything was quiet as I passed through the plans formulating in my head, hearing only the sounds of my heartbeat and Ruth's tiny sniffles.

"If I kill that sorceress," I asked my aunts. "Will that break the curse?"

They both stiffened like statues, their mouths parting in identical O's.

"Well?" I tried again, seeing as that was the only thing that would make sense. Destroy the one who'd created the curse and kill the curse. "Would that work?" I saw both Emmet and Kaito appear in my line of sight as they went to stand next to Marcus.

Beverly let out a long sigh through her nose. "Have you ever killed a sorceress before?"

"Well, no, but—"

"One that even your aunt Dolores, a power-ful witch, couldn't beat?" she pressed, smiling her dazzling smile, but without the warmth.

I got her point. "No. But that doesn't mean I can't." Though I had never actually killed any-one before either.

Ruth patted my arm. "Tessa. No one denies your abilities. But have you ever killed a living

277

being?" she added, as though she'd pulled the thought right out of my head. "Killing a mortal is a whole other beast. Some never recover from it."

"Look. I understand what you're getting at. I'm not the most experienced witch on the planet, but I'm not going to give up. I'm stubborn as hell. And that bitch will get what's coming to her." I stared at them both. "So. If the sorceress dies… will the curse be lifted?"

"Yes," said my aunts together.

Okay then.

My heart pounded with the realization of what I'd just done and confirmed in front of everyone. There was no backing out now, even if I wanted to. I'd said it. And I would see it through.

Plans formed inside my head. "You said she's beginning to tap into the ley lines, right? Which means she's not all-powerful. At least, not yet."

"That seems to be right, yes," answered Beverly.

"So," I said, my pulse thrashing with what I was about to say. "Then I need to hit her now. Before she continues to draw strength from the lines."

"We're coming with you," said Emmet suddenly, throwing me off. He looked at Kaito for a moment. "We've got a score to settle with that ugly bitch. She's taken three of our brothers. It's personal now."

I gave him a nod. They hadn't abandoned me when things got rough on the bridge. Plus, I'd seen them fight. They were exceptionally good. For what I was about to pull, I needed exceptional.

"You'll need me to watch your back," came Marcus's voice, and I nearly choked on my spit. "I'm coming too."

I opened my mouth to protest, but one look from Ruth had me clamp my big ol' trap shut. If she could have shot laser beams out of her eyes—she would have.

"Fine." That was all I said to the chief. He had saved Dolores. And for that, I could be civil. Though *could* didn't necessarily mean that I *would*.

Beverly wrapped her arms around her middle. "I'm afraid we can't come with you."

"We have to stay to keep the curse from spreading," added Ruth.

I gave my aunts a tight smile. "I know. I didn't expect you to come."

"That sorceress," said Beverly. "She'll be more powerful now that she's been dipping in the town's ley lines. She'll be stronger than any of us. Including you."

"I'm not giving up," I said. "It might seem like an impossible plan. Hell, I love impossible. I strive for the impossible. If she can be defeated, I have to try. For Dolores. For this town." And for me too. "This is my home now, and I will fight for it."

"She'll be using demons again," came Emmet's voice. "Probably more than what we've seen so far. Maybe bigger, meaner ones too. That dragon will be there. You can count on it."

"Probably." I'd thought about that too. But I was way ahead of them. I had a solution for her demons and the dragon. It wasn't over yet. I was going to find this evil sorceress. Bitchslap her a few times—then I would end her.

"This is all great, but you still have a major problem," informed Ronin.

I shrugged. "What?"

Ronin lifted his shoulders. "Do you know where this infamous sorceress is? I mean, she could be anywhere. She flew in on a dragon."

Damn. I knew I'd missed something. I paced the room, rummaging in my brain. "I know," I said, looking at my aunts. "Can't you do a locator spell or something?" I remembered reading about them, though I'd never tried one myself.

Ruth pursed her lips while she thought it over. "We could. But we would need something of hers. And we don't have anything."

Anger seethed, quickly replaced by dread. If I couldn't find the sorceress in time…

The front door crashed open.

I jerked around, holding my breath.

"She took her!" Martha came barreling through the front door and came rushing through the living room, her tiny feet moving extraordinarily fast. Her face was red and wet from tears or sweat. I couldn't tell which.

"Who took who?" asked Ruth rushing over to her friend. She tried to grab hold of her, but the bigger witch flailed her arms in the air, spinning around like a crazy version of a pirouette.

"She's gone, and she took her!" Martha wailed, big fat tears gushing down her face.

The blood left my face, and my gut plummeted somewhere near my feet.

"The sorceress took Sadie?" I blurted, meeting Marcus's eyes. His face looked troubled, but I could tell he'd made the same connection.

Marcus pushed from the wall and stepped toward Martha. "How do you know she did for sure? Sadie's always sneaking around. Maybe she went to explore—"

"This!" Martha shoved a piece of paper in Marcus's face.

The chief took it, his gray eyes intense as he read it. Then he looked up, not at Martha, but at me.

I frowned. "What?"

"Read it," he said as he handed me the paper.

I snatched it out of his hand just as Ronin appeared at my shoulder peering down at the paper.

My heart thrashed as I read the note.

Little Tessa Peep has lost her sheep and doesn't know where to find her.

Leave her alone, and she will come home, wagging her tail behind her.

If you want to see the kid again, come to Devilwood Thicket. You've got one hour, or the kid dies.

Samara

"Well, now we know what to call her," said Ronin, leaning back. "Though I much preferred psycho red-eyed bitch. More of an authentic ring to it."

Knowing her true name was useful, very useful. Having her name gave me some power over her. She'd known that, but she'd done it anyway. Either she was stupid, which I didn't think, or so damn powerful it didn't matter.

To beat her, I'd need some extra magical strength and some superpower.

I looked at Emmet and said, "Do you have an extra cape?"

CHAPTER
25

Turned out Emmet did not have an extra cape. Either that, or he didn't want to share.

After we'd all crammed into my aunt's Volvo station wagon, me behind the wheel, it had taken us a whole twenty minutes to reach Devilwood Thicket from Davenport House.

Devilwood Thicket was just as creepy, dreary, and ominous as it sounded. Located in Cape Elizabeth, the next town over from Hollow Cove, it was eight hundred acres of dense, dark forest, that elicited feelings of dread. Every half-breed community had one or two of these kinds of forests and woodlands, not because they chose to make it creepy and filled them with the most "undesirables" of our races, but because most of the undesirables preferred to live there, in a secluded forest and away from the rest of us.

Rogue werewolves were infamous for abandoning their half-breed packs to live more like their beast and among other wolves and creatures. Elves were also another more secretive group who preferred to live in complete isolation from the other races, off the grid, and where their magic was strongest.

This secretive nature came to birth many other fairy tales and legends over the years in the human communities that were close to these half-breed forests. Forests became haunted, and more legends were born there. Humans made claims of seeing ghosts in some of these forests. And they'd be right, of course. There were ghosts. Thousands of them. And worse things too.

When I was little, my aunts told me the story of a family of shifters that resembled large ape-like creatures. They enjoyed a regular holiday in the forests up in the Champlain Mountains, where they'd spend months in their shifter forms, living off the land and enjoying the peace and tranquility of nature. They'd happened upon some hikers—and then the Bigfoot legend was born.

And on and on it went.

Yes, dark and dangerous things lived in Devilwood Thicket. You'd be mad to enter.

Guess that made me mad. And maybe just a little stupid.

As soon as we hit the first line of trees, I felt it.

The constant drumming pulse, like a giant heartbeat. The thrum of magic, and the paranormal.

"Where do we go from here?" Ronin's lanky form appeared to my right. The half-breed vampire had surprised me when he'd volunteered to come along on this magical excursion, especially after his history with sorcerers.

There was no telling where the sorceress took up residence in Devilwood Thicket. But it didn't matter.

"This way," I gestured with my hand to the right between two large oak trees. "It's this way."

I wasn't pointing to a path. There was no path. I was pointing toward where the magic felt strongest. Where, without a doubt, Samara was pulling on the ley lines.

I knew Emmet could feel it too as he trudged forward before anyone else, snapping twigs and clearing a way for us. Kaito following closely behind him, her right hand resting on the hilt of the sword at her waist. As a fae or elf, she could probably sense the magic as well.

I trekked forward behind Kaito, and Ronin fell in behind me, still to my right. Marcus was

content with taking the rear and keeping everyone in careful view.

I hadn't spoken to him since we'd left Davenport House. He hadn't tried to speak to me
either. I wasn't sure why he wanted to come.
Maybe he felt guilty about not being able to
save my aunt from being cursed. Or maybe,
like me, he wanted to protect the town from
this crazy sorceress.

We'd left the house seven minutes after
Martha had barged in with her letter from the
sorceress. I'd rushed up back upstairs, put on a
bra (thank you very much) under a black T-
shirt and leather jacket, with a pair of jeans and
some sturdy flat boots for hiking. We were going to trudge uphill with underbrush, roots,
and miles of rocks and trees. If I wore heels, I'd
likely kill myself.

I couldn't run in heels. Women who can run
in heels are my heroes.

Even though it was only half-past one in the
afternoon, inside the forest it felt like midnight.

The sun was high in the sky above us, but
we couldn't see it. Oak and ash trees as tall as
three-story buildings loomed over us, shielding us from the sunlight. Slips of soft yellow
light sneaked through leaves, but just barely.
Leaves rustled, and a wind blew through the
trees, brisk and cool and unnatural. The smell
of moist earth and damp leaves rose up with
the wind, and for a moment it did almost feel

as though we were walking through a natural forest. But the thickening scent of sulfur and rot gave it away. There was nothing natural about this forest.

"I wouldn't be surprised if there were two or three more dragons when we get there," came Ronin's voice as he trudged next to me, his long limbs stepping over a large tree root and making it look easy.

I heard a series of quick steps, and then Marcus appeared in my line of sight to my left. He angled his head toward me, probably so he could better hear our conversation. A bubble of guilt—a *very* tiny one—formed in my gut. I might have gone a little hard on the chief back at Davenport House. I wasn't perfect. I was high on emotions, and after seeing my aunt Dolores lying in the bed like a corpse, I'd lost it. The guilt wasn't enough for an apology. Hell no. If anyone needed to apologize, it was Marcus. Especially, after the way he treated me when we first met. I still hadn't forgotten, nor had I forgiven him for that.

"I know," I answered, watching Marcus. "It's why I brought a new toy." Marcus's attention snapped to me and I looked away.

"You know I'm getting some interesting visuals," commented Ronin, a smile in his voice. "If you pull out a vibrator, I'm going to be really confused."

I rolled my eyes and pulled out a big green leather-bound tome from my bag. "This," I shoved the book at him. "This is my new toy, dumbass."

Ronin jerked back like the book was crawling with spiders. He eyed it suspiciously. "*How to Conjure and Train your Demon*? Since when are you into Dark witch stuff?"

"Who's into Dark witch stuff?" Emmet's large body waddled over. "You? I thought you were a White witch." He snatched the book out of my hands before I could stop him.

"White. Dark. It doesn't really matter," I said, never fully understanding why witches treated their magic separately. "Magic is magic. What changes is the magical practitioner. They decide how to manipulate their magic. You should know. You're a witch."

Emmet flipped through the pages. "I am. Never trusted the Dark arts. All that demon conjuring. You can't trust demons. Why would anyone want to trade a part of themselves for a little of their magic? Nah. I'm happy with the elements. With a bit of ley line, I'm good. It's enough."

I grabbed my book from him. "It wasn't enough for my aunt. And she's been a badass witch for a lot longer than you or me. We'll need all the help we can get. If it means I need to dabble a little in the Dark arts, then I'm gonna." I had no idea how to do that, but they didn't have to know.

"You've done Dark witch magic before?" came Marcus's voice near my ear making me jump.

I glared at him. "How d'you do that?" When he just raised a skeptical brow, I added. "I've never actually done it before. No. But how hard can it be? Right? It's just about following the instructions—"

Marcus's eyes bugged out of his head. "Are you crazy?"

"Possibly."

"Dark magic can kill you."

I slipped my book in my bag, not appreciating his tone or his lack of confidence in my abilities. But then again, he didn't know me. "Are you an expert in Dark magic all of a sudden?"

Marcus loomed over me, his face flashing into alarm. "I know that if you say the wrong word, or even just mess up a sigil or a rune, it can kill you. I also know there's a reason why White witches don't do it." He inched forward a little until I could smell his aftershave, which was a very pleasant smell. "It's dangerous."

I didn't move an inch. "I don't mind a little danger from time to time. What doesn't kill you makes you stronger. Right?"

Marcus gave a mock laugh. "And what will your aunts think when you don't come home? You think gambling your life away is fair?"

"Since when do you care about my life, anyway?" I ground out. "You've made your sentiments very clear since I came here." I gritted my teeth. I was not having this conversation with him in this damn forest right now. No way.

"Back off, Chief," said Ronin as he pushed a finger on Marcus's chest, forcing him to take a step back. "If Tess says she can do it, she *can* do it. Capiche?"

Marcus's face tightened, and he exhaled slowly. "I might have misjudged you when you first came here. I'm sorry for that."

Now *that* was unexpected. I felt like doing cartwheels.

His gray eyes searched my face, making my heart race a little. "I care about your aunts and my town. I want nothing bad to happen. You have to believe that."

I stared at him and pulled the strap of my bag higher on my shoulder. "Well, at least we have that in common."

"I hope you know what you're doing." With his jaw set, Marcus turned away.

"Me too," I whispered. Guess we were about to find out.

"Don't worry, Tess." Ronin patted my shoulder. "I know you've got this."

Emmet snorted and started forward again with Kaito behind him like his killer shadow. Ronin and I followed next with Marcus picking up the rear once more.

The five of us marched in silence. I strained my ears for any sound of movement coming at us, knowing the others were doing the same in their united silence. More than once I thought I saw glowing green eyes next to some trees. Then another pair of eyes flashed in the shadows of the forest, like things that never quite could be clearly seen. I blinked and they were gone. Nothing came at us, so I kept walking.

It went like this for another half-hour. The deeper we went into the forest, the colder it became, and the stronger the magic pulsed.

It got to a point where it was like I was standing below an electrical power station or a giant beehive.

Emmet was feeling it too. His shoulders kept getting tenser, and he kept reaching out and grabbing his cape, as though it was giving him the strength to keep moving. Now and then I'd catch a glimpse of him muttering to himself. Spells. He was getting ready to throw one.

Even Kaito was on edge. She'd pulled out her sword and was now using it like a machete to cut down branches and underbrush that got in the way.

Ronin was whistling a tune. Either he was enjoying himself, or this was a cover because he was nervous.

We were all on edge. We'd all seen what this sorceress could do, and that was before she'd tapped into the power of the ley lines. And who's to say there was only one sorceress? My gut told me The Church of Midnight had more members.

I was angsty and nervous, my pace a little slower as I went over the power words in my head. For some reason, the thought of Marcus kept interrupting my thinking.

He obviously didn't care about my wellbeing. No, he was here for the town. That was certain. Maybe he cared about my aunts. He needed Ruth to keep making those vials for him, so I doubted he wanted harm to come to her.

But he had apologized…

Yes. He'd apologized for being a dick. It was hard to keep holding that against him now, seeing that he was risking his neck for Hollow Cove and possibly my aunts. My ex never apologized. I didn't even think that behavior or emotion existed in him. I didn't know what to make of Marcus now. I wasn't sure I hated him anymore.

I sank into a quiet measured gait through the woods. I was so involved in my own head that when we stepped into a sudden clearing, I froze, Marcus bumping into me from behind.

All my thoughts evaporated.

The clearing in the forest was the size of a football field. Paths wound in and around structures made of tree roots that could have been small huts. Flaming torches held by poles flanked the sides of the paths. Some paths had human and animal skulls dotting the trails like gruesome marker stones. A garden sprawled to my left. Though it wasn't a vegetable garden but a garden filled with poison ivy, stinging nettle, hogweed, and a variety of poisonous mushrooms.

The moon reflected on a pond, its silvery water rippling in a slight breeze. It couldn't have been more than two in the afternoon at the most, yet it was gloomy and dim, and there was no sign of the sun. It felt like it was midnight. Only magic could create a perpetual night. Powerful magic.

My eyes moved to the end of a winding path. A fortress sat in the middle. Four stories high, it was a gothic, church-like building with turrets, spires, and towers, all made of tree roots, branches, rock, and mounds of earth twisted together into a gruesome and creepy construction.

The Church of Midnight.

The grotesque way it was built wasn't what had my insides tightening into a ball, but the power that oozed from it. A heavy thrumming filled the air where powerful magic moved and flowed into motion. I knew that power. I recognized it.

The ley lines.

The power of Hollow Cove's ley lines was being pulled into that fortress. Like they were slowly being sucked into it, as though the structure was some giant vacuum capable of drawing in ley lines.

And sitting right before the entrance, on a small boulder, was Sadie.

Maternal instincts shot through me, and I was running. I shot past Emmet and Kaito and made a beeline for the little girl.

"Sadie! Are you hurt?" I asked as I stood over her, searching for cuts and bruises but finding none. "Are you okay?" She was still alive. I took that as a good omen.

Sadie looked up at me, her big blue eyes glistening with a wicked delight. "I am now that you're here. I knew you'd come, Tessa."

The last part sounded like a laugh. But I was more astonished that the little girl had spoken. "You're talking?" I asked unsure. Maybe the sorceress had drugged her?

Sadie jumped off the rock and started laughing. Not a cute, little girl's giggle, but a mature, evil harsh laugh that should not be coming out of her throat.

"Creepy kid," said Ronin, appearing next to me to my right.

Kid. My blood froze. I took a step back and then another, pulling Ronin with me as Sadie continued to howl in laughter. I knew that laugh.

The skin around Sadie's face shifted and rippled grotesquely as though it was made of hot wax, yet her creepy laugh never stopped.

"What the hell is happening to her?" came Marcus's voice from behind me somewhere.

The scent of vinegar and sulfur was thick, and a sheet of black mist wrapped around Sadie as she continued to laugh until she had disappeared under a blanket of shadow. The shadow collapsed, and a shape emerged—a much larger and taller one with a dark, heavy robe wrapped around the shoulders of a bald head with scarred, pointed ears.

Gone was the cute, innocent girl. And in her place stood the sorceress Samara.

I swallowed. "Fuck me."

CHAPTER
26

I had a temporary freak-out moment because seeing a little girl morph into a butt-ugly sorceress would do that to a person.

"You're Sadie?" Go with the obvious when you're suffering from a mental fart.

Samara smiled, showing off her pointed teeth that looked like they'd been filed down to resemble those of a cat. "I knew you'd come for…" she made a pout and sad eyes, "poor little orphaned Sadie." She let out a wet cackle. "Pathetic. Really."

I heard a low growl as Emmet and Kaito emerged to my left, both hunched and poised like they were about to tackle the sorceress. Hell, I wanted to do it too.

"You're a sick bitch. You've been her this entire time," I said, more of a statement than a question. And then everything snapped into place. "You were there, in the street, the night Avi was killed, and when the pixies had their meltdown. The ward in the library. It was you. It's always been you."

Now, come to think of it. Sadie had been at all three places, but I would have never made the connection. I felt like a fool. I'd stopped to help Sadie in the library, thinking the sorceress had hurt her, but the girl had played me. I was a giant fool.

"Let's take her now," whispered Emmet. "She's alone. She's vulnerable. We won't get a better chance."

"Not yet." I had to disagree with the big Unseen. I doubted very much Samara was alone and vulnerable. A bitch who filed down her teeth into pointy needles and self-mutilated her ears to look like a Vulcan was crazy, yes, but not isolated or defenseless. Looking at her now, it was probably *the* exact opposite.

The fortress shuddered as it sucked in more ley line power.

The vision of Dolores lying in her bed with black veins covering her face swam in my vision. "What do you expect to gain, apart from taking Hollow Cove's ley lines? What do you want?"

"Gain?" Samara laughed. "All of it, silly. I want it all. To be all-powerful. The Church of Midnight will rise and we will put an end to all nonbelievers. The non-magical will die. They are weak. Technology will die with them, but magic… magic will rise. Just as it once was. The rise of technology, the rise of humans, forced all magical practitioners, among other creatures, to live in hiding. But the earth's magic, the ley lines, all were here before technology. And when all the ley lines in the world point to this place"—she flung out a hand and pointed to the fortress— "once all the magic's concentrated here. We will squish the human world and its technology with it."

"I think you should ease up on the crazy pills," I mumbled. "I knew you were the skitzo type, but I thought I'd double check."

"The bald bitch is crazy," said Ronin. "No one can control all the ley lines of the world. Right? Tell me I'm right, please."

I couldn't because I had no idea. "She seems to think she can." If she could, we were all dead.

My skin pricked like I had thousands of ants crawling up my back. Something felt wrong. Off. Samara *wanted* me here. Hell, she'd practically drawn me a map to get me to this place. But why? She'd already destroyed the town's wards and tapped into its ley lines. So why me?

I stifled a shudder. "Why did you want me to come here? What exactly do you want from me?"

"Finally," drawled Samara, rolling her eyes dramatically. "I thought you'd never ask." The sorceress skipped around the boulder, swinging her arms, as a little girl would. "I'm a curious creature by nature."

"You've got the creature part right," muttered Ronin.

From the corner of my eye, I saw Marcus standing farther away from us to my left. He was crouched low, his knuckles touching the ground. He was either getting ready for a hundred-meter dash, or he was about to do something stupid.

"And when *you* came to Hollow Cove, you intrigued me," continued Samara. My attention snapped back to her. "Not just because you were the new witch in town. There was something different about you. Something special."

"I have that effect on people," I answered, a hand on my hip. Power vibrated from the earth through the soles of my boots just as the air fizzled and crackled with energy. Power thrummed in this place. The ley lines were being pulled here, right where we were. If she could use them, then maybe...

I reached out and tapped into the ley lines. Magic swelled, and my body trembled at the sudden influx of power. I felt my hair rise off my shoulders.

Samara halted, and her face cracked into a grin. Her red eyes grew wide and practically reached over her hairless brows. "Yes. The magic is potent. I know you can feel it." She pointed a scarred finger at me the nail completely gone. "But you don't know how to use it. Do you?"

"I'm a fast learner." Total lie. I might be a slow learner. But once information got into my thick skull, it stayed there forever.

Samara's smile twitched. "You showed great resistance to the demon's fire. Uncommon for a White witch, especially when the witch in question is barely a witch. You are weak. Unprepared. Unschooled."

I raised my brows skeptically. "Really? If that were true, I wouldn't be here, now would I? No. I think you know I can kick your ass and you don't like it. That's why you set this up. You thought you'd bring me here and what? I would let you kill me?"

Ronin laughed. "Fat chance, baldy."

"You cursed one of the few people I care about. I will end you," I told her, feeling brash and crazy, the fueling of the ley lines making me nuts.

Samara sucked in air through her teeth as she spread her mouth into a wide, manic grin. "You can't beat me. You are special, yes, but not that special. Who are you kidding? The force is in *me*."

"This isn't *Star Wars*, freak."

The sorceress showed me her pointed teeth and hissed like a cat. "Oh. But I *will* kill you." She brightened. "Such a useless scrap of magic contains you," said Samara, her voice high and clear. "Trivial, and yet it shapes you. And you will die tonight, Tessa. This time your magic won't save you."

"I'll take my chances."

Samara's eyes moved to Emmet and Kaito. "I will kill you just like I killed the other Unseen." She giggled. "I can still smell their burnt flesh and hear their cries for their mommies as they died. Quite the show. Too bad you missed it."

I looked at Emmet. A giant vein throbbed on his forehead, and his lips were pulled back in a snarl. Damn. That was bad.

As he stood there, Emmet's face seemed to take on a different cast, the shadows under his eyes growing to make him look ill.

"You're dead," he said. His voice changed, became more resonant, and somehow echoed in my head.

In a blur, he rushed forward, his hands dripping in green magic. Latin flowed from his lips.

"Emmet! Wait!" I howled, but it was too late.

I felt a buildup of ley line energy, rising until it was almost painful. He was tapping into it.

Sparks of green magic soared from the Unseen. With a flick of his wrists, he shot them directly at the sorceress.

It was a perfect shot. Samara didn't move. Hell, it looked like she was waiting for it.

I held my breath as I watched the green energy hit—

Samara vanished on the spot, as though her mere presence had just been a trick of the light.

Emmet stumbled to a halt, a feverish gleam in his blue eyes.

"Am I dreaming? Or did she just pull a Houdini on us?" asked Ronin.

Marcus shifted on his feet. "She's here somewhere."

And then the laughter started.

Loud and echoing, it sounded like thousands of voices at once—but all hers. Samara's laugh rose around us as though she was everywhere at once.

"Where the hell are you?" roared Emmet.

"There!" Kaito pointed with her sword at the fortress.

Samara stood at the bottom step of her fortress. The smile on her face was truly beastly, and she looked like a demon.

Suddenly, the ground shifted beneath my feet. I could all but feel the soil shifting and roots settling as the forest shivered, like it wanted us out.

"Why do I get the feeling something bad is about to happen," Ronin said shortly.

As if in answer, The Church of Midnight opened its doors, which looked at least twelve feet high and carved from tree roots. A mass of dark-robed, bald figures came rushing out, spilling down the steps in a swoop of darkness, as though the fortress had vomited them out.

Evil sorcerers and sorceresses on their home turf were boosted with ley line magic. I had barely survived a battle with just one of them, and now I was staring at about fifty. They would hit us in less than twenty seconds.

I let out a breath. "I knew this was going to suck."

CHAPTER
27

I watched the robed figures spilling down the front steps, moving with the speed and precision of predators.

"Man, I hate sorcerers." Ronin cut me a glance. "What's the plan, boss?"

"Don't die," I told him.

The plan had been to kill Samara, but now, seeing her army, I wasn't sure it would happen. Too late to turn back now.

The sound of something ripping behind me had me spin around.

Marcus stood there, shirtless, as he unbuckled his belt and yanked off his jeans, ripping them at the same time.

Holy.

Mother.

Of.

God.

I glimpsed a very fit, golden-brown body, rippling in muscles because there was no room for anything else. I stared because, let's face it, why would I look away from a very naked and well-endowed Marcus? I never thought I'd be the type of woman to drool at the sight of a naked man. I'd seen my share of naked. Just not like *this kind* of naked.

Drooling. Yup. I was wrong.

And then things got weird.

Marcus's face rippled, a sort of slithery motion just beneath the surface of his skin that stretched his features strangely, causing a widening of his head and a slight elongation of the jaw. He let out a growl, and when his mouth opened, it revealed carnivore teeth the size of my fingers. There was a flash of black fur, a snarl, a horrible, tearing sound, and the breaking of bones. And then, instead of a man, stood a four-hundred-pound silverback gorilla.

"Well, scratch my balls and call me Beryl," exclaimed Ronin. "The chief's freakin' King Kong!"

I couldn't help but stare at this magnificent and yet terrifying beast. The muscles on his chest flexed, as he stood on all fours, his front hands resting on his knuckles, a posture I recognized from watching the National Geographic channel. I also knew gorillas were the largest of the primates, and the strongest. Nine times stronger than your average human male, I thought I remembered. You did not want to piss off a silverback gorilla.

Marcus, or rather, the gorilla looked at us with gray, intelligent eyes. Marcus's eyes. He roared, shaking his head, and I found myself taking a step back. You would have too. But his sudden aggression wasn't aimed at us. It was a "get your asses ready" kind of roar.

"Yes! Yes!" Samara clapped her hands. "Kill the witch bitch and bring me her head. Ha-ha!"

"No way," I said, tapping into the ley lines. "I like my head."

"Me too." Ronin's eyes flashed to black, and he wiggled his talons, looking like the vampire version of Edward Scissorhands. "Here they come."

With my heart in my throat, I watched as Samara's army circled us until we were surrounded.

Like a storm of wild magic, they exploded into motion.

"For Kirk, Bill, and Taylor!" cried Emmet as he vaulted forward with green flames spewing from his hands. Green light flooded around him as he hit three of the enemy. They fell like logs of flames before they countered.

306

Kaito ducked, spun, and came up with a great swipe of her sword, slicing off the wrists of about five sorcerers at once. They let out choked screams of pain and shock as blood fountained from their bloody stumps. If the wounds didn't kill them, the blood loss would.

Kaito caught me staring and flashed me a smile. "No hands. No magic."

Smart. Though I knew some practitioners didn't need the use of their hands to conjure magic, but I kept that to myself.

She kicked at the falling bodies, making an opening and scattering them for a moment while gaining some much-needed space.

A flash of dark robes caught my attention to my right, and I twisted around. A group of sorcerers came at me like a great black wave.

The gorilla pounded his fists on the ground, and with a powerful thrust of his back legs, shot forward and rushed to meet the onslaught of robed figures. I heard a cry and the sound of tearing flesh. Marcus the gorilla tore at Samara's subjects with voracious rapidity, his powerful body a killing machine on steroids.

Sparks of red magic hit the gorilla in the chest. He faltered for a moment, and I hissed through my teeth. He shook his head and then pulled back his lips and roared, flinging himself at the sorcerer that had attacked him. In a flash of fur and muscles, the gorilla grabbed the sorcerer and lifted him as though he

307

weighed nothing at all—and split open his torso all the way back to his crooked spine.

So, Marcus was somewhat resistant to magic. Interesting.

He'd also protected me.

The gorilla tossed the dead sorcerer like you would a chicken bone and lunged at another just as four robed figures rushed us.

"Ventum!" I shouted the power word, and a burst of wind slammed into the oncoming sorcerer. I staggered back, not ready for the influx of power from being at the center of all that ley line magic. I gritted my teeth when pain flared as though my insides were aflame.

I looked up in time to see the sorcerer I'd struck flying back. A combination of surprise and relief rushed through me. I hadn't been entirely sure that my magic would work on the sorcerer, after seeing Samara immune to my fire. Perhaps my magic hadn't been strong enough when I'd faced her, or maybe her subjects weren't as strong. But this guy hit a tree trunk at fifty miles per hour. The sound of his head smashing against the tree, similar to the sound of a tomato thrown against the wall, should have made me ill. But I barely registered his death as another came at me.

Female this time, she moved with liquid grace with red magic coiling around her arms like bracelets, the same color of her eyes. She snickered at what she saw on my face, probably a combination of horror and fatigue.

I could still feel the pain of my latest power word coursing through me, though much less. I rolled my shoulders, trying to force myself to relax. It didn't work.

"Urt 'Zaq!" she bellowed, flinging her palms at me.

Red rings of fire burst from her outstretched hands, and my face flamed from the heat of her magic.

"Inflitus!" I shouted, flinging my hand as a blast of kinetic force knocked her magic rings away, ten inches from my face.

Anger. Fear. Pain. The tidal surges of my emotions had propelled me, fueled my magic, and I would use it.

I didn't want to hurt or kill anyone, except for Samara, but this was self-defense. Kill or be killed. And the bitch had tried to kill me. Now I was pissed.

Her lips moved in a dark chant, but I was way ahead of her.

With the power of the ley lines still pounding through me I cried, "Accendo!"

A shoot of fire burst from my hands, high into the air, spinning and spreading orange and red light while catching the sorceress on the left hip.

She let out a cry of fury, and then I heard nothing but the sound of flames burning her robe and her flesh.

I barely had time to catch my breath as another black-robed figure leaped my way.

A flash of brown hair appeared in my line of sight. With a torrent of vampire speed, Ronin pivoted smoothly. With a swipe of his talons, he sliced the sorcerer across the neck.

"No!" gurgled the sorcerer, spitting up blood from his throat. And then he fell.

"Nice," I said, keeping close and readying myself for the next onslaught of sorcerers. "You been working out? You look good."

Ronin's sharp canines flashed in a quick smile. "I don't need to, baby. It's called genetics—" He broke off as a sorceress made a mad dash for him, but Ronin was faster. She was down on the ground, her head detached from her body and rolling off to the side, her lips open in her unfinished curse.

I got an occasional glimpse of the whirling masses that were Emmet and Kaito, fighting side by side while a massive gorilla roared. He slammed his body against the sorcerers, picking them up and crushing them together. Their skulls snapped like smashed eggs. Marcus leaned steadily in one direction—to kill the threat. He was impressive to watch, but I didn't have time for that.

The sounds of battle blared in a combination of cries, shouts, and the boom of magic, making my ears whistle like I was at a rock concert.

I lost sight of Samara under the throng of battle, but I knew she was here somewhere, watching.

More importantly, it looked like we were winning. The Church of Midnight's army was reduced to a mere ten, and we were all still alive. Maybe luck was finally on our side. We were a mismatched band of misfits, but we were beating her army.

We can do this. I can do this.

Filled with a renewed sense of valor, I dashed into the fight. The power words spilled from my lips as though I'd been using them for years.

I let the magic course through me. My will, the ley lines, all of it. I felt like a different person. I felt strong. I felt like a badass. I felt like a real witch.

The more I pulled on the surrounding magic, the more my body felt it had been in the meat grinder. My insides were assaulted by the pricks of the needles, but I fought it. My pulse throbbed, but I never stopped as another burst of my fire struck a sorcerer. He went down in a wailing scream of fire and ash.

The pain was still there, throbbing, but my adrenaline covered it nicely.

Then sudden silence hit me. Panting, I wiped the sweat from my brow and looked around.

I stood in a sea of black, lifeless robes. Everywhere I looked, bodies of sorcerers and sorceresses lay crumbled, beheaded, burned, and very dead.

"Is that all you got?" cried Emmet, raising his fists in the air to some apparent god. "Ha! That was for my friends!"

Kaito was breathing hard next to him, her face covered in blood, but I was sure none of it was hers.

My eyes found the gorilla. He was thrashing his arms from side to side like he wanted to kill more. He raised himself on his two legs and let out a piercing roar that would have had the average Joe pissing himself. He pounded his chest like I'd seen gorillas do so many times in a show of strength, which he did have. Loads of it.

He fell back on all fours. Our eyes met and a strange, warm thrill vibrated in my belly.

"We did it," said Ronin, pulling my eyes away from the magnificent gorilla. "Don't everybody thank me at once." He gave me a brazen smile. "She's finished. Without her army, she's done."

I felt done, but I wasn't going to tell him. My body shook as the adrenaline rush left me. Truth was, I doubted I had anything left to give, in terms of magic. I knew if I continued to use more of that ley line, it would kill me. Maybe that's what Samara had meant by my not knowing how to use them. She was right.

Dizzy, I took a deep breath to cover my sudden weakness. It was a miracle I was still standing.

I turned and looked toward the fortress. Samara stood on the same, exact step as before. She hadn't even moved.

I smiled and gave her a finger wave.

She smiled back.

That was unexpected. "Why is she smiling back?" I asked uncertainly, a sudden chill killing my mood.

The sudden beating of wings brought my attention to the sky.

A gigantic dark shape skimmed over the treetops of Devilwood Thicket. The shape, a speckled gray and red body covered in a leathery hide, soared toward us and landed with a resounding boom right next to the fortress. Its leathery wings unfurled to the length of a small plane.

I swallowed hard. The demon dragon was back.

"*That's* why the bitch is smiling," answered Ronin.

CHAPTER
28

It appeared dragons were my lot in life—that and stupid ex-boyfriends.

Crap. This was bad. All the way down the crapper bad. We were all exhausted and our energies spent.

My frown settled down near the bridge of my nose. "Not really playing fair. Are you, Samara?" I said, raising my voice, though I knew it wouldn't matter.

Her black robes furled around her as she climbed the steps of her fortress. All around her, the energy of the ley lines kept pouring in, sucked through the doorway behind her. When she reached the top platform, she turned. Her eyes closed, seemingly getting a feel of the ley lines, as though they were feeding her their power at the same time, or she was sucking it in. All of it. She staggered like a drunk, though drunk with immeasurable power, and leaned her back against the wall of the fortress. Her arms were splayed like she was trying to hold on.

When she opened her eyes, they were a bright white, gleaming like tiny stars.

Ronin whistled. "Now that's buckets of crazy."

"The bitch is trying to absorb the ley lines," said Emmet, reading my mind. "She wants them all for herself. Their power."

Fear twisted my gut, and I felt Marcus's gaze on me. I looked at him. The giant silverback gorilla's face was pulled back tightly with worry. His gray eyes shone with fear. He was strong, but he knew a dragon was out of his league. It was out of everyone's league.

I looked back at Emmet. "Can it be done? Can she absorb all the ley lines' power?"

Emmet pursed his lips. "I don't know."

What I did know was that I couldn't let that happen.

The demon dragon dipped its long head in Samara's direction, its wings furling against its body as it waited for its master's instructions.

"Yes! Yes! I take it all!" cried Samara. The ground shuddered under my feet.

There was a flash of white light, the ley lines visible for a mere second as they poured into the fortress and into Samara before disappearing.

And then the weirdness got weirder.

Her face rippled and stretched. Her limbs pulled and shifted, elongating to abnormal lengths. Then, they intertwined with the roots of the fortress walls, twisting and molding into a single entity that looked like a giant squid and some kind of unnamed tree creature with too many limbs and great, white eyes.

It was as though Samara was slowly becoming a part of the fortress, or the fortress was consuming her. Either way, I nearly threw up. It was the most disturbing thing I'd ever seen in my life. I'd have nightmares for years.

Ronin's shoulders twitched in sudden tension. "If I wasn't scared shitless before, I am now."

My pulse fast, I had no idea what kind of transformation Samara would turn out to be, and I wasn't stupid enough to wait for it either.

My eyes moved back to the massive dragon. It was watching Samara with narrow, hateful eyes. I knew we couldn't beat the dragon, but I didn't want to hurt it either. Unlike the other demons we'd faced, this demon was being controlled. It had no choice but to obey the one who summoned it.

I was weak, maybe, but I wasn't defeated. Not yet.

And I still had a card to play.

"Emmet," I called, and waited for the large Unseen to turn around. "You got a protective shield that'll keep the dragon from burning us? I'll need a few minutes. Can you do that?"

The redhead grinned. "Yeah. Yeah, I can."

"Good. Do it," I told him, swinging my bag around my front and pulling out the green book.

"I'll need everyone to get a little cozy with each other," said Emmet as he gestured with his arms. "Like real close."

Kaito and Marcus both did as they were told and moved in until the five of us were in a tight circle, shoulder-to-shoulder tight.

"What are you going to do with that?" asked Ronin, leaning over.

"Plan B," I answered, my heart hammering so hard I was sure it would soon drill a hole through my chest and spill on the ground.

There was a sudden scent of animal and musk and I blinked to find the gorilla in my face. Shaking his head, Marcus pulled back his lips, a deep growl thundering in his throat.

I stood my ground. "You can growl all you want, you big monkey… but this is the only way." I stared at him in challenge. "You can't speak. Can you?" Not having dealt with many shifters, I had no idea if they could speak in their beast forms. Or was he a wereape? I wasn't sure of the nomenclature.

The gorilla slammed a fist down on the ground and shook his head again, his eyes narrow and filled with defiance.

That was my answer. "If you don't want to end up as a gorilla shish-kabob, you will get out of my way." The book shook in my hands. "I have to try."

Marcus met my gaze, and his eyes narrowed. For a second I thought he would throw another tantrum. But then he stepped away from me and positioned himself on all fours right in front of me, shielding me with his massive body. It was a nice gesture. Hell, it surprised me, but I doubted his resistance to *some* magic would work on demon fire.

"Burn them all!" came Samara's cry, her voice deep and rumbling as though the earth itself had spoken. "Burn them to ashes! I command it! Do it! Do it now!"

The demon dragon turned our way, its red eyes fixed on us.

Ronin shifted nervously. "If you're going to do something, Tess, now's the time."

"Right." I tossed my bag on the ground and fell to my knees, the big book on my lap as I flipped it open. I blinked the sweat from my eyes, a burst of nausea making the writing on the pages blur.

"Watch out!" cried Kaito, and I looked up from the book to see her in a crouched stance, her sword in her hand but staying close to Emmet.

The demon dragon opened its maw revealing yellow, curved fangs, and released a jet of fire.

"Protego!" shouted Emmet, throwing up his hands, his cape billowing behind him.

A green, semi-transparent half-bubble rose around us, just barely encircling us all a split second before the dragon fire hit us.

Boom.

Fire roared as it roiled and billowed, pressing up against the protection bubble. Heat seared my face like I'd placed a hot hair dryer over it. Ronin cursed, Marcus hissed, and for a horrible moment, I thought Emmet's protection shield wouldn't hold.

But it did. For the moment.

"Hurry up, witchling!" shouted Emmet, beads of sweat forming on his brow as he held on to his magic, his body shaking with effort.

With trembling fingers, I flipped to the page where I'd put a bookmark earlier and set the book down next to me. Next, I grabbed a small knife from my bag and drew a triangle-shaped sigil in the dirt and wrote the name Imipt in Latin in the center. So far so good. Next, I knew I needed to protect myself, even with Emmet's protection.

Breathing hard, I carved a circle in the dirt a few inches behind the triangle, wrote five archangel names around it within a coiled serpent, and stepped into it, my body shaking with adrenaline.

"What is that?" shouted Ronin over the blaring roar of dragon fire, pointing to the name.

"Hopefully the dragon's name," I shouted back.

Ronin's eyes widened. "Hopefully?"

I shrugged, sweat pouring down my face. "With the dragon's true name, I can control it." Or so it said so in the book. God, I hoped I wasn't wrong. If I was, we were all burnt toast.

"Best do it now, witchling," cried Emmet, his face twisted in pain and his fists shaking with controlled force of his will. "I can't keep holding on. This beast is fierce."

"It's a bloody dragon," cried Ronin. "Not a goddam chipmunk!"

"Hurry up," shouted Kaito, as though I hadn't heard Emmet.

Working fast, I tapped into my will and recited the incantation, channeling the magic from the ley lines. "With this triangle, I bind you, Imipt, demon of the Netherworld, to be subject to the will of my soul." And then I added with more conviction, "I command you to stop!"

I waited, expecting to feel the pain of using this Dark magic. Magic always gets back what it's owed. I felt nothing apart from the scorching heat.

It didn't work.

Whoops.

Ronin stared at me, eyes wide. "It didn't work!"

Marcus let out a deep rumble in his throat that sounded like "no shit."

I leaned over my handiwork, inspecting all the letters, sigils, and lines. All were done exactly like in the book. The only thing different was the name.

With my right hand, I wiped the name in the triangle and quickly wrote another.

"What are you doing now?" shouted Ronin.

"Another name, that's what." I swallowed as another wave of nausea hit. "There are *three* dragon names here. It's gotta be one of them."

"And if it's not?" said Emmet, his face red like molten lava. "Many demon dragon names don't exist in books."

He was right, of course. I started to get nervous, my stomach beginning a slow twist that made aches lace out through my arms and legs like slivers of ice.

But this was all I had. I couldn't lose faith now.

Ignoring the mounting fear in my chest, I took a breath and choked on the lack of air. I cried, "With this triangle, I bind you, Atreur, demon of the Netherworld, to be subject to the will of my soul. I command you to stop!"

And again, the dragon continued to spew out its fire at us.

Kaito screamed as the green protective half-sphere warped and shrank around us until it was touching her head.

"It's coming down!" yelled Ronin as he moved to hold on to Emmet, who'd nearly fallen to his knees. This magic might kill him in the end.

I wavered on my knees, blinking the sudden black spots away from my vision. Fear threatened to take over my mind, so easily if I just let it. I slammed my fist on the ground, not unlike how the gorilla had done before.

I will not let this be the end. I will not let a crazy bitch with mutilated ears kill everyone I care about.

Cursing, I conjured every bit of energy I had left in me, wiped the name again, and wrote another.

With all my will, I hurled the last of my energy into the spell and cried, "With this triangle, I bind you, Obiross demon of the Netherworld, to be subject to the will of my soul. I command you to stop!"

A rush of energy flooded my aura. My breath came fast as another torrent of energy surged in me—larger this time—with a force that sent me shaking.

The spewing of fire cut off.

I blinked as everyone stared at one another with wide eyes and uncertainty.

"Holy shit. It worked," said Ronin, beaming. "Look. It's sitting like a dog. A giant dog with wings. It looks like it's waiting for your next command."

Through the haze of the sphere, I could see the dragon was sitting, its red eyes searching for me.

I smiled. "What a good boy." Or was Obiross a girl?

With a pop of displaced air, the half-sphere fell.

Emmet staggered but pulled himself straight. He cursed and said, "Looks like the bitch's been busy while we were working on saving our asses."

I looked across to the fortress, and it was my time to curse.

Samara, what was left of the sorceress, looked like someone had carved a ten-foot, grotesque version of her into the fortress's exterior front wall. There was no telling what was Samara and what was the original fortress's wood structure anymore. It was a seamless, perfect creation.

Groaning, I tried to stand but fell, and if it weren't for the fast reflexes of a furred arm, I would have fallen flat on my face. I blinked into the gray eyes of the gorilla. I leaned against him for support and turned to stare at the Samara-fortress.

"Cauldron help us," whispered Emmet. "Only a god could beat her now. Look at her."

My mind was working. During this whole time, Samara was lost, drunk on the power the ley lines were feeding her. She'd forgotten about us.

That was her first and last mistake.

"How the hell are we supposed to defeat her now?" asked Ronin, his smile vanishing.

My eyes fell on Obiross. "What burns wood?"

Ronin's face shifted into a huge grin. "Fire, baby."

I took three steps toward the dragon, at a slow pace, Marcus holding me up. What a nice gorilla.

When we reached a safe enough distance, which was a hundred feet, I raised my voice. "Obiross. I know you don't know me, but I'm not your enemy. I would never harm you. I would never ask you do to something that you don't want to do. I know you've been hurt. And I know she won't stop." I swallowed. "But if you do this one thing for me, I will release you. And you will never be summoned by her again."

Obiross lifted his head, blinked twice, and slashed his tail behind him, like a happy dog. I took that as a yes.

I took a breath and said, "Obiross. I command you to burn down the fortress and Samara with it."

It took half a second for the big dragon to spin around and start spewing his fire at the fortress. It took a little longer for it to catch and burn, but it did.

The ground shook and a horrible wail rose in the air as the first wave of fire hit the fortress.

"*No!*" wailed Samara's voice. "No! No! No!"

The fortress shifted, and I could hear Samara's voice rising above the flames as she conjured her magic.

But it was too late. The dragon's fire was too strong, and Obiross poured it out as though he were pouring out his hatred for the sorceress. Ooh. He really hated her.

The flames burned through the roots and through what was Samara faster than any normal fire could. Like a giant bonfire, the fortress burned. I waited, watching in silence like the others as the top turrets and towers fell, listening to the cracks and pops of the burning fire.

Obiross had stopped spewing out fire and sat on his hind legs, his eyes on me, expectant, and wondering if I'd hold my end of the bargain.

I took three steps back, the gorilla still supporting me, and wiped my boot across the triangle in the dirt. "I release you, Obiross," I said, my voice barely a whisper.

With a huff of his nostrils, the massive dragon leaped into the air, and with a great beat of his wings, he disappeared over the treetops into the night sky. I didn't know where he was going, but I was certain it was far away from here.

"What now?" asked Ronin, as the last of the tower fell, leaving only ash. "Samara is dead."

As soon as the fortress fell, I felt a release, like the forest, suddenly let out the breath it had been holding for years. The sky brightened and I could see some blue through the leaves.

"Home." It was all I could say. My eyelids felt like lead, and I could barely keep them open, let alone hold up a conversation.

I could feel the payment for using Dark magic in my gut. I could feel it stirring, moving, licking its chops, and eyeing my organs with malevolent glee. It would start tearing my body soon. Then, I didn't know what would happen.

I felt my body start to fall.

That was going to hurt.

I braced myself for the fall. My face would hit first because I was too tired to stick out my hands.

But it never happened.

Instead, my feet left the solid ground and I was suddenly lifted in the air. My head lolled sideways, and I felt something warm, hard, and smooth against my cheek. Blinking, I stared at a golden, hairless chest.

Well, hello there.

My eyes lifted and met gray ones.

"I've got you, Tessa," said Marcus, his deep voice rumbling through his chest and my cheek, not unpleasantly.

Okay, when did this happen?

I flicked my gaze around. Ronin, a big smile on his face, walked in front of us, next to Emmet and Kaito. Kaito glanced over her shoulder, stared at Marcus below the waist, and then looked up and winked at me.

Marcus had changed back into his human form, but I'd never noticed. What I *did* notice was that he was buck naked with me in his arms.

And he was carrying me.

Naked.

I felt myself blush at the idea of my flesh on his. Weird that I didn't want to be anywhere else at the moment.

Did I mention he was naked?

I felt myself rise and fall as he walked. He held me close, and heat pounded between us. I won't lie, it felt nice, more than nice, being in his arms, feeling the arms of a strong man wrapped around me tightly.

I met his eyes again and my heart did a few kickbacks. His gray eyes danced with an intensity that had me feeling like Obiross had spewed some of his fire on me.

Marcus—strong and mysterious, and as dangerous as a poisonous snake. And yet I felt comfortable and natural being in his arms, as he held me gently and protectively. Strange. This guy *hated* me. He *did* hate me. Right?

Slowly I pulled away, not understanding what I'd seen in his face.

The deed was done. Samara was dead. She couldn't hurt anyone anymore. This also meant the curse was lifted off of Dolores, and our town was safe.

Smiling, I closed my eyes and let my head fall onto Marcus's nice, warm chest. Yes, it was a *very* nice chest. Why the hell not, right? It might never happen again. Might as well enjoy the ride.

And so, I let a very naked Marcus carry me all the way home.

And I liked it.

CHAPTER
29

I stood on the shoreline, listening to the rolling of waves as the wind stirred the water, sending my hair off of my shoulders and into my face. The wind itself felt restless, charged with delight and excitement as it stirred in and out around the coast. I closed my eyes, feeling the sun on my face and drawing the energy from the surrounding elements—the water from the ocean, the earth beneath my feet, the wind on my face—and the ley lines.

Power flowed into me, twisting and churning with a shuddering life of its own. I took a breath and focused it with my thoughts, shaped it, telling it where to go. A gust of wind slammed into me, and I took a step back, laughing.

Easy now, I told it. *You don't want to knock me off. Do you?*

It was an incredible feeling to bend wind to my will or to create fireballs with a single word.

But I could do it now. And then some.

"There you are. Honestly, Tessa, I'm beginning to think you're trying to hide from us."

I turned to see Dolores marching my way with a glass of red wine in her hand. Her back was straight like a sergeant major, the way she was coming, and it was a miracle she didn't spill any on her white, flowing linen skirt. The other miracle was you could hardly tell that only two days ago she'd lain dying in her bed from a deadly curse.

After Samara's demise, I'd come home to a newly restored Davenport House, with its gleaming white siding and perfectly refurbished kitchen, walls, and ceilings. There wasn't even one speck of plaster dust. It was as though the house had never been affected by Samara's drain on its magic, as though it hadn't been crumbling to pieces.

Granted, I'd been in pretty bad shape when I'd arrived. I could barely remember Ronin sitting behind the wheel of the Volvo after we left Devilwood Thicket, or when Marcus put me to bed. But he did. And every time I thought about it, I blushed.

And it was often.

"Come now. You're being rude to our guests," said Dolores as she handed me the glass, shaking me out of my thoughts.

And by guests, of course, Dolores had invited half the town.

I looked at her face. With her rosy cheeks, her red lips and her hair pulled into a high messy bun, she looked great. You'd never have thought she'd been close to dying.

Dolores had thrown a party in "celebration of life" as she'd called it, but to us, it was more of a "the bitch is gone" celebration.

I cast my gaze around the grounds. Five large garden pavilions had been stockpiled with tables stacked with food, every alcoholic beverage you could think of, and giving shade to those who were firing up their grills and were singeing meat. Happy chatters filled the air and music played from several locations.

I spotted Ronin next to one of the pavilions, chatting up a pretty dark-haired woman, who was batting her eyelashes at him, her hand on his arm while he put on his vampiric charms. I laughed and wondered if this was one of the women he was dating, or if she was new prey.

Marcus stood with a beer in his hand, conversing with a red-faced Emmet, whose voice kept getting louder with every downed drink. Not too far was Kaito, performing the art of slicing watermelon with her curved sword to a happy audience.

331

I hoped she'd rubbed some disinfectant on that sword.

I'd never expected my aunts to welcome back two of the same Unseen who'd wanted to take Davenport House from them and invite them to this very party. A lot had changed, and I was happy about it.

It was a grand party. And it would cost a small fortune, but I couldn't bring myself to talk about our lack of funds at the moment. Dolores looked so happy. I couldn't do that to her, not after what she'd suffered. Tomorrow was another story.

Together we started back toward the house.

I took a sip of my wine. "Can I ask you a question?"

Dolores glanced at me. "Yes. Of course."

"I'm from a family of White witches, right?"

"Yes. Davenport witches are White witches."

I nodded. "Which means we draw power from the elements and occasionally ley lines."

"Yes. Yes. Is there a question in there somewhere?"

I halted. "I told you what happened. I could control the demon dragon."

Dolores stopped and faced me, her eyebrow arched. "Ah. I see where you're going with this."

I chose my words carefully. "The thing is," I said, catching Marcus's eye across the grounds, which sent my pulse beating a little faster. "I had this feeling that I *could* do it. That Dark magic to me, well, it's just that. Magic. Just another branch of magic, but magic all the same." Was he trying to eavesdrop?

Dolores nodded. "It's rare, but some witches can do both. White and Dark. One side will always be dominant, say more White than Dark, but the witch can use his or her multiple gifts. Tap into Dark magic whenever it's necessary. A witch can favor the magic of the elements but still manage to summon and control demons to some degree. Like you did with the dragon demon."

"Obiross," I said. "He was cute, you know. Deadly. But cute."

Dolores laughed.

"So what does that make me?" My heart pounded as I waited for her to answer, hoping she had an answer.

Dolores's dark eyes flashed, and she said, "You, my darling niece, are what we call a Shadow witch—a witch who can dabble in both."

"A Shadow witch," I repeated, testing the words on my mouth, and for some strange reason, they didn't feel foreign at all, but rather familiar.

A smile crept on my face. "I like it."

"Gilbert!" cried Dolores suddenly, her eyes on something behind me. "I need a word." She marched over to the smaller man, who frowned at the much taller witch.

I laughed as I made my way to one of the pavilions. I was ravenous, and I knew I needed to get some food into me before the wine hit.

Ruth looked up as I approached. She'd braided some flowers in her hair that matched her floral-patterned dress. "Here try some of my mushroom puffs," she said as she lifted a plate with bite-sized pastries topped with dark mushrooms.

I grabbed one and stuffed it all in my mouth in one go. Delicious flavors burst over my tongue as I swallowed.

"Wow," I said. "You should open your own restaurant someday. These are fantastic."

Ruth beamed, a slip of her teeth showing through her pink lips. "Have another one. Go on. Take one."

I did as she instructed. "You look happy," I said, between chews. "Like you won the lottery happy. Have I missed something?"

"We're back on the town's payroll," exclaimed Ruth, her cheeks pink. She reached out and took a large sip of her white wine because I was sure it wasn't apple juice.

I choked on my mushroom puff. "We are?" I looked over my shoulder to Marcus, who was laughing at something Emmet was saying. I turned back around, frowning. "Well, they should have never taken you off the payroll, to begin with. That was a *huge* mistake."

"Us," corrected Ruth. "You too, Tessa."

"Right." The town's income was very welcomed for me too. Not that I knew what that would look like since I just started here, but with some website designs and book covers on the side, we could be comfortable again.

"We all make mistakes, dear." Ruth popped a mushroom puff into her mouth. "It's about learning from them," she said around her mouthful. "And owning them."

I washed down some of the pastry with a sip of wine. "So, the other members of the council voted against Marcus, huh? Guess they all realized what a huge mistake it was to take you off in the first place."

"But they didn't," informed Ruth, pouring herself another generous glass of white wine. "Marcus reinstated us. Such a nice young man."

I spit out some of my wine, and it went flying across the table to land somewhere in the grass. "Excuse me?" Marcus had put us back on the payroll?

"Yes, that's right," continued Ruth. "Marcus apologized for taking us off. Was very nice of him to do it in person, too. Poor thing. He could barely look us straight in the eyes. You could tell he was all torn up about it."

"Sure he was." I resisted the urge to turn around again and look at him. Guess he realized he needed my aunts, especially after what he'd witnessed with The Church of Midnight.

"He was. It was so strange." Ruth laughed. "He thought we took on jobs from other cities. Can you believe that? Don't know whatever gave him that idea, but he didn't know he had ruined us when he dissolved our contract with the town." She laughed again.

I wasn't laughing. "When did this happen?"

Ruth put a hand on her hip. "You were there, silly. At the town meeting."

"No," I started again. "I mean, when did Marcus come to you. When did he bring the news?"

"The morning after the library incident," answered Ruth. "While you'd gone out to look for Ronin. You let him in, remember?"

So, that's why he'd showed up at the house.

"Girls!"

I spun around to see Beverly swinging her hips in a red dress that hugged all her curves.

"What a glorious day to have such a glorious party," she beamed as she neared. "Here you go, darling," said Beverly as she handed me a stack of cards.

"What are these?" I asked, turning them over.

"Your business cards," she smiled. "Can't be a true Merlin without cards."

My mouth fell open as I read the inscription:

MERLIN GROUP
Magical Enforcement Response League Intelligence
Network
TESSA DAVENPORT
Davenport House Division, Maine, USA

The sound of the kitchen's back door slammed shut, pulling my gaze toward the House.

Three men stepped off the back porch. They shared the same dazed expression, like they were lost, throwing their heads around like they did not understand where they were or how they got there. I watched as the three men went around the house and disappeared toward the front.

A light went on in my head. I recognized them. They were the three men Beverly had thrown down the basement and locked the door behind them. I thought I'd never see them alive again.

I looked at Beverly. "I have to ask. What is it with these men? What happened to them? Why were they in the basement in the first place?"

Ruth snorted and looked away.

"Davenport House is a beast. And all beasts need to eat." Beverly tapped my hand. "Don't worry, darling. No harm done. And they will *never* harm anyone ever again. That's a promise." She let go of my hand and sashayed her way into the throng of guests, in the direction where males were more dominant.

I had no idea what to say to that. Maybe I wasn't supposed to say anything. Maybe they got what they deserved.

I sighed and looked at Ruth. "I think I'll go mingle before Dolores spells my face with acne," I said, making her laugh.

I'd taken only five steps before I was assaulted.

Martha bounded into view and hooked her arm around mine. "Tessa. You should have let me do your hair, hon," said the larger witch, pulling me along. "Every woman needs a little pampering."

"I'm not the pampering type. Besides, I do my own hair and makeup."

"It shows," said the witch.

I frowned at her. "Do I look that bad?"

Martha flashed her teeth. "You can always look better, hon."

Not exactly the answer I was looking for. But I was glad she was steering me away from Marcus and heading toward the bar.

Martha caught me staring at him. "I know the two of you are at odds with each other, but he's been a godsend to this town."

"I know," I answered as we stood next to the bar. "I just wished I knew why he hates my mother and me so much. I'm part of this town now. I could make this work if he wasn't such a dick."

"You don't know?" questioned Martha.

I wiggled out of her grip. "Know what?"

Martha let out a dramatic breath of air. "Well, I hate to be the bearer of bad news," began the witch, which I seriously doubted with that smile on her face. "Two years ago, your mother was here, working with her sisters while you were in New York. I believe your father was on tour somewhere and your mother couldn't go, for reasons I don't know."

"What does this have to do with Marcus?" I asked, my voice low because I had a feeling he could hear.

I thought about my mother and Marcus having an affair and quickly dismissed the idea. He was way too young for her. She loved my father too much to even look at another man.

"Marcus was working a case," continued the witch. "Very much like what's happening now. Demons. Deaths. The town was a mess. Your mother was charged to work with Jason, one of Marcus's deputies. He was also Marcus's best friend, from the same clan of shifters before they came here." She paused for a second. "Things happened, I'm not sure of the details, but while they were in the middle of it..."

My brows rose. "The middle of it?"

"Yes. Jason and your mother were battling a demon, right on the Hollow Cove Bridge. Something terrifying, I'm sure."

"Okay." I wasn't getting any vibes why Marcus was such an ass. So far, my mother had had a partner. What was the big deal about that?

Martha's expression shifted. "And then your mother got a phone call from your father."

The blood left my face.

Martha sighed. "She left. She left Jason alone with a demon. Marcus found what was left of him hours later."

I shook my head. "How do you know any of this is true?"

"Your mother told her sisters, darling. Unaffected by what she'd done. Didn't even shed a tear or look guilty. Nothing. A bit of a flake, that one. How could she do something like that?"

"Because she would," I whispered, remembering all the times she'd forgotten me in the parking lot at school because she'd been off to see my father. Too many to count. "My mother would do something like that."

And then it all clicked into place, why Marcus hated me, why he didn't want me here. He'd lost someone close to him because of what my mother had done. He had trusted her, and she'd let them down. She'd let his best friend die.

It all made sense now, why he'd treated me this way. Hell, if that had been my friend who died because of a foolish and selfish witch, I wouldn't even be talking to him.

But still, he'd helped me. He'd protected me. He'd carried me all the way out of Devilwood Thicket, held me in his lap while Ronin drove us home, and had put me to bed.

"Are you okay, dear?" asked Martha. "You look a little pale. I have blush in my bag. You could use some lip gloss. You should never leave the house without lip gloss." The witch opened her purse.

"No, thanks." I forced a smile as she let go of her purse. "Thanks for telling me."

"My pleasure, hon." Martha squeezed my hand and moved to face the bar. "I'll have a strawberry daiquiri with a bit of…"

I barely heard what she was telling the waiter as I walked away, my heart heavy with dread.

Of all the stupid and mindless things my mother had done, this was the clear winner.

Faces blurred as I walked around them, their voices distant, like hearing them from a radio far away. I stood for a moment, emotions high, as I wiggled my bare toes in the soft grass.

I turned my gaze on Marcus again, my heart suddenly pounding a lot faster than before. My chest contracted, like my intestines were playing jump rope in my gut. I took him in. All in.

My eyes rolled over him, slowly. I saw the confidence, the broad, wide shoulders and muscular arms and that hard chest I'd been lucky enough to feel, to his trim waist and smooth face.

Marcus's gaze snapped to mine, as though he felt me staring at him. Our eyes locked, and I found myself incapable of looking away.

We held each other's gaze for a moment, my body prickling and reacting to the heat between us.

Perhaps I'd been wrong about him this whole time. Perhaps he wasn't the giant dick I thought he was.

Perhaps he was something else entirely…

Don't miss the next book in The Witches of Hollow Cove series!

ABOUT THE AUTHOR

KIM RICHARDSON is the award-winning author of the bestselling SOUL GUARDIANS series. She lives in the eastern part of Canada with her husband, two dogs and a very old cat. She is the author of the SOUL GUARDIANS series, the MYSTICS series, and the DIVIDED REALMS series. Kim's books are available in print editions, and translations are available in over seven languages.

To learn more about the author, please visit:

www.kimrichardsonbooks.com

Printed in Great Britain
by Amazon

87312024R00201